A Novel by

Shirley A. Hawe

COPPER DUST

Karen,
Enjoy
Love, Cousin
Dr. Shirley A. Hawe
11-06-06

Copper Creek Publishers
139 NE 130th Place
Portland, Oregon 97230
website: www.copperdustnovel.com

For information, address:
Copper Creek Publishers,
139 NE 130th Place
Portland, OR 97230
www.copperdustnovel.com

Printed in the United States of America
ISBN: 0-9627076-0-0

The story is fiction.
The characters are imaginary.
Butte is real.

All characters in this book exist only in the imagination of the author, and are visualized by pure fantasy. The names were invented without role model, or from anyone existing outside of the author's inner thoughts, and bares no relation whatsoever to any other person using the same name.

Butte, Montana is a real place, with real street names, and business names, and locations—at times, referred to in the book.

All events, happenings, and some places, are as phony, fake, and unreal, as the people that live inside the pages of the book are.

I wrote this story for me.

Therese Martin, deceased, edited the book. She had the last word.

I think she is perfect.

Any mistakes she made are there on purpose.

I dedicate the book to

The Blessed Virgin Mary

and

My husband Jack

They both know why.

Prologue

30,000 feet above the Rocky Mountain range within the boundaries of western Montana on Flight 411

Caitlin O'Shaughnessy believes she's returning to her small hometown to turn her life around for the better. The short of it is, somewhere between analyzing handwriting strokes, dots, dashes, and lines, and leaving Butte, Montana to work in Europe for two weeks, she experienced a life changing miracle, that'd complete her existence.

Or, so she thought.

What's about to happen to her on the airplane, and when she returns home, will be far more eventful than successfully completing a forensic handwriting assignment. Upcoming events will change her life in unimaginable, explosive ways. And, carry everyone she knows along with her.

Upon landing at Bert Mooney Airport, she'll start her future by dragging into a fiery day, on a scorching hot afternoon. June, 13, 1990—Miners Union Day. Uncommon weather for Butte's usual mid-June nip, where she grew up without knowing her birth parents.

She expects, like the child of abandonment, she'll silently carry that empty birth with her into the future.

Chapter One

I sat tight-lipped, and squirming impatiently on the last leg of a return trip to Butte, Montana, from Berlin, Germany. It was hot and damp and my air vent wasn't working. Every time the plane bounced, it felt like the pilot was wrestling with the controls to give Flight 411 a joy ride over the Rocky Mountains. I'd discuss my chagrin with someone, but I'd had enough of strangers. I was thinking of going to the lavatory to talk to myself in the mirror when a terrifying scream pierced the air.

"Help! Help us!" a woman shrieked wildly.

"What's happening?" I blurted out, unbuckling my seatbelt. I reached for the flight attendant's call button, and wrenched my head to the seat behind me.

"Sweet Mother of God, help us!" she begged, watching her husband gasp for breath. "My husband's having a hard time breathing. We need help!"

What did I know about helping someone to breathe? I felt powerless to see her husband bent over, and rocking his torso back and forth. All the while he was wheezing and hacking. I panicked when he clutched his throat. While angled cockeyed to find the flight attendant, the plane suddenly swerved sharply to the right, slamming me back into my seat with a thud, and drawing my open briefcase into the aisle.

My head snapped up to see the attendant, a self-assured woman half my age, trip over my belongings as she rushed to assist the elderly couple behind me. "This should help," she said, leaning in to adjust his oxygen apparatus. "The tube got twisted again."

"Is he going to be O.K.?" I asked, surprising her—and me—by tugging at her arm. After completing my assignment in Europe, I had no desire to interact with anyone. Assessing dangerous Third Reich war criminals accused of atrocious acts of terrorism had clouded whatever people skills I owned. My self-protective attitude stood out like Christmas blinkers. In a moment of weakness when I boarded in Chicago, I told the attendant my name, Caitlin O'Shaughnessy. I've made no effort to communicate ever since.

She started to walk away and stooped down to pick up an empty glass by my feet. "May I get you something, Caitlin?" she asked politely. I thought I recognized her voice inflections but I knew she wasn't from around Butte.

"A Seven-up . . . an antacid . . . and one of those donuts you served earlier?" I asked, patting my chubby stomach, thinking a few more hundred calories won't matter. I smoothed my rumpled business suit, and slid my high heels over my toes. I could hardly wait to jump into a shower, and put on a pair of jeans, I thought, listening to the man behind me struggle against another bullish coughing spell.

He bit down hard on the side of his hand to stop from gagging. He left teeth marks around his bloodied thumb before he recovered, and then snuggled his troubled wife to him.

"Mil, we're flyin over the Rocky Mountain range. Nothin to fret about."

As for me, I was born a worrier, under the sign of Murphy's Law. I worried about my safety from the time I left Butte three months ago. I worried every time the plane jerked a bit, which now seemed to come much too often. I looked out the window. There was no hint of bad weather that would cause us to scrape a shadowy mountain, I told myself, gazing at a clear blue sky.

"Will this do it for you?" the attendant asked, leaning in to place a soda and a donut on a tray between my hurry-home attitude and an empty window seat. I narrowed my greenish-blues at her. The way she handed me the antacid and a glass of water reminded me of someone.

"Miss, how long before we get to Butte?" I asked her, realizing that fear was opening me up like a can of jumping beans. I glanced at my wristwatch and watched the little hand swim around slowly without stopping—just like my aimless life.

"We land at Bert Mooney Airport in about an hour," she answered, and whisked away.

Out comes the guilt. I wrapped my mouth over the donut. Sweets are my sedative of choice. I ate them in Berlin to comfort my shocked nerves when I analyzed the handwriting of dead people, heinous assassins that signed orders to do away with millions of people during World War II. It baffled me that a war I considered ancient history, had unexpectedly injected within me, an eye-opening positive attitude about my adoptive mother.

I was wiping crumbs off my mouth, when I looked up at the attendant standing over a May-December couple sitting across the aisle from me. "Sir?" she asked him, reaching up to turn off the call button. Not one lock of her stylish blonde hair cut short to the nape of her neck, moved as she leaned in. "You need something?"

"Two refills," he ordered, pointing at a tiny woman next to him. "The doctor likes to drink on a keep fill basis . . . if you know what I mean." I didn't recognize him, either. He was just another meticulously dressed, snooty executive. And middle age like me—over forty and forgetting the number. "Is the flight air duration consistent with the estimated time of arrival?"

"Coming up . . . and yes Sir," she replied, sweeping her violet-blue eyes at him. "What the . . ."

Suddenly, the plane danced the Charleston. I gripped the armrests just as the captain's bell tolled for her. She hurried forward, scooted into the cockpit, and slammed the door shut.

I drummed my fingernails incessantly on the armrest until the flight evened out. Then, I bent over to gather my belongings from the floor. When did bending become so hard for me, I wondered. I stuffed what I could find in the briefcase. Bundled my long, sweaty red hair, in desperate need of a wash, in a large rubber band, and sat back. Soon my sugar sedative soothed me into a peaceful-in-between sleep state—not quite awake—not quite asleep. While locked between someplace and nowhere, I was suddenly jarred awake by a sharp slap to the side of my face.

"Ouch! Stop that!" I twisted my jawbone back and forth in my hand.

"Caitlin," the attendant called to me.

I shook her arm off my shoulder. "Stop!"

"Caitlin . . . Ma'am . . . you screamed repeatedly," she reported. "You waved your arms, and tossed your head, as if you were sparring with Muhammad Ali." She leaned a tall, trim figure next to my seat. "Both your eyes were locked wide open. You gave no response to my shaking your shoulders."

"Not again!" A spray of guilt sprinkled my flushed cheeks. I motored my healthy sized thighs higher in the leather seat. "I'm so embarrassed."

"You O.K. now?"

"I have no control over a recurring dream. A frightening, colored nightmare, where people I trust tell me my mother never existed."

"Dreams about our parents can be nasty. I have them too, about my mother. They're not pretty!" She stood there while I lowered my head to gain my composure.

I figured my guilty conscience was acting up again.

I was always disobedient about searching for my birth mother. Against Bridget O'Shaughnessy's wishes, my adoptive mother, whom I call Hummy—and against both my aunts' wishes—I've hunted for years to find my roots. Hummy's story, that she didn't know the name of my mother, never set right with me. And, the way she raged wildly at the love of my life, Sam, had caused a rift between her and me.

Ironically, what I learned in Europe made me realize, it should be enough that an Irish legacy was stamped on my round freckled face. That red hair and a worrisome nature were proof of where my roots came from. I pulled my blouse forward to fan some air into my bosom, while mapping a plan to sweep Hummy into my arms and beg her to forgive me. What a fool I've been to treat her with stone-edged indignation the last couple of decades.

Out comes the lower lip.

"Um . . . did anyone complain?" I asked the attendant, darting my eyes to the aisle.

"No," she replied, surveying the couple alongside me, and the two people behind me. "First Class isn't full. Not one of the four complained. They—"

All of a sudden the nose thrust unexpectedly upward. Was the pilot drunk, I wondered. A whirlpool of nausea turned my weak stomach into Jell-O. I hunched low trying to stop from shaking rapidly with small movements. "What's happening?" my voice rattled. "What in the—"

"Stay belted," the attendant ordered. Her voice bounced up and down like that of a Jackhammer operator as she straddled her strong arms between my seat, and the one across from me.

We kept pulling into a climb. We were heading deeper into space instead of flying towards home.

"Oh, God!" I yelled in absolute terror. I was thinking *Murphy's Law,* when the plane started to fly horizontal again. Then I was thinking about the three O'Shaughnessy sisters, brave immigrants from Ireland that planted roots in Butte—an isolated region located far from America's mainline civilization—where Hummy adopted me as a daughter.

"Are you two all right?" I cried out to the couple behind me.

I looked back at the frail woman fidgeting with a breathing tube on her husband's face, and biting her lips. She'd be the right age to be my birth mother, I thought. But, I saw no tiny, light-brown spots living next to freckles—like on my face, and let the thought pass. I felt ashamed I broke my recent promise to stop looking for my birth mother.

Shame on me, too, that during my off time in Berlin, my nosey nature rummaged though mildewed boxes filled with badly scribbled military records, hastily thrust in a basement, and forgotten since Germany surrendered in 1945—as if by some miracle, I'd actually find Irish data that could lead me to my heritage. But, I didn't come up empty.

Surprisingly, I stumbled upon horrible information that'd solve a longstanding mystery in Butte.

"Things are under control," the attendant trumpeted, returning from a conclave with the captain. "Please stay calm." She rushed past me to Coach section to speak with her assistant, a cheerful, dark-haired, medium build, Pollyanna, to assure her we'd be in Butte shortly after lunch.

"Excuse me, Miss," I said, pulling at her skirt as she wrangled back to her station. "Please, can we talk?"

"Caitlin," she motioned me to follow.

I scrambled behind her.

"My name's Dacsu." She held out her hand.

"Pleased to meet you," I replied, shaking her hand. "I threw my business cards away at the front of the trip. What good's a misspelled first name . . . Gattling O'Shaughnessy?"

She laughed. "You on business or pleasure?"

"I'm a small-potato forensic handwriting scientist."

I was thinking potatoes.

"Government work?" The pitch of her voice raised. She noticed my eyes nervously roving the ceiling. "A problem?"

"I'm looking for inconsistencies," I told her picking up magazines that jetted out of the rack when the plane acted up. "A three-year-old would know that something's wrong with the plane. I'm afraid. I saw in a movie to scan the wall for loose screws. Check the ceiling for disengaged bolts. And, to look for cracks in windows."

"We're not in any danger," she tried to comfort me. "Please, continue about your work." Her hips wiggled as she straightened glass cups to the back of a cabinet and gathered tableware askew on the floor.

"In a nut shell," I began. "Due to miscommunication during a telephone interview, I took a job from the Geneva Historical Council in Europe and landed in the middle of some other scientist's fifteen minutes of fame. All that ugly business about World War II, you know."

"Yes, I surely do."

"Hmm? You do?" I wrinkled my brow. We were as far apart in looks as we were in our ages. A contrast, beginning with my thickened waistline. I was no good at small talk, but I was good at reading people. This young kid wasn't going to know anything past the last high school prom.

"History was my major in college." She urged me to my seat. "My master's thesis focused on history of mining in Montana."

"I majored in brain dissection through handwriting, and—" The plane jolted us to attention, once again.

"Don't worry," she said, steadying herself.

"Your words comfort me as much as a parachute would," I replied. "I'm coming home from my first trip overseas, and I'm not used to flying more than two hours."

"We're just fine," she repeated, sitting on the edge of the armrest, not an ounce of fat spilled over the sides. She paused, and waited for me to stick a piece of gum in my mouth. "I tried to get a run to Germany last November when the *Wall* toppled."

"November, 1989 . . . Berlin Wall tumbled." I made a strangling noise with my throat. "That's when East and West Germany combined documents chronicling a war fought before I was born. Or, before you were a gleam in your parents' eyes."

"Were you doing research for a magazine?" She circled her right hand playfully in the air as if she were writing. She didn't fool me. I knew she wrote left-handed. The inside of her left middle finger was indented from writing with a pen.

"I was hired to satisfy curious historians that wanted to re-write history. The current sport of intellectuals these days—anxious to cross a bridge to the past and come back to change history."

"Right," she agreed. "What'd you look for in handwriting?"

"The Council hoped to prove that imposters from other countries in Europe had signed death camp orders to annihilate humans," I said, shifting my weight. "Not solely Hitler's Gestapo or SS officers. They were also looking for motives, other than obeying commands."

Her face showed surprise. "You can't be serious?" she said, stopping to balance her feet. This time the right wing tilted up. We both tipped sideways. While I was hugging the doorway, she tumbled into the aisle. When the plane straightened, she surged to her feet and rushed to the cockpit. I stumbled back to my seat and pulled my seatbelt tight.

"Hmm. What do you think?" a voice shot out. I twisted my head towards a deep toned, male voice across the way. "Has the steel integrity of this massive structure been compromised?" he said, raising his pitch for me to hear, but addressing his seat partner.

I think he said he was worried.

"Do you suspect such repeated impacts could jeopardize the plane?" he said to her, adjusting a crisp white collar. His dark face looked Italian. He sat with straight posture. His thick brows raised whenever he spoke. I knew all the Italians in Butte. None of them spoke with multi-syllabic words.

He caught me sizing him up, and turned away immediately.

"Ugh!" I uttered to myself, wiping perspiration from my neck. I had no patience for a scholarly egghead.

I fished in my briefcase for a candy bar, and came out with a pen, designed by NASA for astronauts to write upside down in space. I squared a notepad on my tray to jot a letter of apology to Hummy—sort of a last Will, just in case. I wanted to write that Butte wasn't a prison from which to escape, and that I love her. But, my nervous handwriting scribbled into a ball of illegible marks, unconsciously sealed to each other.

I scrawled ugly scratches that the holiest of nuns would swear at in disappointment. My thoughts were cramped so tight, all the strokes stuck to each other—like Saran Wrap. Every sweep of the pen hideously fused together in one giant code: LOOK OUT FOR THIS QUIET ONE. SHE'S GOING TO EXPLODE!

"Enough!" I yelped, feeling certain Flight 411 was in serious trouble. I leaped to my feet, determined to storm the cockpit to send a message to Hummy. To tell her that after just learning how untold numbers of families disappeared during WW II, and all their roots and heritage were erased forever, I wanted to embrace the O'Shaughnessy clan with love.

It should have been enough for me to blame God.

I brazenly thrust one foot in the aisle, at the same time Dacsu was briskly forging down the walkway, carrying a bottle of water, a towel, and a worried attitude.

We bumped into each other with a harsh thud.

"Buckle up, Caitlin! Now!" she ordered. Although I had more bump than she did, she shoved me back into my seat and disappeared into the cockpit before I could tackle her.

Chapter Two

1990. Flying should feel safe. This craft moves through the air as if it had a split personality. One minute calm. The next, dipping and diving. Where's that coming from? I pose the same question about my lifelong nemesis—*Megan Pat the Terrible.* They both changed moods like a dimmer switch, and I seem to be at the wrong end of the exchange.

I'm no good at waiting. Grocery lines empty when they see me coming. Dacsu hadn't returned with the status of the plane. My heart pounded so hard, I thought my chest would explode. My stomach swirled. Begged to be emptied. No sick bag. There's one across the aisle. Poking through a seat pocket in front of Dictionary man . . . eyeing me out of the corner of his crafty eye as he heads for the lavatory.

I was single, cranky, travelling alone, and I liked it that way. In between artful looks at me, he acted totally devoted to a stylish senior woman, my mother's age, twisting gaudy diamonds on her bracelet. I'd never ridden up front before. Of course. First Class. Diamonds.

I coyly covered the black rope band of my broken watch with my hand.

Hummy never owned a diamond. She'd always been single. She doesn't drink one Boilermaker after another, either.

I winked. Pleasantly.

Her stylish two-piece ensemble moved gracefully as she bent her small frame over her knees. She saw my outstretched arm reaching for the sick bag and grew irritable, while glaring me into a hands-off squirm.

My nemesis will confirm I'm non-aggressive. I retreated. Unblocked the aisle in time to make room for Dacsu.

"Sorry I kept you, Caitlin," she apologized, handing me two sick bags and a cup of peppermint paste. "This should make you more comfortable."

"Comfortable? When purple molds on my face." I figure Murphy and his band of bad law rebels, boarded without a ticket. Sat in an empty seat next to me to cause trouble. I wiped my mouth with the back of my hand. "I'm worried about these rock and roll maneuvers. Then a complete turnaround to calm. What's happening?"

"That blue sky out there, looks calm. But mountain areas have unstable wind velocity."

"Meaning?"

She tilted her large, expressive eyes to the lit seatbelt sign. Pointed a manicured finger to where my waistline used to be—until it completely disappeared under my rib cage. "You need to buckle up, please."

My cue to worry more than normal.

She fumbled with a tray of hot pasta snacks smelling like roasted garlic in Little Italy on a humid day. I burped loudly.

"Oh, God." I teetered shakily to the lavatory. Jammed five-feet-eleven inches into a tiny water-closet room, designed for children. A lovely sight! Grounded in a foot of contaminated floor space, *Return to your seat immediately,* flashing above my head. Contorted over a midget tidy bowl, my rear end butted up against the door . . . I barfed in Thomas Crapper's innovative toilet . . . red light flashing in rhythm.

What kind of man would think this up?

I splashed cold water on my face. Sucked in my cheeks, for the mirror. The only part of me that has any suck left in it. Swung the door open and bumped into Dacsu. "I must get a couple of messages out, or, I'll go nuts with worry. Please?"

"Captain needs the arms of an octopus, more than another body up there." The way she squared her shoulders as she leaned forward to help, looked familiar.

"I don't want to make trouble. Peace of mind. I need to get two short messages out . . . short!" I'd tell her I spotted a gleam in her eyes that I'd seen before, but she'd think I was coming on to her.

"Write down your message. I promise to pass it along." She handed me a notepad from her pocket.

"Write? Can the pilot read Saran Wrap?"

"That way . . . or, no way. I'll try and help your cause more, as soon as I do a precautionary run." Professional flight attendant code. Hurry—get all the garbage picked up and passengers tightened down. It's going to be a bumpy ride.

She shook out a plastic bag. Flung open a curtain that separated the have's from the have not's. Walked slowly to the back, stopping at each row, while her assistant discussed something with a man seated in the last row. He was missing a limb, and wriggling his wrists, handcuffed to the seat.

The flight wasn't full. Counting the pilot, copilot, her assistant, and me—a little fish in a big pond of personality investigators—there were 27 heads. 54 arms and 53 legs. Except for the Italian spaghetti eater across the way that went to the front galley for seconds on his pasta, and to get the board up his butt unstuck, the group appeared congenial.

Again. The woman behind me shrieked. "Help! Someone help us! He's going to hack himself into a coma if he doesn't get some air." I twisted my head to her round angelic face wrinkled in pain. She pointed to her husband leaning over, clutching his chest.

What do I know about comas and chest clutch? The left wing soared exceedingly high. I vaulted up, close to his aisle seat. The engine revved loud, like a motorcycle gunning its motor at a stop light.

"Move aside," I told his panicked wife, watching him choke his face blue. I girded my arms around his chest. An upward thrust below the breastbone. Pasta dislodged from his throat.

Dacsu stood behind me. Anxious. "Did it work? What did he swallow?" She hovered over the ex-miner's gray brows, cracked deep with age, as he breathed slowly. Kept coughing.

"He swallowed forty years of copper dust," the pale woman whispered.

I moved out of the way. Dacsu leaned in. Spoke in verbs. "Lift your head. Follow my fingers. Take off your shoes. Move a pillow behind your neck. Breathe deep." She turned to his wife. "See that he takes short deep breaths on his own. Then hook him back up. Make him drink this bottle of water. Keep the tube straight." She clamored to check overhead bins for a blanket. Stumbled her way to the back, slamming doors as she hurried along. Moving faster when the captain's bell tolled for her again.

"Honey, will you help me?" his fearful wife asked, standing up behind me by the window. She was barely able to look over the top of the seat. "His oxygen isn't doing right," she moaned, holding a tube in her shaky hand that'd been tethered to his nose.

I cleaned out his mouth with my fingers. Chiseled to the rear of the plane, where Dacsu's assistant pointed me to a spare inhalator. Bounce. Bump. Neck snap. Carnival ride. I balanced between each row like a high wire Empress and hurried back.

"We're coming home from a health clinic in Minnesota. I'm terrified," she said. He can't stop coughing and he's got a bad heart"

"I'm so sorry."

"Mining was Gunner's life for over forty years."

"What'd you mean?"

"He'd go down this day if he could. To the 3600 foot level where the temperature rises over 100 degrees."

"He's not angry about his health?"

"Gunner's angry at the Anaconda Copper Mining Company. All he ever wanted when he came out of Ireland was to own a piece of land for himself. That's what drives the Irish to succeed. It's all about land. Even if it meant getting ill to earn a living. Never counted on a child— "

"You rented?"

"For years. In Meaderville. Until our daughter got sick from poisonous gases that settled over the community. She died. We moved to higher ground."

"I don't know what you mean?" I knew Meaderville. An Italian suburb of Butte. At the base of Butte's famous Hill that had all the mines on it. Eminent eateries on Main Street. Rocky Mountain Café. Aero. Notorious night clubs. And down home taverns like Brass Rail, that opened at 8:00 am daily. Colusa Bar, named after a different mine than the one across the street—the Leonard. Grappo liquor in every basement. Groceries. Miner's Meat Market didn't sell meat on Saturday because of a Blue Law, but drinking and gambling were wide open.

Everyone knew Meaderville. "Poisonous gas?"

She grew calmer as Gunner fell asleep. He slept noisily. I wondered if he could dream, cough, then snore . . . and still get a good rest.

"Lethal stink pots," she shook her head. "Smelter roasted ore outside. Arsenic and sulfurous matter killed our Sophia."

I knew death. You can't live in a copper mining community without becoming intimate with mourning. How to say "Sorry for your loss," without crying. I'm just not good at dealing with it.

"Sorry for your loss," I said, straight faced. I meant it.

"Long time ago." She snapped her hands over her ears to drown out an earsplitting sound from the plane's engines. Strained to speak over the noise. "Bought a small place on the Flats. Vegetable garden. Dog run. Chicken coops."

"Wasn't that a good thing?"

"The Company sells you a home, all right, but not the land it's on. Those gangsters don't sell you the mineral rights. They sell you anger and—"

Gunner's deep throated cough alarmed us. Miner's Consumption. A disease that destroys elasticity in the lungs.

It hurt to watch him choke on his own sticky phlegm. Like my girdle, once it stretched there was no way to get it back. “My two uncles worked underground. Of course you’re worried.”

She nodded, clutching a Rosary in her small hand, touching one bead at a time to pray a Hail Mary on each bright red stone. Rosary. Soon I’d see the three O’Shaughnessy sisters—blindly obedient to their faith. Little did they think, when they pulled me as a child along a Hail Mary road that led to attending weekly Mass . . . the most powerful prayer in the Catholic church . . . I’d end up firing blatant indignation at God.

Why not? Most of me inside died when Sam O’Toole left me standing at the altar. What kind of a God would allow the love of my life to abandon me on the day of my wedding? To let my birth mother abandon me at six months old? Who am I?

Tell me that doesn’t put a knob in the pit of your stomach?

I twisted around to help her scoot over Gunner’s lap. She ambled to the lavatory. Something made me take a quick glance to the back. Wait! . . . I didn’t notice before. Could that be Deputy LB, one of Sheriff Dak’s men, hanging over the side of a rear seat coddling a prisoner? Short and hefty, Lard Butt. Packing the same 300 pounds, since he reached his full height—five-feet-five inches. He sat stuffed in a small seat on the last row beside a prisoner I knew all too well.

One of the mischievous McDoon twins, that tried to rob my house a week before it burned to the ground, was perched next to the window, grumbling in a raspy voice at his captor. “LB, Houdini couldn’t run away from up here!”

"Pipe down."

"Get these cuffs off." He fidgeted with his wrist.

"Consequences, friend. Consequences."

"Promise not to make trouble." He propped his peg leg through the armrest between the seats in front of him. "Please? Huh? Please?"

LB noticed me leaning in the aisle and waved in surprise. He was glad to have some distance between us. Our friendship strained since I threw a large glass vase, filled with summer flowers and floral greenery, at him. The front steps of St. Pat's Cathedral. His misfortune to be Best Man at my failed wedding.

The situation worsened. One day later, his twin brother drowned at a dike near a smelter operation. Obituary: "Mrs. Calluhanan didn't blame anyone. Stated her boy drowned swimming in a lake young people were warned not to swim in."

I knew better. LB, a premier swimmer, would've been racing beside his brother's punctured inner tube, if he hadn't been hospitalized. Concussion. Cuts. Disoriented. Slurred speech, and all because of me. Out comes my guilt. I surged up to speak with LB, and bumped Mr. Dictionary's knee, partly straddled in the aisle.

"Help me . . . hurry! Hey . . . quick, I need help!" he pleaded. His mouth twisted in pain, hot spicy pasta streaming down his lap. "I'm scalded."

"Please tell me, I didn't do that?" Gooey noodles squirmed on the floor next to broken glass . . . and me. First Class section. Real china shatters. I slid my wet shoes off. My feet were puffy, swollen like baked donuts. "Ouch." I stepped on a small St. Christopher medal that fell out of my briefcase earlier. Hummy knew the church fired Chris. That the saint lost his job as a safe-travel consultant. St. Christopher was my friend. We were both on the outs with the church. Why did she, above all people, tuck it in my belongings?

"Please move," Dacsu ordered, plunking my tailbone to the armrest, and stooping to rescue his lap from a plate full of sizzling spaghetti with her bare hands. She trotted off like Man-O-War. Returned carrying a towel, cleaning supplies, and an exasperated look.

"Sir, I 'm sorry," she apologized. "Airline will pay for your cleaning." She mopped up saucy, red soaked carbs, slithering from the top of his muscular thighs down his pant legs.

"Not obligatory." He slanted his eyes towards me. "Untimely shortcoming. Entirely my fault." He spoke as if his emotions were directly connected to his business interests . . . and me.

Navy blue was in this year.

He was wearing an expensive Armani, navy blue suit, white shirt, and bright blue tie, harnessed with a diamond clip. Diamonds were also in this year. Slight outgrowth of his waist. Thick, dark hair, lightly speckled with gray, swayed side to side, as he tried to stay balanced.

"Not again!" The plane dipsy-doodled for the umpteenth time. I seized the armrest. A sick bag. Why didn't the pilot announce something? White knuckles. Worry.

Mr. Dictionary's lady friend had no worries. She passed out from an overdose of Boilermakers.

Dacsu's assistant wrapped a cloth over her hand. Adjusted his soggy zipper cover. Rubbed out stains from his fly. Wiped his designer pants with a rhythmic motion. My face reddened. "Hold still, Sir. This won't take long if we work as a team!"

"I can take it from here," he said, holding his long pant leg to one side, and biting his tongue. "Just give me the damn towel!"

I turned away innocently.

Suddenly, blood rushed to my head. My hind end stiffened like a piano wire. The plane's frightening dance resumed to a more violent pace. Thrashing. Whipping. Groaning. I strained to look out the window at mountain tops reaching up to touch the belly of the plane. Of all the different ways I thought I might die, being speared by a mountain wasn't on the list. Something terrible had gone wrong. Would the Pilot's resume' show he flew space missions to the moon at warp speed? Navigated the Spruce Goose? Flew as a test pilot for NASA as a teenager?

I muscled to the cockpit door, and started banging. "Hey! Hey . . . you in there. Open up this door!" I banged louder.

"Stop Caitlin," Dacsu came out of nowhere. "Return to your seat at once, or I'll put you in restraints." She blocked me with a hard tackle around my waist. Her uniform was feminine, but her arms were like steel. What could I lose? I poised my hand on the knob, ready to crack it off the bolt.

We grappled.

The plane veered sharply to right, as if we were in an air show. I braced my feet like a cement cornerstone. Hugged the entrance. She stiffened her stance. The nose pointed down. Speed increased.

"We're going to roll over!"

"Sit down!"

"Never."

"Captain O'Donovan's one of the best pilots around."

"I don't care if the pilot rode Big Foot."

Our combined weight Billy goaded forward. Walloped us against the door like two paper-dolls stuck together from too much paste. "Had enough?" she snorted. Her body lunged against mine, pressing my face sideways against the closed entrance. Knocking the wind out of my Ma'am bones. Scrunching my round cheeks into rectangles. "Comply!"

"I'm going in!"

"Not!" She shoved her knee, the only bony part on her body, in the crack of my right leg. Then, bent my left arm behind my back until I caved to the floor in total defeat.

"O.K. . . . stop. You're hurting me," I surrendered.

She broke off her crowbar pry. Pulled me to an upright position. Patted me down. Satisfied I wasn't packing a weapon, she relented. Like Sister Agatha Ann, after getting to know me better, she was no longer determined to make me an enemy. She twisted me through the aisle, flung me into my seat, and cut a deal.

"I'll take care of business with the pilot," she decided. "You sit and wait for me to get back to you."

"Make it snappy," I requested politely.

Chapter Three

An agitated Dacsu spiraled from the pilot's pit frantically pinning her blouse shut, two top buttons were missing. Her right sleeve shredded like confetti, and matched a rumpled uniform and wild hair. "Ms. O'Shaughnessy." She bid me to follow her.

I stomped into the galley. "You tell Charlie Lindbergh up there I'm going to speak to him if I have to chew a hole in the door with my teeth!"

Backed against the wall, she looked like a bag lady. She made no excuse as she slid two fingers inside the waistband of her skirt to straighten it on her slim hips. "It's Amelia Earhart . . . and her hands are full."

"Full of what? The two of you up there obviously had a good time." I paused. "Ah . . .no!" My mouth widened. "You're a threesome fooling around?"

"Caitlin," she whispered. She pressed her finger to her mouth. Looked both ways to see if anyone was listening. "Can't let other passengers hear this." She trembled as she squared her jaw. "Got it?"

"I'm a discretion vacuum," I frowned, nuzzling close to her mouth, and raising both hands in the air. "Different romantic stuff doesn't matter to me—I'm a one-man woman. What matters is getting off this plane safely."

"Over the last hour, Patrick the copilot . . . "

She stopped to sip water as my neck went rigid with puzzlement. "Get hold of yourself. What did Patrick do?"

"He was seized by violent spasms that caused chaos in the cockpit."

O.K. I haven't heard this stuff before.

"Patrick's unconscious. Captain's flying solo."

"Isn't she trained for a one-person act in case of emergency?"

"Here's how it played out," she explained. Her eyes, serious and clouded, pierced through my apprehension like an x-ray. "Copilot agonized in pain. Unbuckled himself. Thrust his arms and legs everywhere. He's a big, solid guy. Weighs 190 pounds. She couldn't restrain him, and fly manually over the Rocky Mountain range at the same time. Hence, sharp wing tilts. She managed to ring for me twice. Patrick fought like a lion."

"Catch your breath," I advised, inching towards her. "You're not making complete sense."

"This last time, I struggled to contain him until he conked out. It took great effort to anchor him to his seat."

I stepped back dumbfounded. "What do we do now?"

"Mary O'Donovan's the best. She avoided a dive. Saved our lives."

"*Murphy!*" I mumbled under my breath. I swallowed hard and pulled a hanky from my pocket to tie around her cut arm. "That should stop the bleeding." I leaned animated against the counter. "That explains some of the irregular flying. As well as your long absences."

"Accounts for a short circuit on the call buttons and lights, too," she said, turning her head. "And the shrill noise that scuttled our ears."

"Doesn't spell out the lopsided flying."

"That's the worst of things."

"Flying lopsided?"

Something distracted her to look up. "I've got to help that sweet couple," she said, obeying a panel of buttons blinking for attention. "They're very frightened."

"*They're frightened?*" I rooted through her cabinets for a miniature bottle of liquor. Drank one, tucked three of them in my pockets and waited . . . shaking my bare feet in a draft.

She returned, speaking on fast forward. "The auto pilot was damaged earlier when Patrick first went into spasms."

"Otto plot?"

"Yes, auto pilot."

She opened a closet, shook out a sweater and assisted me to my seat. "Those two looked at me pretty weird."

I was thinking mix-master and looking at her hair. "Otto plot? You mean a device named after a guy called Otto?"

"You're kidding me, right?"

"Whatever!" I huffed, then spoke low. "Are we—"

"Sorry," she said. "I'm very edgy, and you're the only passenger I've confided in."

"Was the plot problem in that maze of buttons and controls in the cockpit?"

"Yes, Caitlin. The auto pilot switch was disengaged . . . maybe deactivated all together."

"Good Lord, you think you . . . or your assistant back there . . . can help to fly this thing?"

"No . . . and, you?"

"Not one lick," I admitted, turning my head to Mr. Dictionary across the way, wondering if he could pilot. "Asking me to maneuver anything bigger than a pickup truck would be like appealing to the Jolly Green Giant to sleep in a sardine can. I overheard the fellow behind me brag of his flying experiences during World War II. Maybe he could act as a second pair of hands . . . or eyes, up there?"

"He's one sick senior battling for every breath he takes." Her voice weakened. "He's very ill." She rolled her eyes to the floor.

"What is it you're not saying?"

"We're off course!"

"What? Over these rugged mountains—"

Just at that moment, the engines flamed with a loud noise, but the captain's bell didn't toll for Dacsu.

"Don't you need to get up there? This is 1990, surely there's navigation help from the airport?"

"The only radar, or scientific know-how we can rely on is the pilot's brain searching for a workable alternative." She darted to the lavatory. I mulled over *workable.* Added the words, disaster and death, and Megan Pat the Terrible surfaced in my mind.

Grade school. Nun disciplined me for something MP did. Made me write JMJ on the blackboard 100 times to honor the holy family—Jesus, Mary, Joseph. The way to Heaven, she ordered. "Write JMJ on the back of all your envelopes."

I'm in the 5th grade. I don't own envelopes.

I shifted my legs and saw the man across the way photographing my every move. He stared intently, like a character in a sappy novel. Admittedly, his dark brown organs of sight were so deep, I could swim in them, just as the author described. I hated myself for drifting into fiction at a time like this. Imagining I could do a backstroke in his large eyes as they ran up—then, down my weighty calories. He nodded repeatedly.

I had my fill. Pounded my fist on the armrest and glared at him. "You got something to say, Mister . . . spit it out."

"You're a long way from home, aren't you, Red?" His voice soft and warm. He raised his shoulders. "I expected you to talk sooner, after executing your quadrumanous effort of full-backing with the flight attendant at the cockpit door. Did she describe possible current scenarios the pilot is experiencing?"

He said *what*?

I elevated my neck over at his seat partner, a beautiful, white-haired senior slumped in a window seat so large it swallowed her whole. Her mouth wide open, she dwarfed her throat with her tiny shoulders. Stared back. Even from a distance her alcohol breath poisoned the air.

Out comes stubborn. "What'd you mean?"

"Your athletic skills at the pilot's door." He counted on his fingers. "Obviously Flight 411 was sidetracked from schedule—"

The engine roared so loud we both pulled at our ears.

He wrote on four yellow sticky notes. Handed them to me.

I retrieved my glasses off the floor. How much of my stuff was lost beneath the seats from the first major tilt and spill, I wondered. Reluctantly, I read the notes.

"Enjoyed anxiety pretense on this flight."

"Your silent treatment performance, excellent."

"Pretending you needed to vomit . . . over the top."

"Now . . . time to come clean, Red."

Written with heavy pen pressure. I sprawled my magnifying glass over the stranger's notes to see if he was an ax-murderer. He printed. Unusual physical strength at his command. Tall t-bars crossed to the right of the stem, trumpeted a pushiness. He controlled his flaws by using the workings of an active mind. Murderer? More like an intellectual looking to vent.

"Well?" he quizzed, not knowing what field I worked in. "You know I wrote from the heart." His chest noticeably pumped hard as he waited. "Red?"

I tore up the notes. "Leave me alone! I like you less than a sauerkraut sandwich." I knew two German words. Sauerkraut was one of them.

"Playing the feisty card?'" he grinned, reaching his long arms to punch the button for Dacsu. He turned up both palms of his hands, and snapped them my way. Energetic people do that to preface a command. "Cease-fire?"

I held my head in my hand, and looked at the floor. Maybe at some other time, a different place, or special circumstances, his advances would have flushed my cheeks. At this moment, I'm reeling from a mental hiccup. Family apologies. Plane disaster.

His companion nudged him. She talked with an Irish accent. Like older citizens in Butte speak. Except her inebriated words stuck like glue on her fuzzy tongue. "Tray rengen fur a wee one, well yeh now, dear?"

"Right away, Dr. Freida." He catered to her whim. Rang again for Dacsu. Lobbed a few chocolate peanuts in his mouth and offered her the rest. "It's been an eructate ride, all right."

Stunned at his worship, I stared in silence thinking her greatest achievements were behind her. That she must be rolling in dough. Otherwise, how could she snag someone my age?

"Aye'll jest bottom oop thes one, Lad . . . now won't Aye?" she announced, pushing the peanuts aside. She clutched her crooked fingers around a nearly empty glass of whiskey neat. Slowly drained the last eight drops into her mouth.

"What's taking that attendant so long?" He looked at me as if I knew. Stepped into the aisle. Peeled off his suit coat, neatly folded it, and brushed his tie straight.

Predictably, out comes my non-aggressive behavior. I crawled over my pride and relented. "She's under a lot of pressure up there—"

Wherein, he amusingly pushed me aside, rolled up both sleeves of his crisp white shirt, and raised his arm high.

I ducked.

"Where could she be?" He scratched his head, and strolled down the aisle.

I cautiously approached his lady friend. "Ma'am." She raised her chin. The light emphasized an uncommonly smooth neck for a seventy-something. "I need to warn you. There's trouble with the plane."

"Yeh hev somthen teh say, now do yeh, child?" She cupped her hand over her ear. Draped her chest over the armrest, crumpling a green silk suit I'd love to own. Her speech twisted with her posture over a curved tongue. She formed an Irish drawl as thick as Dublin Gulch mud. "Wooodn't yeh bay tellen me, lass, straight away. Aye'm joost—"

Her mister returned. Startled her to scoot over to her own seat.

I retreated. Flipped myself towards the window to see endless green mountains below. Deep blue sky beside. The universe above us. Infinity. And, a strong smell of my underarm deodorant that woke me to reality.

"Shay . . ." she snorted, dropping her glass, and loosing consciousness.

"Her hearing aid batteries died. What did you tell her?" he said, unconcerned. He paused. "Red, will we be staying together at ... what's the name of the tallest hotel in Butte?"

A bona fide Jekyll and Hyde. Roll in the hay with him on the tenth floor Penthouse suite at the Finlen? He's been sniffing too much dictionary print. Such forcefulness rocketed me to the 5th grade, again. Unresolved issues I hated to remember.

Last class of the day ended. Changing my gym socks. MP the bully, cornered me. Beat my feet to raw bone and blood, with a heavy backpack. Classmates watched in silence. How could such a gorgeous girl—voted as the most beautiful, intellectual blonde to have ever walked the halls of our Catholic grade school—train all the girls in our class to be her puppets? Shouldn't adults apologize?

It's not as if I was alone back then. I had plenty of support.

Dak Sullivan. Zoonawme. Blessed Mother. She sent me clear messages on how to handle trouble. Every sound and sight talked to me. Within every touch, and smell, I received clues to help me get out of predicaments. The feel of the wind against my cheeks. The sight of someone stooping over. The scent of a room. Finding a clean, sanitary napkin someone dropped behind the furnace, to stop my feet from bleeding.

Zoonawme throttled Megan Pat . . .MP . . . military police, to quit attacking me. Promised more serious lessons, if she didn't stop trying to kill me. I couldn't run my life, or Copper Dust Forensics without Zoonawme as my partner, and Dak . . .

Dacsu interrupted my rambling thoughts.

"Captain and I checked on charts and graphs, to measure the distance between life and death."

"Success?"

"It's totally up to O'Donovan . . . and God . . . now!

Chapter Four

"Captain will make an announcement—soon as the address system works. Entire intercom is down," Dacsu confided, stroking her chin. She turned from me, walked into the galley, and began to write instructions on her tablet, for her assistant. She was unaware of the couple behind me, shouting in a heated marital dispute.

"Mil, old gal, I flew in worse situations in WW II," he told his wife. He planted his baseball hat on his bald head. An insignia, *Tail Gunner,* stitched on the crown. He stopped to cough. "Commercial pilot. We're safe as ridin a bike, Honey."

He was wearing khaki cotton pants, held up by wide red suspenders. Extra large, brown plaid shirt covered his generous stomach, and a flyer's—know it all—attitude.

"From God's mouth to your arrogant ears, eh, Gunner?" she said, clutching a white sweatshirt stamped with a purple logo, *Best Grandma.* She searched for a sick bag. "How can a plane bump up and down? Rock sideways? We're flying in a soft sky?"

He coughed up nasty mucous. Spit into an oversized hanky. "Don't worry." He pried open a sick bag, and handed it to her.

"You look at flying from the rear-end." She'd listened to his tail gunner experiences for over forty years. "I tell you we're going to die in this rattle trap, husband."

I agreed.

I spun around at the sound of a different controversy.

The attendants mined each other for information.

Dacsu grilled her slightly younger, less experienced, upbeat assistant. "What'd you learn from the captain?"

"Mary's . . . feeling her way through these mountains," she said irritably, hushing her voice. She'd just returned from the cockpit. She clutched her chest with both hands. "I'm very, *very* worried."

After a quick caucus they formed a plan and scurried to act.

"While the plane's steady," the senior flight attendant schemed. "We tighten these people down before we have a riot. Start serving the hard stuff immediately. Keep it flowing. And, don't charge anyone in the back, either."

"Right away, but why doesn't Mary—"

Out comes a long overdue message.

"This is Captain O'Donovan, ladies and gentlemen," she told anxious passengers in a deep voice. "We've had some electrical problems. As you can hear . . . things are cleared up." She apologized for any static, blaming the mountains. "Sorry for the irregularities. Please keep your seat belts on until the ride is smoother. We'll be a little late arriving in Butte. Thank you for your patience."

The voice of someone in control was comforting.

Not to Gunner.

"Hear that Mil?" His disagreeable, elderly eyes turned to the floor to accommodate a ferocious cough. No longer robust, or muscular and independent, he was forced to look to others for strength in bad situations.

"I'm relieved." She reached down to pick up his spit bottle.

"Get that Rosary of yours out, woman. Some fool dame's up there tryin to fly this ship. You're right. We're goin to die. A slow-witted, empty-headed broad. She'll fly us into a mountain."

"Please take it easy, old man," she said lovingly. Mildred's round, rosy cheeks spelled friendly, but her tone marked fear. "You know your breathing suffers when you get excited."

I turned to give them comfort and gasped in surprise. How could I have been so caught up in myself I didn't recognize my former neighbors seated behind me? I gazed at Gunner's hazel eyes filled with resignation, instead of concentrating on his oxygen apparatus. He was older. Black rings were painted under his optic receivers. He looked more like a sickly panda bear, than the energetic miner I knew in the old neighborhood.

"Miss, you need something?" his wife asked me.

"Excuse me, but did you used to live by our family, the O'Shaughnessy's? Then later, by me?" She had a soft spot in her heart and a kind twinkle in her eyes. If I had a grandmother, I'd want her to be Mildred. The *good grandma*—that loves you unconditionally no matter what you did. She'd gone from 120 pounds to over 200. And, just like me, most of the fat invasion was hitch hiking on her mid section.

"Punch my back in the middle, Mil," he broke in. Raised his shoulders. "Sometimes it knocks air loose and I breathe better."

She reached her arm out, and aimed at me.

"Sorry Caitlin," she apologized. She was snuggled in a sweatshirt covered by a warm knitted shawl, and tapping me on the shoulder with ice-cold hands. "Gunner's having trouble."

"Mildred, then, you really do recognize me?"

"You went all funny after Sam O'Toole, um . . . on your wedding day. We sat in the back of St. Pat's when you hi-tailed it out. Threw a vase at LB chasing after you. Tore off your wedding gown. And went all private ever since. We didn't think you wanted to speak to us." She paused to adjust her shawl. "Gunner was Erin's best friend, you know."

"Erin O'Toole!" I exclaimed. "Sam's dad was an MIA in the war. I'm sorry for being so stand offish since Sam left me at the altar." A broken heart at twenty-one had changed me.

"Gunner's oxygen isn't flowing," she appealed. "You help?"

"I've tinkered with Aunt Nell's air tank." I contoured up to Gunner, wiggled knobs, inserted a tube up his nostrils. Looked up to see Dacsu standing in the aisle grabbing at her chest.

She screamed. "What in the hel—"

"Dacsu," I jumped to her side.

She'd been hit above the waist with a full glass of booze thrown by Dr. Freida. Black letters on her nametag streamed down her blouse in a puddle of runny ink.

Mr. Dictionary lowered his voice. "I'm so terribly sorry, Miss. are you injured?" He swabbed hard liquor off her face with the back of his hand. Turned to the doctor, and shook his finger.

"Shame on her," Dacsu whispered to me, wiping her eye. "My God, she has to be somebody's mother. Make that the mother of all mothers."

"I'm no expert there. I'm adopted," I answered.

"I'm adopted, too." She dashed to the lavatory.

Mr. Dictionary hot on her heels.

"Please, Miss . . . Dr. Freida wasn't aiming at you." He spoke through the door. "She was aiming at her past." He puffed back to drill his seatmate.

I hunkered low in my seat to observe, and listen.

"Look, Doc, I understand you don't like blondes, but why'd you do that? Ipse dixit of you. Mutinous. Uncouth. Plain mean!"

I don't know what he said.

"Shay looked et may the same way the dumb blonde ded thet worked en Butte's red light destrict . . . now dedn't shay?"

"Hardly seems enough to get violent about . . . at your age."

"Thet tramp ran may out oov town, now dedn't shay?"

He fell silent.

She fell asleep. Yet, again. As if a cogwheel in her brain misfired periodically.

Could this trip from hell get any worse? Would we get home? We were already over an hour late. I missed the Miners Union Day parade. Much of the rodeo. Mostly, I missed making an apology to my Hummy.

Others felt apprehensive, too. Exhaustion swept over the cabin. Except for the roar of the engines, a ringing in my ears, and sweat rolling down my face, I was surrounded by silence. Silence had always been my friend. A way to escape my heartache. My disappointment in God. That is, until silence stood in the way of my impatience. Right now, my sticky, long red hair clung to my neck and cheeks. I saw my hair band on the floor pinched between the heels of Mr. Dictionary's fancy shoes, and stooped closer.

“Hmm?” he grunted.

Politeness entered. “Please, move your feet?”

“What? You say something?” He grinned like a Chesapeake cat. He never took his eyes off me. “Did you talk to me?”

Here comes the persistence. The brown nose. The false sweetness. Soft voice. “Excuse me, my hair band is near your feet.”

Immediately, his nimble fingers swept the floor.

“A little to your left.”

“This it?” he laughed. “Some sort of a band, all right?”

I reached out.

“Yes Siree, Ms. whatever you call yourself . . . it’s a band all right.” The tsk’s flowed. He slowly spooned up a dainty pair of green silk, thong underwear in his large hands. An extra pair—as a joke—I promised Hummy I’d keep handy in case of an accident. At least one of her holy badges wasn’t stuck to it.

“Umm . . yes.” I reached out. Wondering how many other small town women, make an effort to impress a medical staff with superior hygiene habits, at *their own* accident.

“Madam . . . your band.” He draped Victoria’s secret playfully over my left arm. Elbowed his muscular body out of his seat, then hog-tied my right arm.

I gasped in surprise. “Get your mitts off me.” The more I pulled away, the tighter he clamped. All the while his intensive brown eyes stared at my crimson cheeks steaming with mean. “Move away.”

His face close to mine, he counted each puckered pimple on my neck. Then he squeezed, released, squeezed, and released my arm as if taking my blood pressure. “Red, I’m elated you're sitting across from me. Ingenious. Time to cease and desist . . . we're almost in Butte."

My cousin Mike, and I learned to speak five languages. None of them came to mind. "You jerk-head encyclopedia." Simply because I haven't dated in years, doesn't mean I don't recognize a man putting moves on me. I feigned a karate hand stance. "You let go this second, Ape Man!"

"Game's over," he scolded. His playful tone turned serious. All the while, both hands clung firmly to my crumbling arm. "You know what I'm talking about, Sarah Bernhardt."

"What game? I liked it better when you and your girlfriend were ignoring me." I whipped sharply to one side to release his grip. Tobogganed into leather as I broke free. "Stay away."

He kept after me and came closer, wide, Dick Tracy eyes trained on my stubborn face. His strong fingers formed a tourniquet over my wrist. "Touchdown?"

"Get your creepy paws off me, Casanova. Or, I'll decapitate your manhood!" I raised my knee, threatening to wound his privates with my right foot. Maybe it was an unconscious lash out at MP, but I felt determined to defend myself for a first time in my life.

"You wouldn't?" He didn't back down. Slowly . . . ever so slowly . . . he moved his hand from my wrist and slid it up to my elbow, as if he'd done it a million times before. All the while he inspected my freckles. Memorized every tiny wrinkle on my furrowed brow. Made mental images of all 20,000 clammy pores on my face. His journey ended by glaring at a tiny, heart shaped mole throbbing on the right side of my neck.

At that point, he stopped abruptly and dropped my arm like a hot branding iron.

"At last!" I yelped, looking up the aisle for Dacsu.

"My God . . . I can't believe this!" he shrieked.

"I'll do it all right. I know exactly where to aim. And, I've got a lead foot when it comes to protecting myself." Another first.

"No," he choked. "All this time I thought you were . . . it's uncanny. It's—"

"Why don't you saddle up your big words, Ace, and leave!" I protested, smelling damp body odor. His and mine. Still sitting down, I stiffened my right leg to the aisle although my groin hurt, my persistence strengthened.

He didn't leave. He stood stone still. Slapped his hand to his forehead. Softened his voice. "Just can't believe this!" He fell back. His long legs hung over the edge of his seat into the aisle as he straddled the armrest.

"You bet your boots I'll do it."

"Honestly, I thought you were a beautiful red head I know. You both have the same large, sparkling green eyes."

"You call them green?" They were mostly blue with a tiny hint of green. Maybe all brainiacs were short a few cards from their deck! "So, you twist her arm for fun and games?"

"Let me explain. She's extremely special to me. Surprises me from time to time with extravagant foolery." He reached into his pocket. "She'd book a seat near me. Disguise herself. Coyly pretend not to know me. Go so far as to wear an unwashed wig. Like yours. Act snobbish and rude . . . the same way you did."

He's got the hair right. He'd have to be blind to think I was someone else. "Wig? I scowled.

"You're a few seconds away from understanding." He raised his hip, pulled out a billfold, and rubbed his large thumb back and forth over expensive black cowhide.

"Please, just leave me alone."

"Give me a chance? A few seconds?" He waved a white handkerchief.

"Then, will you leave me alone?" I asked.

"I promise."

"Go ahead. Tell me." I waited for him to say that he saw me and the face of Christ on a tortilla.

"First. Erroneously, you concluded I'm a pervert that abused your privacy. I must legitimatize my unintentional arrogance before a misadventure controls our destiny!" He looked up when the doctor moaned, and he reached over to prop a pillow behind her back. "Secondly. A fresh start before I show you proof of my honesty?" He paused to extend his hand. "Name's J.P. Palagretti . . . Jeep for short."

At last, words I can understand.

"Caitlin O'Shaughnessy." We shook hands cautiously.

"And your girlfriend?"

"Dr. Freida's not a girlfriend," he laughed. "She's a retired physician returning to Butte. Claims she was run out of Butte years ago. I wouldn't want to be the one to knock off that chip on her shoulder. We met in Chicago. She's helping me on an investigation to provide legal documents that could change my life . . . and my wife Orla's."

"You originally from Butte?"

"No."

"Your wife?"

"We've never been to Montana," he said, stroking his chin. "Help me out here, Red . . . I don't want to start up again . . . but would you answer one question?"

"I hate to be called Red."

"I apologize," he tipped his head.

"Your question?"

"Is the heart shaped mole on your neck a tattoo?"

"A birthmark."

He sighed. Held his wallet in his hand as if it were a communion host. He snorkeled his index finger at a small wad of photos, and shook his head in puzzlement. "See, this explains—"

At that moment, Dr. Freida woke up. Clumsily climbed over his legs, snatching his wallet from his lap as she stumbled. Then, she poured into the aisle like spilled Guinness.

"Aye'll bay rate back."

"My wallet?" He was unable to pry it away as he steadied her onto a seat back. "She's really a nice lady once you get to know her."

"Perhaps." I took a breather to glance out the window at Montana's big, blue sky. Light wispy clouds were turning gray as the sun shifted lower. I looked up as Dacsu bristled by.

She cupped her hand over my ear. "Keep your fingers crossed."

What did that mean?

"Do you know what's happening in the cockpit?" Jeep grilled.

"Yes. The plane's off course," I confessed. I'd gone straight from impatience to absolute fear. The longer we were in the air, the less chance we had of getting home. "God's not going to help. Dr. Freida must be smart. You think if we sobered her up . . . she could read maps?"

"Were not lost in these treacherous mountains?" He paled. "Our miracle won't come from a woman pushing ninety."

She returned without his wallet, and fell into her seat. "Ded yeh arder may anoother one?"

He reached up to widen a defective air vent over her. Hurried to the lavatory for his wallet. She fell unconscious before he returned.

"A Catholic, eh?" he commented.

"How'd you know?"

"Public school kids don't blame God for stuff. They blame their parents." He glared at a Rosary around my neck.

I pulled it off. Bent my arm under and slid it to Mildred. "I forgot, I found your Rosary on the floor."

"You find all your papers?" he asked.

"Hope so." I answered. "Are you Catholic?"

"I'm Italian."

"I'm sorry."

"Don't be." A wide grin stretched his square jaw oval. "Our people own the Vatican . . . and it's chief occupant."

Gunner tightened his hand to his mouth to muffle a succession of coughs. He spit in a bottle. Pulled at my blouse. "Geesh-us cripes, girl. Mildred said you're part of the O'Shaughnessy bunch that lived between us and Erin O'Toole?"

"Yes sir."

"Little Missy," he spiked. "You're goin to want to hear this." He moved a toothpick from a back tooth to a hole in his front spacer. "I got somethin important to tell you about the night your house burned!" He coughed. "Yup. Real important."

Chapter Five

For all that happened this day, it seemed later than 3:00 o'clock in the afternoon. "You that shy Bridget's kid?" Gunner asked. Small talk. Butte's way to get things done. Thirty minute lead in. Five seconds to nail the point. It worked.

"Shy as an ostrich. Aunt Rose took care of all the family matters for Hummy."

"Is Hummy a fourth sister?"

"Bridget's my mother. I call her Hummy."

"No respect for parents from you young ones." He stared at my chin. A coughing spell. Recovery. Water. "Mil . . . where was I?" She scratched her head.

I twisted uncomfortably. Impatiently. But, he deserved my respect. He served in the war. After that, he dug up the red metal of antiquity—copper—within a maze of horrid tunnels in the recesses of the earth.

"Bridget," I answered. "We were talking about the old neighborhood where she adopted me at six months old. Strange how people say I'm a spitting image of Aunt Rose. Ridiculous. She's not even my real aunt."

Her name started a war.

"That loathsome schemer! Vulgar grandstander," he charged. He rubbed a tattoo on his arm, where a WWII airplane would move when he flexed his muscles. The infamous *Enola Gay.* Inactivity had softened his muscles. The bomber seemed to ripple on water when he scratched. "I'd be ashamed to call her a real relative, too."

"Why would you attack my family?" My voice edged in defense. No one criticizes them, but me.

Out comes his down and dirty, rough miner language.

Why was there a special language among men? Talk mean. Howl louder than anyone in the area. Hunker to the ape man stance. The lower the hunker, the more contaminated the sound would appear. Gunner's voice had faded due to Miner's Con. All he could do effectively, was to swear weakly, and bend from the waist. Cough hard, and spit.

"Gunner, I'm very sorry to upset you." He was old, quasi helpless. I toned down. "Aunt Rose was—"

"Rose O'Shaughnessy . . . that miserable, no good dame stole my house. My property. She should be put to sleep!" He stared blankly at the ceiling. He was somewhere back in the war during August, 1945, readying to pummel Hiroshima, Japan and wishing to drop the first atomic explosive device ever detonated in the world—on my aunt.

Mildred squeezed his hand. Her voice cracked. "Calm down, sweetheart. Be kinder about Rose. She just likes to live loud. It's not this sweet child's concern. It's between you and Rose." She helped him to the lavatory.

"Ugh!" I turned to Jeep while I waited. "Gunner's sitting on some information about my house fire. He wouldn't bring it up unless it was hot."

"Soon as you're done, Caitlin. Urgent to converse with you," he replied with a chuckle.

The couple came back as I was running my fingers through wild hair. Tossed like a salad. Fizzing upward from static I collected rummaging beneath the seat. "She does look like Rose. 'Cept Rose's one pain in the a—"

"Stop that," Mildred ordered. "It's old business. You keep quiet. Your heart needs a rest."

Ethnic superstitions coursed rampant in Butte. Bad luck if a woman wore the pants in the family. The math added up. Aunt Rose, intelligent and innovative, was denied admittance to the Montana School of Mines. Estrogen oozed from her soul. She found other ways to support the five O'Shaughnessys. Hummy, Aunt Nell, Mike, and me. She was the first woman to work underground in the mines.

Then, black-listed by a Labor Union that wouldn't allow her to join.

Mildred slid forward. "Caitlin, child . . . we know Rose took care of your family after your Uncle Tim died. Gunner and me went to his funeral. We helped the three sister's bury their twin brothers, Shamus and Sean."

History. I leaned back. This was now. How to resume my thirty minutes with Gunner? "Aunt Rose took good care of us."

"Yeah . . . and everybody else." He snorted microscopic filaments of copper poison into his kerchief. "I hate that broad."

"Gunner, you know something about the fire that burned my house down?"

"Huh? Oh, yeah. Early mornin after the 4th. Walkin my dog by your small place."

"Yes?"

"A flamin inferno," he laid bare. "Went up in smoke minutes after I first saw it start."

"You saw it start up?"

"Sure did, little lady."

What's he leading up to? "Gunner, did you turn in the alarm?"

"Nope," he continued. "And I know for certain that woman didn't pull it either. She was runnin pretty fast."

"Woman?"

"Dak ever question her?"

"What woman?" My face shocked purple. It'd been four years since the fire and this was the first I heard of a witness. "You see who she was?"

"Don't get all riled," he choked. "No dame's smart enough to be Butte's serial arsonist. Most likely she was a hooker. It was 3:00 in the mornin . . . she was high tailin it away. Likely sneakin out of some married guy's bedroom near your place."

Butte's a small community hidden far from mainstream America where everyone knows your name, has a clear picture of your history, and knows your business better than you do. It's a cinch he knew exactly who that woman was.

"Gunner," I smarted. "You're telling me this because you do know the woman! You suspect she did—"

"Caitlin . . . go down memory lane later," Dacsu chided, summoning me to bandage her arm.

Chapter Six

Dacsu acted less confident. She stowed a medical kit. An odd twitch in her stern face confirmed. I'd seen her before. Where? "Poor Patrick's going to feel terrible for what he did to me . . . and to the plane," she told me.

"His condition?"

"Unconscious," she reported. "It's getting near evening. Do you pray?" She bolted her head to Jeep, and gritted her teeth.

"I do now." One pilot. Treacherous mountains. Damaged mechanisms. No navigation help. "Ouch! Ouchie!" A piece of broken glass prickled my toe. I limped to my seat.

"Caitlin," Jeep said, kneeling beside me. He handed me an envelope. "Found this under my seat. Yours?"

"Thank you."

"The writing on top is some kind of ugly."

"It's German. Says, Confidential."

"By your expression, the document appears to be disputatious and controvertible."

"Where I come from, we speak English."

"Is it one helluva piece of data?"

"The answer to a longstanding mystery in Butte. Over forty years." Private O'Toole was Gunner's good friend. After I get things sorted out with Hummy. Apologize. Gravel. He'll be the first person I tell, that Erin was no longer missing in action. I squeezed the envelope. "Another of God's injustices."

"Hmm?" His wallet in hand. "Are you on a business trip?"

"Forensic Handwriting Scientist."

"You teach people how to write?"

"Measure handwriting for legal evidence. Analyze behavior."

"Inexplicably interesting proclivity." An expression of Tom Foolery veiled his face.

"Our communication isn't going very—"

"Why not just throw a buck in a machine like at the County Fair?" He wrote his name in the air with his finger.

"The Fair only comes around once a year. I'm available twenty-four, seven." I wrote my name in the air with my nose.

A mischievous gleam, twinkling in his eye, gave him away.

"Jeep, you're putting me on."

"You're too serious, Caitlin. Faith. We'll land safely." His after shave lotion smelled manly. I hoped it lingered. There's something comforting to think a man's around to help during a crisis. Even one dressed in a Boardroom suit, lacquered hair, and a dictionary tongue.

"My friends say that, too." I was unaware of my sullen mood. Laugh? How long has it been? Releasing endorphins all at once might kill me. "You know about handwriting science?"

"Our law firm hires such experts for forgery cases. And other matters. To disrupt white-collar crime syndicates." He shifted his knee.

Hmm. A lawyer. Butte has too many now. We could use a another doctor. More specifically, a cardiac surgeon to replace Megan Pat the Terrible. "You have something to show me?"

He immediately opened his wallet. "Small talk. Then specifics," he said. A smart lawyer. Maybe we do need him. "This will explain everything. You must see for yourself tha—"

Right at his point of revelation, hiding like a sniper in a hollow spot, Murphy's gloomy law swept into our lives, and seized control of the airplane. Jeep barely buckled me in, before a swift change of motion forced him to grip the seatback.

Engines gunned. A tumultuous sound split my ears. Hurt my head. Cabin lights flickered. Again, the ears popped. Bled. 10,000 leprechauns pounded on the inside of my head. Being hit with Ireland's Burren rock, would have been softer.

Mildred screamed. "Ooh. Help!" Gunner's neck tightened. He coughed up blood. Choked on his own phlegm.

Dacsu disappeared. An overwhelming pressure thrust my head upward. My back stiffened. A forceful shaking leveled Jeep's show and tell to the floor. He straddled in the aisle.

Dr. Freida slumped.

I braced myself to meet destiny. I needed forgiveness. Not from Hummy. From God. I was more afraid of losing my soul, than of losing my life. I prayed.

"Jesus, Mary, and Joseph! Envelope!"

"Jesus, Mary, and Joseph! Envelope!"

"Jesus, Mary, and Joseph! Envelope!"

Chapter *Seven*

"This is Bert Mooney Airport . . . Flight 411 . . . do you copy? What's your position? Repeat . . . your position? Bert Mooney—"

Jake's capable voice broke into a dejected rattle.

A married man of fifty, slim waistline, affable smile, qualified to work all the jobs in the control area, had been on the job from sunrise, covering for Hambone who called in sick.

The air, clear and crisp. No reports of bad weather in the region. The kind of late afternoon he'd take his two sons fishing behind the Nine Mile after work.

Today was different.

Flight 411 was already two hours late, and communication with the craft ceased over an hour ago.

It ended with a *May Day* distress call.

The bartender from down the hall came in to help out.

Bill, a portly fellow, stocky in a Mel Gibson sort of way, usually scoffed at Jake for jogging five miles a day. "You want me to man the phones while you run a few laps?"

"I keep praying I'll pick them up on the radar screen, any minute now," he responded.

Bill jiggled a large silver, empty coffee pot, beneath a sink faucet in the corner, and set it on a table. He yanked up his Wrangler jeans and whacked the side of Jake's control table with a size fourteen foot, and a helping attitude. "Works on our TV."

"I wish the problem was with our equipment." Jake's breathing slowed. He tried to ignore a small switchboard lit up like the Fourth of July. Mounted with little squares that kept flashing with unanswered inquiries about Flight 411. "Why can't those callers stop peppering my conscience?"

He watched Bill load a card table with candy snacks, potato chips and hard boiled eggs. "Too many people!" Bill said, looking out a window from the second story.

A private phone rang as Jake plugged in the old coffee pot, that leaked as it brewed. He shuddered. Smoothed his bald head, and picked up the phone. "Yes, it's true. It's running late. Where'd you hear about it? How'd you get this number? Stay off the line."

"Whew! Here comes the law," Bill announced, spinning to the door, and leaving the room.

Dak stormed in, his husky voice rang out. "Don't tell me the whole town knows already?"

"Give the Sheriff some room," a deputy ordered, motioning a large number of people to step aside. And, to move their vehicles, stacked bumper to bumper in the airport parking lot.

"Judging by the growing crowd, we're going to need assistance from Anaconda," a newspaper reporter decided.

He took copious notes from people that didn't know a thing about Flight 411. "Human interest."

Dak elbowed his way through a packed waiting area, catching the edge of his uniform sleeve on a door knob. He untangled. Rushed over to Jake's desk to seize the microphone. "Hand me that speaker," he mandated, his clean shaven face tightly drawn.

"Yes Sir," Jake responded and stepped aside.

In a resounding voice, he probed for signs of communication. "Mary . . . Dak here! We're not receiving you by audio. If you hear me, we're on Red Alert. We're asking every port of flight from here to Mars, to help guide you here . . . you know what to look for!"

"God! This can't be happening!" Jake gulped. He controlled his eating habits better than he controlled his fear of a plane going down on his watch, for a second time.

"What's been done?" Dak asked him, wiping his brow. His concern for the plane's safety went far beyond duty.

"I sent out an air-net over a five-hundred mile radius," Jake answered, his tired face grim with worry. "Checked our equipment. It's tip-top." He sat on the edge of a swivel chair with wheels attached to the bottom, and rocked back and forth.

"Jake, things will work out." Dak rested his hand firmly on his friend's shoulder, and looked up at the sky. "This isn't your fault."

"You think I should do something else?"

"Keep calm."

"Heard LB's up there?"

"He's transporting a prisoner," Dak said.

By now, more people filed into the control room without permission.

Dak swaggered his medium build to a window. He was better proportioned and more healthy than men half the age of his mid-forties. "Clear the room. Except for personnel." He wiped his brow. "This job's for a younger man."

Until recently, his work had been his life. Caitlin was a major part of that life. Now, he talked about retiring. Financially he couldn't. He stared at a childhood scar on his wrist. A scar the same as Zoonawme and Caitlin had. They were blood siblings.

"You heard from Zoonawme yet?" he asked Jake, shaking his head no.

Ten minutes later, Bill returned carrying Cracker Jacks and diet Cola from a counter near where an ambulance dropped off Megan Pat. "Chief of Staff's coming. Maybe the hospital heard something?"

"Let's hope so." Jake turned his head to the floor momentarily, to stop his heart from fluttering out of his chest.

"Hope?" Dak gripped the speaker so tight his knuckles whitened. He remembered countless times he rode shotgun for Mary in the military. She flew *Hail Mary* missions under fire. Better than any other flyer that rescued injured soldiers in the jungle. "She piloted helicopters patched with glue, pasted together with duct tape, and four-inch bolts. In the darkness of night, without lights," he told Jake. "Through thick fog and heavy rain. Brushing tree tops brimming with unfriendly snipers shooting hot lead to disable the rotary blades. She'll bring her in."

"I might have heard a crackle." Jake's eyes widened. He snapped off his headphones. "Just a crackle."

"Give me those," Dak muscled. He listened with one ear. "Mary! Give me a Roger, Dammit!" He handed the receiver away, adjusted his revolver holstered on his hip, his favorite Smith and Wesson, model 19. No one else on his force carried a .357 magnum. He wanted to keep it that way.

Megan Pat, an icon of heart surgery skill, and lifesaving abilities, jogged around the far corner of the airport, sweating expensive perfume. She ran inside the building wearing a size six, turquoise blue pant suit, softly draped over tiny hips.

"Any news?" she asked.

"No word from the plane since the *May Day* distress call . . . well over an hour ago," Jake reported, powerless. "They're two hours late for arrival." He hung his head.

Megan Pat was as much an anomaly in Butte, as her breathtaking beauty. A deviation from the rule. More successful and wealthy than every male in the city. Her ticket to the Old Boy's Network, was being a miracle worker. Successfully infusing new life to worn out hearts.

Bill, Jake, and other men prowling the control room, stood by, ogling the goddess. A female deity with a 38" bust, 36" hips, and a slender 26" waist, a man could wrap his hand around.

"Dak, I heard you call her Mary?" she quizzed. "You know the pilot?"

"Highly decorated. Military helicopter pilot." He dropped three red colored sugar cubes in his coffee.

"Number of passengers?" Her nose twitched.

"Twenty seven aboard." He scrolled through an inventory sheet. "LB's up there bringing back Slippery McDoon."

"There's one screw ball prisoner that flew your coop," she remarked, wishing she hadn't. Instinct told her to back off. Not to say what she was really thinking. Or, that she had a connection to him. *If that loony hadn't escaped from the jail, he'd be safe behind bars instead of saying his last prayers, she told herself.*

Dak was distracted by Jake. "Megan Pat, what did you say?" By far, she was the most beautiful woman he'd ever seen, yet he wasn't romantically drawn to her. He poured her a cup of coffee. "Sorry. You were saying?"

She tossed her blonde, shoulder length hair from her face, looking more like a New York model than a small town resident. "My team's lining up in front of the terminal." Irritated at his disinterest in her, she pushed the coffee aside. "I use real sugar, not cubes shot up with red dye by an employee with too much time on his hands."

Dak pressed his nose to the window.

The weather was cooling down after a hot day. Steam from his brew fogged the window glass. June 13. Summer officially hadn't arrived. When the sun started to set in the mountains, chilly weather took hold. He fingered a big "C" through the vapors. His mind was on the plane and the passengers.

"Dak?" She poked him. "Have you formulated a plan?"

"Caitlin's on that plane," he answered.

She lowered her violet eyes, that'd loved Dak Sullivan since she was in the 5th grade. She prayed her enemy would die on the plane. "Didn't know she was out of town."

"It was in the paper?" he commented. "She's been gone too long. Working her butt off in Berlin for the past three months."

"Must have skimmed past that article," she said, turning green with jealousy. "With fishing and camping season open—broken limbs, burns from campfires, knife wounds from fish-gutting, two gun accidents, and, five heart attacks over the past few weeks—I've been swamped at work." She had the voice of an angel and the soul of a devil when it came to Caitlin.

She stepped back to make way for Zoonawme who came rushing in quietly. Like a soft wind. "Any updates?" he asked with a baritone voice. "Dak, did your deputies inform you of a traffic jam on Airport Road?"

"None . . . and no," Dak answered.

"I brought Caitlin's family with me. They're in the bar." He adjusted a dinner-plate, silver buckle, askew over blue jeans, that stretched comfortably around 230 pounds of three-dimensional muscle. "You know how worried our three women can get."

"Hey, Compadre," Jake hailed the Blackfoot Indian. He was glad he came. He laid a microphone down and held out his hand. "Long time, no see."

Nothing about Zoonawme, except his lucky belt buckle, was pretentious. They shook hands. "How're your boys?"

The private phone rang. "I copy that," the sheriff frowned at the caller. "Keep this line open! Next time, call me on my cell." He cradled the receiver.

"News?" Zoonawme hid his fearful emotions. He didn't want to go through another airline disaster. "What kind of news?"

"False alarm," Dak said, staring at a clock and scratching his head. "Dead end."

"Any news from your network, Megan Pat?" Zoonawme figured she had connections all the way to the White House. "You've got excellent contacts."

"I have no idea what will be coming to my hospital," she said somberly to Caitlin's protector. She garnered as much use for an Indian, that throttled her within an inch of her life in grade school, as she did for a poisonous rattle snake. "I'm prepared for whatever comes."

"Our Caitlin's up—"

"As you've said, Zoonawme, our dear Caitlin has nine lives," she interrupted. She wore expensive shoes, and a bizarre hatred for Caitlin beneath her smooth outward behavior. A fact that Zoonawme and Dak knew all too well. "She'll be just fine."

Dak paced the room. "I'm counting on Mary to bring the plane in safely. She's one helluva brave pilot."

"You must be very close to this woman? She important to you?" Her stomach churned hearing him compliment another woman. He never gave her a compliment. She hid her resentment, and crowded Dak's space. "Of course, she'll get the job done."

Fifteen minutes passed. Zoonawme flipped his long, black pony tail off his neck, and broke the awkward silence. "Captain O'Donovan tell you what's in the package she's bringing to you?

"We didn't spend much time on the phone."

"Somebody explain to me," Megan Pat said. "Weather's clear. No clouds. No Bermuda Triangle near the vicinity. An experienced pilot like Dak's friend should be able to find a landing strip, even without radio contact."

"That'd be plan A," Dak replied.

"Of course," she agreed, sharpening her cynical knife. She'd slice a piece of Zoonawme's feelings in a clever way that appeared naïve. "I recall those horror stories. Over there on the east mountain in front of us. While I was away at school, a plane went down. Crashed. Killed everyone on board. Last thing we need is a repeat tragedy."

Just then, Bill came in carrying cookies his wife made. They smelled like Grandma's freshly baked chocolate chips. He hurled them on the table. Nudged MP sharply on the arm as she started towards the window. He pointed silently to Zoonawme.

"What?" she shrugged. Annoyed. "What is it?"

Bill put his finger to his mouth. "You forget, Dr. Megan Pat?" He squeezed her arm. "Did you forget . . . or what?"

"Oh, no!" she feigned in surprise. She covered her lips with her hand. Turned abruptly to Zoonawme. "I'm so very sorry. What was I thinking? You lost your wife, Zakhooa, in that crash!"

Jake took exception, and scowled at her. He'd been on duty the night Zoonawme's wife died in that crash. He did all he could to make way for a safe landing, and failed. His voice crackled. "I don't know if I could live with myself if another crash occurred."

Zoonawme kept silent. In control. Of course, the mention of the love of his life hurt him deeply. He knew Megan Pat for what she was. Her back stabbing would never penetrate his resolve.

Suddenly, a newspaper reporter flipped his head to the sound of a radio playing music. He called out to the others. "Hey . . . catch this!"

He was listening to a disc jockey spin Englebert Humperdink's 1988 hit tune, *Embraceable You*, when the broadcast cut short for a news report.

"Listen up!" He turned it up louder to hear Butte's favorite local announcer, Sticker Noon, charged with excitement.

"Flight 411 has just been sighted southeast of Butte."

The room filled with both tension, and apprehension.

"Here's our next step," Dak commanded, tapping his pencil on the desk. He firmed up Plan A with a deputy over the phone. "Clear all non-personnel people from the building immediately."

One of his deputies was to stick like glue to Jake and report minute by minute to a central command post in the lobby.

The rest were to keep the area clear. Disburse every car and unauthorized vehicle lined up on Airport Road. Make sure fire trucks and emergency equipment were in position. Direct traffic. Keep pets, especially kids, away from the area.

"You want us to assemble folks waiting to greet the plane? Put them in a holding tank—the bar on the second floor of the building?" a deputy interrupted.

"Good idea. And, just as we practiced for crises, prepare to assist Dr. Megan Pat to deplane passengers." He reminded his people of plan B, the worst of all plans.

A rescue, without rehearsal.

He walked down the hall behind Jake, making his way to the restroom to throw up. He caught a glimpse of Bill behind the bar, mumbling while he set up bottles of beer and booze on the counter. "At a time like this . . . let them pour their own drinks!"

Zoonawme didn't need instructions. He'd be attached to Dak's hip. They rushed to a viewing stand. Cranked their heads toward the sky. Waited to sight the plane.

Dak elbowed Megan Pat. "Order your people away from the field until the landing is completed. Situation could get dicey."

She rolled up her sleeves and made a phone call.

You could smell uptightness in the air, as two volunteer fire departments stationed their rigs east of the runway, and waited for orders. Dak was pleased that cars parked along the highway, to view the landing, were chased away.

Zoonawme prayed to his Indian gods. Dak didn't believe in God. He trusted the human element, and environment, to run a safe course.

They waited.

Chapter Eight

"Oh, God, help us!" The plane lunged through dead air space at merciless speed, threatening me, and 26 others with death. Like Star Trek Voyager, Flight 411 had been snared into the eye of turbulence. Pocketed in a gigantic black pouch of nothing in Montana's big sky, without a safety net.

A sudden drop at blinding speed stung my stomach like a lightening rod. My heart stampeded through my mouth. I reached out for Jeep, stranded in the aisle, fending for himself. His strong hands vigorously digging into a seatback. His terrified eyes met mine. In one abominable second, acceptance of doom mirrored each other's face.

"Please, God! I want to live!" I cursed myself for leaving my faith. We kept going downward, yet, stayed horizontal at the same time. Descending like a lead pancake—dropping flat—thousands of feet to God knows where. Shrill, obscure voices cracked with fright, begged for mercy. I begged for life.

"This mother . . . "

"You son of . . . "

"Sweet Jesus . . . "

I cursed Murphy. Gunner cursed the pilot. For an older, delicate woman—pinched rigid against her husband's side—Mildred's yell for help could shatter glass.

"I won't let anything happen to you!" he promised, pulling off his air hose. He smothered her gray head to his chest to muffle her fear. Suddenly he raised both hands to swat off a glass plate that spiraled to the ceiling. "Incoming shrapnel!" he warned weakly, and coughed.

Unanchored items zipped past me. I crouched as low as the seatbelt would allow. Jeep's wallet, two snapshots, and my favorite pen—a cheap, plastic freebee from the bank—were plastered on the ceiling.

"Jeep! Take hold of my arm." A powerful energy pinned me to one spot. All I could clutch was his shirtsleeve. He loosened his firm grip. His body started to rise. Whatever wasn't bolted down was being towed to the roof.

The faster we dropped, the more pull from above.

"Caitlin! . . . the doctor . . . " Barely hanging on, he nodded her way. Even if I could move, his contorted frame blocked my sight. All I could do was to face front, where I saw Dacsu crouched near the garment cabinet. Tackling my lead-heavy, suit bag, hanging on the inside of the closet. Like a line backer increasing pressure on a practice dummy, she draped her legs around the bag and squeezed tight.

An oxygen mask covered her face.

"Do it now, LB!" Slippery's raspy voice fog-horned at his captor. He wrestled helplessly to free himself from handcuffs.

"Old buddy," LB wailed. "I can't move around in my seat. Key is my pants." He bit down. His lips bled like his kind heart. "I'm so sorry!"

Amazingly, at a time of peril, tough guy Slippery McDoon, grinned the wicked grin of a felon. He'd been on the wrong side of the law the better part of his life. He lied to the cops all the time. But, never to his good friend, LB.

"Don't matter, Lard Butt," he strained. "I'm more of a stupid, bumbling fool, than you are a fat, over weight, lard ax! You're the best damn tracker in the business. It was stupid to break out from Butte's penal system." Their voices faded.

"Oh, my God!" I shrieked. "Help!" My seatbelt tightened like a wet rawhide strap, drying quickly under a hot, summer sun. Squeezing my nauseous insides, from a Missy size, extra-large, to a high school thin. At the same time, Jeep's silk shirt tore from my grip. In a single wink, his lanky legs buckled like broken matchsticks.

Was I dreaming? A merciless magnum force grappled him from the aisle, propelled his strong, muscular frame to the ceiling as if he weighed five pounds. He went up, as the plane plummeted towards majestic rocky mountain peaks, that towered over my treasured home state. I was powerless to help.

In the shadows of late afternoon terror, I spied Dr. Freida's 90 pounds buckled tightly to the inside seat. Two pillows strapped to her lap. Pickled in alcohol, her senses were turned off. She had no way of knowing that Jeep was out of his seat and beached on the ceiling above the aisle, battling for his life.

Freaky. My jaws chattered involuntarily. Uncontrollable. Hitting my chest and rising, as the seat reverberated like a cheap bed at the Mile High Motel. More terror followed.

The upward suction that siphoned Jeep, came after me. Trying to scoop me up and paste me on the dome.

"Oh, please God! . . . Blessed Mother?" I clattered. I was a helpless human starring in a Steven King psycho flick, and calling out to God after a couple of decades of turning my back on Him.

"Forgive me my sins!"

"Jesus, Mary, and Joseph. Envelope!"

"Jesus, Ma—"

I experienced gravity that failed. Both my feet rose two feet off the floor, without my help. Same with my arms—involuntarily pitched straight up, suspended in air like two stiff goal posts.

Outside, daylight prevailed, but darkness swept over the cabin. Through dim chaos and a buzzing head, I glanced at pint size emergency lights bordering a floor that no one could get to. Overhead bins exploded off their hinges, and the doors flew upward. Luggage popped out. As did jackets, a backpack, suit case, and a carefully wrapped, special package holding hundred-twenty-proof whiskey I bought under the table in Germany, for my Aunt Rose.

A drop down lifesaver directly above me, burst out of its holder. Instead of nudging my face as it automatically released, the yellow turncoat, designed to give me air, came out of its compartment, and flew straight up, next to my paralyzed arms.

A trapeze artist couldn't reach the oxygen mask.

My time was running out.

I had no bargaining chips to make a deal with God.

I felt ashamed, blaming Him for passing me by, when the good-feely stuff of love and companionship were handed out. Ashamed of my actions toward Hummy.

The second I accepted, that I had nothing to give Him as penance in return for my salvation, my thinking waned. Breathing slowed from a fast beat to a drowsy crawl.

All my concerns, and aches, miraculously disappeared, as I surrendered my soul to God. I felt pleasantly lightheaded and peaceful. Unfettered by anxiety and desperation.

To my surprise, the deal was sealed when a hard object wielded a solid hit to my shoulder—swishing air from my lungs like a stepped on milk carton.

I felt no pain, as I was piloted to an unconscious black void, with no way to swim out.

It didn't matter.

I had absolutely no desire to leave.

Chapter Nine

"Caitlin . . . O'Shaughnessy, kid! You hear me?" Gunner's voice shouted over and over. "Answer me!"

My eyes were crusted together with dried tears. I pried them open. "Did we crash?" My voice bounced to myself. I fumbled to wrench an oxygen mask off my face. Fanned with a magazine. A fake breeze might stop my cranial nerves from pounding my head when I spoke.

"Air turbulence!" Gunner reported, coughing through a nasty smell of jet fumes that fouled the air like spoiled cabbage. "Pilots in these parts understand how to fly over Rockies laced with air disturbances. That pip squeak woman . . ." He caught himself. "The broad flyin this junker wasn't so bad after all."

Mildred shoved a damp cloth over the armrest, and pointed at a trail of blood trickling down my cheek.

"Wait. How can . . . hmm . . . last thing I remembered was dropping down to China." I wiped metallic tasting saliva from my chin with the back of my hand. "We were descending at blinding speed—"

"You got whacked by one mother hay-maker." He blew his nose. "A laptop thingamajig—knocked you unconscious. You blacked out before we hit a brick floor."

"Whut? Why did we drop? Why didn't we crash?"

"Air pocket disturbs a natural flight of a plane. One of them zingers . . . um . . . air pockets . . . lassoed us . . . locked us in place, then dropped our as—"

"You promised not to swear," Mildred said, looking over the top of her glasses to calm him down. "You're getting too worked up. Tell the child what happened without sugar coating facts."

"Yes, Mil," he winked, scratching his bald head. "Hold the sugar, dish out facts." He coughed. Looked down near his feet for a missing spit bottle, and dribbled spittle into a hanky. He had a slight snap to his voice, and lighter shoulders. He understood, more than anyone, that we escaped the dangers of turbulence. "That stewardess over there," he pointed to Dacsu's assistant. "Said we hurled toward ground for thirteen seconds."

"Thirteen seconds?" Am I Rip Van Winkle. "Surely the disaster lasted an hour? My entire life flashed before me."

"The dame at the controls handled the sticks like a man," he added. "We were goin down. She jolted this bucket of bolts to fly, like it was a javelin. Felt like we hit a brick floor. Then bounced into a flight pattern."

I adjusted my eyes to the light. Looked over at Jeep's empty seat. Frail Dr. Freida lay stone-still, carefully propped beside a window. Harnessed beneath rumpled blankets and small pillows. Covering all but her vulgar, snoring mouth.

"She's out colder than an ice block," Gunner hissed, tipping the brim of his baseball hat to salute her.

My shoulder throbbed reaching over Murphy's seat. I raised the shade to see that a blue sky had faded to a hazy, light gray. "Late afternoon," I said. "Long overdo for a landing. My family would be worried." I wet my lips. "You folks hurt any?"

"Mil's got a cut on her arm. I got sore muscles," he grinned. His teeth were white. Not yellow like some seniors. He seemed playful. "And . . . a bad cough."

I couldn't see Dacsu or Jeep. Out comes the neck stretch to find them, and survey the damage. "What happened here?"

All around us loomed the aftermath of a free-for-all on a Saturday night at Marty's Bar and Bowl.

Like the morning after a wild barroom brawl—the place was wrecked and not one person was left standing.

"Real bad," Mildred said.

I peered through dim folds of an ugly curtain—hideously bright red, and fluorescent yellow fabric, like a bridesmaid would be forced to wear. Deputy LB, a reformed goof-off, stood in the back holding a Rosary. His serious head lowered. Shoulders slumped.

Slippery sat like a statue, without cuffs, his head slightly tilted. Peg leg bolstered on a pillow. I hadn't seen him or his twin brother since a week before my house burned down. I was on a handwriting case in Helena the night they tried to rob my place. Sheriff Dak showed up, shots were fired. The heist was foiled. Slippery went to the hospital for leg amputation, and Sledge was trotted to jail.

During five years attending Boy's Catholic High School, LB and his twin brother, were close buddies with the Antichrist twins, the McDoon goons.

Their pranks were legendary. Their spiteful mischief, and lack of good sense, caused three holy men—teaching Brothers, dedicated to proper attire and dignity—to shave their heads.

However, LB turned to his faith when his brother died. He now wears religion proudly on his sleeve. I started for the back when Dacsu yelled out. “Caitlin, wait!”

She was two rows away stacking a pile of cracked bin doors in an empty seat. I twisted over rumpled clothing and men’s shoes. Saw my St. Christopher medallion hooked on a broken hinge above her. I swear the medal winked at me.

“Where’s Jeep?” I lipped, piling clothes on a seat. I looked down at my open briefcase. My green silk thong looked back at me, trumpeting I’d been in an accident, and that I could definitely use clean underwear. No argument from me.

Except, real people don’t wear sexy thongs. They hang them on a bedpost and recite a mantra of discontent.

“Follow me,” she insisted, whisking away bits of debris from her blonde hair as she tilled forward.

“Water?” I asked.

“Most of the bottles exploded from pressure.” She handed me a half full bottle of spring water from a pocket in her apron. I choked it down. We reached the galley where Jeep lay motionless in a puddle of warm, red blood. His tall body tightly wedged low in the center of her mangled kitchen. His face up. Eyes swollen shut.

“No movement since I drug him here.” She tooled her way around his crumpled legs. Passed me a bottle of beer to douse my raspy throat, and moved aside. I slithered down. My legs stuck to spilled whiskey, beer, Vodka, coffee, and unspecified sauces running wild, as I squatted on the floor. I felt his neck for a pulse. I was never good at finding one—even on myself.

“Is he? You know . . . is—”

"He's not dead." She ran her hand over his hot, sweaty forehead, then edged away. "Hasn't spoken or moved. Do what you can." She touched me softly on the shoulder. Walked off.

The air was thick with heat. I wanted to take all my clothes off. "Jeep! Wake up! . . . speak to me!" I held his head tenderly in my lap. Dripped a few sips of beer down his dry throat. Screamed loudly. "You stay with us, Mr. Palagretti, you hear?"

I startled him to consciousness. "Ooooh," he moaned. He instantly knew he wasn't in a good place. His eyes twitched. He gradually pursed his lips. "Where…" his voice faded.

I felt his neck and chest for broken bones—as if I knew what I was doing. "Stay with me," I said, hearing him mumble. Did he say, "Orla, Honey?" I stroked his chest. "Jeep. It's Caitlin. We've been in an accident."

He tried to get up. "One helluva of an interval to dower me a feel." Audible enough to understand. His eyes opened wider. "What transpired, Orla?" He gazed at my face and saw his wife.

"Save your interrogation for a courtroom," I told him. "I talk, you listen." In a micro-second the lids of his eyes grew heavy. He fell unconscious. Didn't hear the bleat of the Captains bell.

"Ladies and gentlemen . . . Bert Mooney airport is preparing for our arrival. About forty minutes," she announced. "For your safety, stay belted, and no smoking please!"

I heard clapping. Dacsu stepped out of the cockpit. Hovered silently over the two of us. We exchanged glances.

"It's a miracle the captain got her engineering stuff up there to work," I said.

"All the equipment is not functioning," she brought to light.

"Meaning?"

"No contact. Our trust is in divine intervention."

Why does everyone speak in riddles?

Ten minutes later, a voice rang out. "What's that below?" A passenger that sat in the middle of Coach section, adjusted his horn rimmed glasses, and peered through powerful, thick binocular lens. A rare combo making it possible to see whiskers on a deer from up here.

"Pipestone Pass? Silver Star?" Someone else saw it too.

Optimism showed its face. I walked a gamut of broken glass, mixed with a wild concoction of putrid food, and funky liquids, to reach a window. If he saw Pipestone Hot Springs nestled on a back road in the mountains, a broken-down, most unpopulated area in the world, that my family took me to as a child, we were definitely on a trajectory that led to Butte.

Without Superman vision, I imagined the peewee complex. A dilapidated, old wooden tavern next to a run down, three table restaurant, and a small house. Tucked in a remote mountain area and built next to a covered swimming pool. Where the three O'Shaughnessy women drowned in a bottle of Jack Daniel's, a six-pack of beer as a chaser. Telling stories of Ireland while waiting for me, their ten-year-old, to tread water in a pool of steaming, natural hot springs.

"Jeep." I squeezed his hand. The soft hand of an educated man. He tried to lift his head. I patted him to be still. "We're on course to Butte."

"Orla . . . ." he moaned. "Cigarettes . . . in my pocket." He hung onto his clever humor. "A blindfold, too."

"Die? No!" I snared cigs and a lighter from his shirt. I quit smoking the day I was left standing at the altar. I puffed a couple, and placed the gray and white poison in his mouth. The taste of tobacco was like kissing a lover from my past.

Too weak to smoke, the cigarette ladled from the side of his mouth. "Dr. Freida . . ." He was disoriented when he looked me in the eye. "Ah. Yes. I met you in law school. You're Caitlin."

"Unless you went to Montana State University, or the Forensic Academy of Handwriting Science in Washington, D.C., we never met in school." I shook a Charley Horse out of my leg, and folded over a stained blanket.

"Ohhh . . ." he whispered, as I covered him. "You operate a crooked machine at the County Fair—"

Mildred was cautiously working her way to the lavatory and offered to help. She pulled her shawl higher over her chubby neck. "Why'd you broadcast to the newspaper about what my cousin did? Were you mad at her too?"

"I was mad at God, and took it out on people," I defended. "I know I'm wrong. Forgive me for whatever you think I did."

"My cousin's having a hard time looking people in the eye since she finished her prison work-program for the County."

"I don't know your cousin. But, sometimes Butte's gossip grapevine gets things wrong."

"You exposed her for forgery last year."

"You mean that pretty lady that wears flashy, tight clothes, high heel stilts, and heavy makeup? The one that forged Sister Agatha Ann's signature on bum checks for eight hundred dollars, at the Shady Sleep Motel?"

"My cousin's not too bright." She faded into the lavatory. I cornered her when she came out.

"How's Gunner doing?"

"He's doing better than sweet LB, in the back, praying the Rosary."

"Whut'd you mean?"

"See him?" she nodded. "He's standing over that hoodlum, Slippery McGoon."

"McDoon," I corrected. "LB's bringing him back to Sheriff Dak." I cranked my neck. "Gosh. He's been glued to that same spot for a long time."

"He's in shock. Praying . . . over Slippery's McGoon's dead body!"

Chapter Ten

"Flyin over the Divide," Gunner said, peering out a small plastic window on the exit door, and exercising his knees. Like me, he was thinking how the water run-off sloshes over winding paths, passes through grooved trenches, and floats to the oceans. We both loved the splendor of outdoors in Montana.

"The Divide?" Dacsu frowned at a panoramic view of lush, green mountain tops. "A watershed?"

"Twin watersheds on Continental Divide's mountains," I replied, imagining a site coming up, haunted with a bitter image of wreckage. Carnage. Death. "Water sends down both sides to the Pacific and the Gulf of Mexico." I visualized Zakhooa flying over this route. Coming home to her husband, Zoonawme from a Blackfoot Indian Pow-Wow and how the airplane crashed with Butte fully in sight. "We're getting very close to home."

"Our captain's amazing," she sighed. "So far."

"How long you staying in town?" I asked her.

"Got ten days off, a mini vacation."

"Family?"

"No. Meeting your Sheriff."

"Dak?"

"Dak Sullivan's the reason the captain requested I work this flight," she said, trying to tidy her hair.

"Dak?" I repeated.

"He'll be waiting at the airport when we land so we can be introduced. I'm up for the challenge."

Nah! Dak wouldn't. What'd this kid know about challenging a Don Juan that was way too old for her? I asked for a safety pin to fasten the zipper on my polyester slacks. "Dak's been one of my good friends for years."

"I heard he's handsome. What kind of man is he?"

"Hard nosed and stubborn." I stretched my zipper together and bent the safety pin out of shape trying to clasp it shut. "You don't want to get on his bad side."

"He's single, right?" Her wide, violet eyes were shadowed by dark circles under them, but she beamed a smile on her face.

"Married to his job," I affirmed, clamping my teeth over the pin to straighten it. "He's been making headlines as a tough career cop. . . long . . . long, long before you were born. Come to think of it . . . he's been around longer than most of the mining community's landmark buildings—many of them gutted by fire over the years."

"Captain's a long time friend of his. She talks about him like he's a Greek god."

"He's full Irish," I said, remembering Dak's admiration for a female pilot in the Viet Nam skirmish. "He's spoken kindly of her many times. What a coincidence she's the pilot of Flight 411."

"You don't really believe in coincidence?" She wiggled her hips uncomfortably. Wiped sweat from her brow.

"Dacsu . . . why're you acting so nervous?"

"The landing gear's stuck shut, Caitlin. Still, no contact with Butte!" She scooted into the cockpit, just as Jeep's arm quivered. He was unconscious, or in a coma. All I could do was fan his face with a newspaper, and dapple beer on his tongue.

"Please, Jeep, hang on!" Close to the floor, the engine sounded loud. There's a chance he could hear me? "Do you know that Montana's state flower, the Bitterroot, showers mountain perfume on dark evergreen trees?" My own words changed my mood. "Actually, I hate those blossoms. Partly because they choke my throat and close off my breathing. Mostly, 'cause they grow wild next to where Zakhooa's remains are buried."

Dacsu's assistant crouched beside me to help me stand and see the sunlight fading. "Ma'am, do you know what that enormous monument in the distance is?"

"The Blessed Mother. Sitting on top an 8500 foot mountain—shining like a beacon of hope from the east ridge. She's welcoming us home."

"What a wonderful thought," she said. "I heard it would be huge."

Gunner was excited to see it, too. He rallied his breathing from calm to eager. Shoved his oxygen aside, and draped the window with his face. "Mil," he tugged at her sleeve. "Take a gander at the Eighth Wonder of the World. Now, there's one overweight Mama—her fat tonnage planted like a church icon in a 400-ton concrete base."

"Don't see a thing, husband." She shifted her weight.

"Over there, Woman," he churned impatiently. Held a napkin to his nose. "Blind Helen Keller could see it, for cripes sakes. How can you miss a fifty-ton holy shrine?"

"Now, Gunner," Mildred pleaded, lifting her glasses to rest on the top of her head. She tucked a book in the seatback, and scolded him. "Take it easy, old man. I'm gonna need your help with the luggage."

"You can see her from the moon," he went on. "Look over there. That mother soars ninety feet high for Chri—"

I looked down to hear Jeep moan softly. He heard Gunner's voice rattle with mucous and excitement. "Caitlin." He pointed through the wall. "Orla's future and mine revolve around that lady and—" He whimpered to unconsciousness.

"Little lady," Gunner called to me. He pointed to the statue. "Women don't have no muscles, but didn't you volunteer with a million other fools to grind out a passage to the top?"

I rubbed my callused hands together, remembering how I shoveled dirt. Ran big equipment. Handled hard rock. "You're right. I'm a fool. It wasn't a job for a woman. I could kick myself for spending many weekends, plowing a narrow path up the side of that steep, dangerous, and winding grade. At the finish line, my back was in as many pieces as the Lady of the Rockies, that arrived by helicopter in segments."

He was too busy schooling his wife, to hear me. "I've got to get you up there to see that mother." He gave a bad description of a concrete icon molded from our own hometown sculpture's dream. "You're gonna see how it overlooks mountain peaks and low valleys—for a hundred miles to the south and west of Butte."

"You didn't get me to ride up to the second floor at Burr's Department store when they put in the only escalator in Butte. You ain't getting me near that statue—"

Just then Dacsu let out a wild shriek.

"Not now . . . oh . . . God . . . not now!" She flapped her arms. "This can't be happening!"

Every passenger aboard hogged a window to see the statue only inches away. *Inches.* We swooped close enough to reach out and touch her shining robes stitched in eggshell white. So near we saw strips of golden rays coming from Mary's radiant face, blowing a current of air on the plane's tail as we flew by.

Dacsu rushed to the cockpit to see if Patrick woke up and was hindering the captain again.

"That fool dame." Gunner exploded with his *woman thing.*

"Unlike your thick skull," Mildred yelled, her blood sugar count as high as the plane. "Anyone who flies backwards while shooting at the enemy . . ." She slapped her hand over her mouth. "Please, leave the pilot alone, you old fo—"

"Attention passengers," O'Donovan cautioned. "We're flying low. Forced to circle Butte until a ground crew can clear a couple of deer from the runway. Stay belted. We're working on getting the air vents primed. Thank you for your patience, once again."

"Deer don't get within gunshot of the airport," Gunner blustered. "They ain't stupid. Bert Mooney's got a permit to shoot up to ten deer a year if they wander on the property. Most guys in town pack ammo and a rifle on the window of their trucks. Those deer smell trouble. They ain't goin to wander no place in the sights of guns."

Minutes later.

"That's where I live," I pointed to the Big *M.* "Built an A-frame near that huge letter *M.* It's lit up in white blocked letters, cemented on the side of that mountain."

"I studied about the dormant volcano, in college!" Dacsu's interest in Montana history surfaced. "The *M.*" She reeled information in her mind. "Is located high on Big Butte, established by the former Montana School of Mines."

"Volcano?" Mildred's head animated in a succession of no-no's. "Town knows you live next to the 13th letter of the alphabet. Nobody said nothin about a volcano. Why not just live in a cemetery and call it a day?"

"Everyone prepare for landing," Dacsu broke in.

"We O.K. now?" I asked her.

She shook her head to signal me we were still in trouble, and to pray for divine providence to step in, again.

Chapter Eleven

I craned my neck, making sure Mildred got to her seat safely, and saw Deputy LB. His meaty thighs were catching on the seats as he scraped between them to get to me. Why isn't he buckled in, and preparing to land?

"I'm so sorry about Slippery," I said. "I'm assuming you stayed friends?"

"I don't dump my friends," he replied, refitting his sweater and twisting the belt on his pants. "I don't try to change them, either, just because I got religion and went straight!"

"How can I ever make things up to you?" I talked to a deep scar on his forehead.

He was too big to fit in the galley. He peeked in and stared at Jeep. "The whole point of faith is how you treat other people. You make things right with yourself, and God, Caitlin. I'm always going to be your friend." He stretched his neck down. "Is he from Butte? How bad's he hurt?"

"He's from Chicago, and he's hurt bad."

"There's some minor casualties in Coach," he reported. "But, I didn't come here to talk about the plane. I wanted to make sure you were all right. Friends have to stick together."

I felt small. Stupid. Looking into the eyes of a man overflowing with love in his heart. "So terribly sorry. Slip—"

"Nonsense!" he assured, pointing through the ceiling. "Can I help out in anyway?"

"LB," I need to apologize. It'll make me feel better. I suffer guilt about the night the twins tried to rob my house. Faulty basement stair. Slippery snarling his leg. Cracking it almost in half when he tumbled to the bottom."

"The boys had no idea Dak would be house-sitting while you were away. Dak's a good man. A great boss. A friend. He fired that shot because it was his job. Slip lost his balance, because God had a reason for—"

"Why rob me at all? I'm not wealthy. I never liked them. Sure as cow chips in a barn, they didn't like me. If Slippery wasn't in the hospital, and Sledge wasn't in jail when the fire broke out, I'd have blamed them."

He clasped his stocky arms tenderly around my shoulders. Guided me to a window alongside him. "Honestly, they never thought of you at all. I have to tell you something important Slip said about that night."

"Water under the bridge."

"I wish that were true. However, today's water will never wash away for me," he confessed.

"How do you mean that?"

"Why'd he die, and I didn't?" He looked down at the terrain as we circled the city a second time. "I just couldn't free him from the cuffs."

"I have no doubt you did what you thought was right."

"He'd be alive if that were true."

"How could that be?"

"My plenty-plus size prevented me from wriggling keys out of my pants pocket." He hesitated when I looked away. "I was sure I'd be killed when the seat in front of us tore from its hinges, thrust back to crush Slip's neck."

"I'm deeply sorry for your loss." I stapled my eyes to the window. My heart hurt for him. And, I'm no good at dealing with death. "But, I'm extremely grateful you didn't get hurt. Your survival must have happened for a reaso—"

"God, Caitlin," he gasped in horror. "Look down there."

"It appears an enemy bombed the region!"

"Never seen such stuff from the air."

"Me either," I answered, twitching my back.

Sam's best friend wiped his hazel eyes with his sleeve as we flew low. Over a destroyed canyon located three miles east of the city, where a beautiful summer retreat used to thrive.

Out comes the ghost of the Columbia Gardens.

Followed by moans of ire from passengers staring at a nightmarish sight caused by the Anaconda Copper Mining Company.

"How could they annihilate a well maintained landscape, once carpeted with deep feelings of rapture?" one man cried out.

Another said, "The place's blanketed by ugly, deep craters. Hilly mounds of copper-color dirt."

"LB, where was I when they destroyed one of the most important landmarks in our town's history?"

"Wallowing in self-pity," he said warmly. "Pretending that Sam left you at the altar." His round jaw streamed understanding. "It was a bad time for all of us."

I telescoped beyond his weighty face directly into my past.

I wasn't thinking about riding the roller coaster at the Columbia Gardens. Flying high on a by-plane. Straddling my favorite horse on a carousel. Pumping my arms to propel a cowboy swing. Or, eating Licorice ice cream, waiting to go home on a free city bus, at 4:00 p.m. every Thursday during the summers.

"I'm thinking about the Ladies' room at the dance pavilion," I blurted, staring below in wonderment.

"Huh? Ah, come on Caitlin, I don't need to hear this," he said. His faced flushed red. He turned away. The plane was as much of a hot house, as what he was thinking. His shirt stuck to his skin. He pulled at it.

"I'm talking about the Senior prom."

"Oh. Yeah. Well, I never could get a date to a prom."

"The night started out in the Ladies' room just off the dance pavilion," I told him. "I spent as much time primping in a dark, kelp-green room, lined with wooden stalls, and a worn, flowery linoleum floor, as I did dancing. I'd gaze into a full length mirror. My formal . . . skin . . . hair . . . shoes . . . gazed back in a puke-icky, thick green reflection."

His testosterone rose in embarrassment.

"Caitlin—way too personal for me. How can you remember that stuff? That was twenty-five years ago."

His oversized paunch, stubby, hooplike legs, and chipmunk cheeks, masked a man of integrity. Two years younger than me, he knew exactly who he was, and where he was headed in life.

"LB, we're circling the city again." I refuse to burden him about faulty landing gear. Or, loss of communication with Bert Mooney airport. But, he kept talking, as if it'd help soothe his breaking heart.

The more we talked, the more our memories grew.

Like a series of grass fires. We'd stamp out one, only to discover three others popped up.

"The first adult dance of the rest of our lives . . . or, so I thought," I told him. "Me and Sam. Danced the innocence of our eighteen years on a polished wood floor. Swirled under a magical cluster of a large ball, flashing beads of light over a dance pavilion larger than a football field. We were hypnotized by Glen Miller's music."

What I didn't know then, at a time of knowing it all, and of knowing nothing—was that glassy, fake crystal ball, its diamond shaped specks beaming brightly like the Aurora Borealis—bounced light off the balcony into the middle of our inexperience, to hide a dark future from us!

"Let Sam go, Caitlin. You can't change your life by reliving memories."

"Bittersweet memories!" I proclaimed. No matter how different things looked from the air, my memories of Sam were fresh. "Sam proposed to me behind the master gardener's potting shed."

"Disgusting, Caitlin."

"I was thrilled."

"Not that . . . the devastation!" he said. "Sam did tell me how the shrubs, groomed into playful animal shapes, urged you to say yes." A boyish smile. A hint of mischief. "He said, too, that you didn't tell Bridget right away."

"You know how much Hummy hated him . . . my God, LB . . . we can't even mention his name now, or she goes ballistic, and—"

"I need you both to buckle up, now." Dacsu approached us. The east canyon faded behind. Instead of positioning for a landing, the plane continued to circle. Big Butte showed up again. "What? I'll check things out with the captain." She darted to the cockpit.

"How'd you ever buy property there," he asked. "ACM owns every mineral right in the city."

"All, except for Big Butte," I said. "Aunt Rose threw her weight around. Ran the sale through—all legal like—before officials got wind. Sure enough. I own the mineral rights, and she has the last laugh!"

Gunner heard me. His antenna churned with resentment.

He'd worked in Butte all his life and didn't have a dime to show for it. "Only thing my kids will inherit is funeral bills," he threw his voice. Again with resentment. "Me . . . everybody else, could buy our house, but not own the ground."

"Please, hush." Mildred looked worried. "Please, Gunner, I can hear a dangerous anger in your voice that could set your heart to . . ."

It was no secret that his anger about property went far beyond malcontent at the Company. That long ago, Aunt Rose won his cabin in a poker game. His property was located outside the county, and her owning mineral rights was part of the deal.

"You're right about that, Gunner." LB felt sorry for him. I did, too. But the situation was awkward. "Owning a home in Butte is like sitting on a pile of manure . . . and, being told it's against the law to smell it," he stated.

"More like the ACM forced us to eat it." Gunner got a kick out of his quick comeback. "Caitlin, tell your Rosie that—"

"Soon as you tell me the name of the woman you saw running from my house that night."

"My goodness. I'd of spoken up sooner, but I thought Dak knew all about it. Seein as how you're all so close with her. Why, when you think—"

The Captain's somber voice came over the speaker. "Flight attendants, prepare for an immediate landing."

Dacsu caught my eye. She glanced through the floor, to where the landing gear lived. I had no idea what she meant, as I hunkered beside Jeep.

She quickly re-strapped Dr. Freida. Winked slowly, twice, at LB. "Deputy, please return to your seat. Buckle up immediately. We've got one more sweep over the city, then, we land. Do everything exactly the way I outlined, and you'll be O.K."

He smiled. Winked back at her. A long, steady wink, as if his left eyelid had been glued shut. He spoke to me over his shoulder. "I must talk to you. Slippery told me extremely important info." He started for the back of the plane. Hesitated by Gunner's foot in the aisle. Pointed to their window. Then, clumsily ricocheted his lumpy thighs down the aisle. Bumping, grinding, and tip-toeing over debris.

"Jeep, we'll be on the ground soon," I told him.

One way or another.

Chapter Twelve

Gunner's eyes fired crimson red, the instant he saw a shiny lake fertile with poison chemicals, covering land where the richest hill on earth once towered.

"Snakepit Lake," he called, hacking and spitting. "The ACM might as well have detonated an A-bomb."

"Please keep calm, Sir," Dacsu ordered from a front seat, tightening her seatbelt. "Stay buckled, bend over a little, and hold those pillows in front of you. We're landing in a minute."

"What'd you think?" I asked her, lifting my head as I leaned into the aisle from the floor.

"About the Pit?"

"No. About the landing."

"Keep your fingers crossed . . . it might be rough."

"Dacsu, can you see the Pit from your window?"

"Looks just like the Historians wrote . . . after the Company decapitated the Hill, they dug one of the largest holes in the world searching for copper." She turned towards me. "I read where a Super Fund was established to decontaminate the area."

I propped my back to the wall and cradled Jeep's head, thick beads of perspiration soiling my lap. "Super Fund or not, Butte's survival has been more resilient and successful than any other mining town in the history of mining."

"Hmm . . . there must be a statistic for that—"

The louder the engines roared, the slower we seemed to nose down.

"Is it possible we're slowing down?" I asked her.

"She has to get it around 100 knots."

Whatever that meant. "This'd be Gunner's cue to comment," I said, calling down the aisle. "Mildred . . . is he O.K.?"

"Never saw him this enraged in all our fifty years together." His neck veins enlarged as he tore off his oxygen tube, and grasped his left arm. "Caitlin!" she shrieked, as I lowered Jeep flat to the floor and crawled uphill to help. "He won't let me put the tube in his nose."

"Gunner?" I gasped, looking at his eyes bulge wide open. He clutched his chest. His face turned blue. His jaw clenched tightly shut just as I pushed Mildred aside. He collapsed forward into my arms.

Was death taking another practice run, or was this for real?

Mildred shrank farther back into her seat. Her face as pale as a discarded wedding gown. "He's going to be all right, isn't he?" I didn't need a pulse read to know that Gunner was definitely dead. That I was as helpless as Mildred, with no way to comfort her. No way to stop her watery eyes from gushing, or keep her heart from breaking—when she learned her lifelong partner had died.

I wouldn't be the one to tell her that their fifty years of togetherness had ended. That his suffering was over and hers was just beginning. Chicken-heartedly, I propped his head on the seatback, re-attached his oxygen tube, and turned on the noisy machine.

"Please hang tough Mildred," I advised. "Why don't you just sit back until we land? We'll be on the ground soon." I pointed to the window where the sky was getting smaller and the ground was growing larger, then harpooned my way back to Jeep, and cramped my legs next to him.

"Gunner?" Dacsu cabled to me across the aisle.

Out comes the dreaded head shake.

In comes my long lost spiritual sensibilities.

Please help these passengers to safety," I petitioned the Blessed Mother. "And take care of the three O'Shaughnessy sisters that'd be waiting at the airport."

I rubbed a scar on the inside of my wrist. It made me feel close to Zoonawme and Dak. As close as the day we mingled our blood.

I waved my thoughts at them.

I was dead sure they'd be waving back at this moment.

Chapter Thirteen

Sheriff Dak's heart raced wildly as he stepped forward to the fence to watch his friend complete a second low flying loop around the city. He cropped both hands tightly to his neck, and exhaled. "She'll bring all 27 people safely down. She's amaz—"

He ducked, as did Zoonawme, as the belly of the plane passed over the airport, much lower than the first time.

"She's not coming in yet, I don't see wheels down," Zoonawme said with a concerned look.

Inside, Bill tightened the snaps on his bartender apron and hovered over Jake. "No radio response yet?" He glared at the plane. "What's up with the landing gear?"

Jake's white shirt was dripping with sweat. He stripped down to his tee shirt and scratched his face. "She's coming in too low!"

"She's cutting it thin," Dak acknowledged, watching the plane roll closely to the Lady of the Rockies without touching it. "She can fly a saucer through a needle."

"She supposed to fly that low while circling?" Megan Pat pinched her fingers in links of the fence. Her face was powder dry, but she appeared clammy and cold.

"What did you say?" Dak asked.

"You think she knows about Butte's strange wind patterns?" She motioned to a huge man-made gap breaking a continuous chain of mountains that surrounded the city. "Over there." She pointed to the disappearing Columbia Gardens that'd drastically altered wind velocity into the town.

"Of course, pilots are briefed," he throttled in a deep tone.

Inside the terminal on the second floor, Bill piped into the control room holding a triple shot of Tequila in his hand, and a scared attitude. "God help them."

"No drinking in this work area," Jake reminded.

"I'm not drinking it. I'm holding it for you . . . for when the plane's . . . umm . . . on the ground."

"If those bozos hadn't carted away tons of dirt, one truckload at a time, to mine copper topside, there wouldn't be a gigantic break in the natural flow of the environment," Jake mumbled, rooting his face to a panel of instruments. "She doesn't need communication to find the runway on this clear evening."

"Why does she keep circling ?" Megan Pat asked Dak. "And, without wheels down?"

Zoonawme weighed in. "That baby's loaded with fuel . . . she's trying to avoid a Hindenberg disaster."

Dak's heart thumped like a ball peen hammer. "We haven't identified what the problem is. Or, why she's not lowering wheels. We're certain she's mired in a catch 22, and flying by the seat of her pants."

"For heaven's sakes, why not just come in?" Her knowledge of flying, compared to her medical wisdom, was like stacking up a juicy Cuban cigar to a lady's puny, lightweight Tiparillo.

"Look, Megan Pat," Zoonawme informed, stepping further away from the fence to survey. "It's like landing with a bomb. She's got to calculate fuel consumption. We know she's flying low to burn fuel. We don't know if she has to dump any."

Dak chimed in, stretching his neck up. "She'll get one chance. Nobody's going to wave her off. It's her call —"

Zoonawme's noiseless footsteps glided closer to the gate. "Ground crews are mounting up."

"Shouldn't we all be inside the building, or something?" Megan Pat bit her lip.

"If she gets this far," Dak said, keeping an eye on the wings bobbing up, then down, before the plane leveled off. "And something goes wrong, it won't matter where we stand." His eyes tooled away from the sky to focus on two ambulances backing up to the gate.

"She's coming in," someone yelled. "Wheels are down."

Dak stuck his chin out, turned on his squawk box, and fired orders. "Ground Zero! She's on final approach. Harry, move those fire trucks to the north gate. Megan Pat, show time . . . jack up your support staff."

Edgy about his team's ability to tame their emotions, he walked briskly to his car parked near the runway, looking over his shoulder for Zoonawme.

He didn't need to hear orders. He wasn't a cop. Never worked for the Sheriff's department. The two men would give their life to protect each other. He followed Dak to a brand new Sheriff's car that took an act of congress to buy. That . . . and eighteen months of waiting for a one-of-a-kind, special order to be filled.

Dak felt uncomfortable that his men were as fired up, and over-excited, as spectators. He recalled a horrible crisis situation that he couldn't control the outcome, and clasped a speaker from a state-of-the-art communication system. "All civilians evacuated from the terminal?"

"Roger that," his team answered dutifully. They'd been trained for emergencies during long hours of overtime that Dak donated, after a fire burned J.C. Penney's to the ground, almost taking one of his men with it.

"Security, you're not going to mess things up again!"

Zoonawme scraped a long burn scar on his arm as he opened Dak's car door. He remembered the night two deputies disobeyed command. Jumped a fire line, attempting to rescue a fireman that was already dead. Stairs connecting the first, and second floors collapsed, trapping one deputy. The other deputy got out safely. Immediately, Dak and Zoonawme raced into the inferno to save him. "They know to sit tight until you give the all clear this time!" Zoonawme said, hoping he was right.

Dak thrust his right leg into the car, and started the engine before he was all the way in. "Of course. . . I trained them myself. They'll do their job right."

Chapter Fourteen

Landing in Butte was like landing on the flight deck of an aircraft carrier. You clear one last mountain that surrounds the city, and drop immediately onto a short runway at the edge of town.

"Hang on, Jeep," I ordered, tucking up my legs as giant wheels hit dry pavement with a thud. My neck wrenched backwards. He was unaware I held him tight, as we bounced up and down—off the floor—on the floor—then jolted on a sideways slide. "We'll get you help soon." I nudged his cheek, imprinted from a button on my blouse, as we surfed over a coppery dust that settled on a warm asphalt runway. Taxied behind a trail of light gray smoke puffing from the tires, until the plane came to a complete stop. "Thank you, God!"

Jubilant passengers exhaled in unison. Like a well rehearsed chorus they shouted loudly. Cheered. Hollered. And clapped enthusiastically.

"Yeah!"

"Wow!"

"Lavatory opened?"

"Gonna sue!"

"Quick, a sick bag!"

"Ladies and gentlemen," the captain spoke. "We've arrived at Butte. Please remain in your seats until we get the wounded deplaned—"

Thunderous cheers for her—hip, hip, hooray—rang out. Three times, while she spoke, drowning out all reference to two dead passengers, the injured, and destroyed luggage.

"Ouch," I moaned. It hurt my back to unwind my cramped legs. I maneuvered to my feet. Snaked to a window, shuffling over mounds of debris that'd shifted. Just in time to see daylight drift into evening. And, to spy my family in the distance. Three worried seniors, silent and stiff bodied, clung to a chain link fence on the far side of the main terminal.

Jeep moaned, but didn't regain consciousness.

I looked over at Mildred, crying. Then back at my family's worried faces. It was an unusually hot, sizzling day, but when the sun goes down, crisp mountain chills nudged two of them into fleece lined jackets. The other into a long coat.

Aunt Rose classed up Bert Mooney airport, wearing a full length mink coat, and a broad smile, that had nothing to do with June 13th—Miners Union Day. The local holiday repulsed the O'Shaughnessy clan. Strong immigrants from Ireland, that were seasoned in adjusting to hard times over the years. They were casualties of death. The mines killed their twin brothers, Sean and Shamus, in a cage accident at the Belmont—Uncle Tim died at the Anselmo.

Aunt Nell's husband fell hundreds of feet down a mine shaft. Her Tim survived long enough for deadly copper poison to seep into his wounds. Of course, the ACM compensated her.

They patted my three-year-old cousin Mike on his curly red hair. Swept him, and my aunt, out of the Pay-office door like dirt, carrying a $500 dollar death benefit check, and two broken hearts. With no man to depend on, it followed, that Aunt Rose worked as a waitress to support the lot of us.

Small wonder the girls call the observance of Miners Union Day—"MUD Day."

Out comes my shame. What kind of person would push such tender, loving hearts to the edge of their advancing years by wallowing in self-pity about a lost love? Or, boldly search for my birth mother when Hummy loved me like a daughter? "I'm going to make up for my selfishness," I mumbled, practicing an apology to Hummy. I pressed my nose to a window where two ambulances motored past, and parked in the middle of the field. Others saw it, too.

Silence filled the plane with a deep serenity as rescue vehicles advanced closer. Parking, one by one, in an orderly fashion. Trained professionals hopped out alongside unskilled volunteers, packing equipment, and fear as they came closer.

I cleared my throat. "I see my partner."

"You didn't mention you were gay," Dacsu blurted, inching to the back.

"Partners in Copper Dust Forensics," I corrected. My heart pounded louder than a bass drum in today's parade that I missed. He was poised in the front seat of Dak's new car. Holding his ten gallon cowboy hat on his lap, and waiting for a portable stair ramp to brace against the plane's exit door.

In the distance, two deputies were detaining people that'd filed anxiously into the terminal, ready to storm the plane.

I saw Dak waiting. He stood with one leg in his car, the other was balanced on the ground. He was holding a phone in his ear.

"Get those over-achieving vehicles off the range," Dak shouted to his men over the phone. "Clear the area of civilians."

"On it," a deputy replied.

"How'd you allow that wild crowd of sightseers to jump the Safety line?" he snorted. He knew the minute folks sniffed trouble, they'd ban together like vigilantes. Interrupt their fun at the rodeo grounds half a mile away, to come help.

"Sorry, Sir . . . the line's breaking up," a nervous deputy lied, turning to his partner. "Geeshus . . . Dak told us before to keep the Security line so tight that a popcorn fart couldn't squeeze through it."

Zoonawme didn't wait for Dak to tighten ranks. He stepped out of the front seat, streaked his large silhouette against a mountainous background, and raced like a Titan warrior towards the plane.

Dak lifted his arm off the open car door, moved his right hip towards the front seat, and crouched his head to enter.

"What the—"

Whizzz! . . . Swoosh!

His pant leg blew in the after breeze of a souped-up, green Chevy sedan, as it whistled by like greased lightening. His temper flared. "Watch out you crazy bugger . . . arrest that maniac!"

Zoonawme heard a screech, instinctively grappled a small handgun into his fist, and surveyed the area with his radar eyes. He carried a gun ever since he was shot at in the hospital parking lot by an unknown assailant. No doubt, a prejudiced citizen that ignored Webster's Dictionary, labeling him an American citizen.

Dak shook his fist at the car as it made a U-turn, then steamed back—close enough to heat up the paint on his new vehicle. "Get that nut off the field, now! Teenagers! Nah . . . all kids are worthless. They just take up space." He brushed dust off his car door as the Chevy tore across the field with a deputy's car chasing after it. "That damn fool narrowly missed me."

"Steady, friend, I've got your sorry back covered," Zoonawme threw his voice. He holstered his piece in a shoulder sheath. Glared at three more cars that broke the Security line. "Unbelievable!"

A number of people in town had no tolerance for a Blackfoot Indian. Dak respected him. Ennobled a nick name that only a close friend could get away with. "Yeah, Keno Savvy . . . and I've got your regretfully ugly front . . . umm . . . " He stopped to bark orders at his men. "Holes in the protective shield are as big as the pit! Use your mother-in-laws if you have to—just keep that damn line tight!"

Zoonawme pushed ahead of a medical team jamming the ramp. Bolted through the door into a nasty domain that smelled like a horse stall. He sloped down. "Cat Woman!"

"I'm over here."

He craned his neck for a second, then pressed cagily forward. “You all right?”

“Uneasy,” I admitted, wedged awkwardly next to a window in the second row, my body bent in a half-standing position.

“Who’s the man on the floor?” Long buck skein fringes on his tan leather jacket flapped, as he reached down, and tightened his arms around my thick waist.

“A new friend. He’s hurt bad—”

“Wait. Move closer to me.”

“Whut’s going on?”

“MP’s coming.”

“Caitlin? Is that you?” She acted friendly, but her ice-cold, violet eyes pierced my spine. “I’ll be over to help in a minute.”

“She can see through dead people,” I whispered, cringing with fear at the sound of her hypocritical voice. “I’m not hurt.”

“She’s a toothless tiger,” he said, sidestepping a pile of magazines with gloss-polished, square toed, brown cowboy boots. “You’re off limits to her since the toilet stall caper, when she dunked your head in the bowl and hammered your butt with a stick, until two nails poking through, drew blood where it wouldn’t show at your 5th grade picnic.”

“Nonsense, Caitlin,” MP said, hovering close to Jeep’s legs, twisted in spasms. “You’ll need to be checked out for airline insurance purposes. You come see me!”

She opened a black bag. Examined his face, covered in blood. Ordered her team to immobilize his neck in a cervical collar. Helped adjust the neck brace. Straightened his legs on a gurney. Backed away, colliding with my shoulder.

"Oomph," I exhaled, wincing in pain. Zoonawme directed me to the wall to allow two ambulance staffers angle by the cockpit, and anchor the copilot onto a carrier.

"Sorry, Caitlin," MP said spiraling a dark smirk. "I'd say you luxated your shoulder. When you get to the hospital, I'll tend to it personally."

Luxated, all right. You'd think a serious conflict kindled in grade school would have gone up in smoke by now—instead of fuelling her obsessive passion for Dak . . . or, was it her hatred for me, into an endless war.

"Copilot's secured. Take him to an ambulance waiting at the bottom of the steps," she ordered. She picked up a piece of broken bin, and gripped it tightly, as she glanced at me with a subliminal threat.

We held still while MP helped a vigilant pair of underlings transport the copilot from the cockpit onto a makeshift rickshaw. "The rest of the town sees her as a beautiful, talented do-gooder. I see her as a schemer trying to kill me."

"She's not going to harm you," Zoonawme insisted. "I told you about the day I hunted her down and throttled her sweet, innocent looking neck until it turned blue. She knew I meant business when I threatened to re-shape her virtuous looking face into the devil she was, if she didn't leave you alone."

"I trust her like I'd trust a pit bull in heat!" I countered.

"Give me a minute." He stretched his bulky neck to see the rear of the plane. "Dak said LB's bringing Slippery home on this flight. Mountain interference fouled up cell phones . . . as *you* know."

I blushed. "Those bulky gadgets are too big to catch on. I was relieved when the battery died weeks ago in Berlin."

"Is that LB and Slippery I see in the back row?" he asked.

"Yes, it is."

"Slippery might need my help. His wooden leg, and—"

"Please step aside." Walter, an employee of Duggan Dolan's Mortuary appeared busier than a cashier at a suit sale. He untangled his arm from Zoonawme's long fringe, and barreled to the back.

"Wait, Zoonawme," I pulled at his arm. "Poor Slippery was killed during the accident . . . is his brother waiting outside?"

"Sledge and his family moved to Helena after he served time for robbing your house," he said. "I thought you knew." He paused. "What kind of accident? Place looks like it exploded."

"I'll brief you later." I nodded to Mildred slouched behind a broken seat back, sobbing uncontrollably. "Gunner died too. Shortly before we landed."

"His lungs finally gave out? His heart?" He slowly swept his eyes around the plane for other casualties. He detected Dr. Freida, sprawled helplessly across two seats, camouflaged under a stockpile of flight blankets and he vaulted over to help.

In comes a Mea Culpa to the patron saint of guilt. "I'd forgotten about her," I confessed, watching the humble son of crafty thinkers—a descendant of a 2000-year old lineage of sixth-sensed, cunning Blackfoot minds—bend over to peel her covers away.

"Ma'am," he shook her tiny, frail frame gently. "Ma'am . . . you need to wake up."

"She's been drinking like a fish the entire flight," I said, twisting my mouth to one side.

"Don't be frightened," he told her.

Her voice rasped. "Get yur stenken hands off oov may!"

"Medical help's waiting." He supported her weight. Dusted smatterings of food crumbs from her clothes. Cautiously helped her into the aisle. Then, he placed her purse in her hands, and lifted her to the exit.

Her sarcastic, white pimpled tongue rolled over her dry lips. "Aye'm bloomun thar-stee. Whare's me frand Jeep? Wave gat empartant besness, yeh know."

He pointed to the open door. Cocked his wide-brim hat forcefully back with two fingers. "Please rest at the top of the steps. Folks are coming to assist you."

"Now . . . doon't yeh bay tellen may whet teh do . . . yeh flunken Red Skin. Aye'll bay getten down bay me self." She lunged her fists at him as if he were an attacker.

I suppose everyone has a reason for keeping people away. If the solid strength of a six-foot, seven-inch man, towering over her didn't intimidate her, then nothing would.

I hobbled to the door to see her rifle through her purse. She drew out an antiquated gold cigarette carrying case. Then, as if she were Greta Garbo in the old glory days of fanciful women, she tacked a cigarette on an extended gold holder, and lit up a smoke.

I corked my humor, as she clamped the apparatus between her teeth, and swished it to a corner of her mouth. Hung her purse around her neck. Plunked her butt down on the top step. And, grasped the right side railing with both arms.

Next, she rotated one foot forward onto the step below. She worked out a system to bump her feisty behind down to the next step.

She stopped to take a long drag on her cigarette.

Then came the two-armed rail grip again, before she dropped her fanny down to the step below. Jouncing and sliding one cheek at a time, until she reached the step before the bottom, where Sheriff Dak's broad shoulders waited to help.

Chapter Fifteen

Dr. Freida looked past the airport. She saw the familiar community, where'd she'd become independently wealthy, and felt like she never left Butte. A mile high above sea level. Where her own history once glowed, as brightly as the city beginning to light up in the distance. The golden senior had been run out of town years ago. Quickly. Silently. Mysteriously. She came back sizzling for a challenge, she thought, as she reached the bottom of the ramp where Dak approached her.

"Ma'am." He cautiously extended his arms the second he saw her unyielding glare. He hoped to scoot her inside the terminal and get on with his job.

She pulled back. Spindled her small neck up at Dak's six feet and looked at his face. "Hmmph," she sneered.

He's experienced with women. Divorced three times. Instincts told him to get out of the way when a woman pitched arrows of hate at him. Yet, he tried again. "Ma'am, you hurt? Please let me help you inside."

"Yeh'll bay laven may alone, now won't yah!" She reared back. Drew in a long drag on her cigarette. Unscrewed the cap of a silver flask, and put it to her mouth anticipating a swig of courage.

Ka-chink!

He made a clumsy attempt to swing his arms around her shoulders, and bumped her flask to the ground.

"Look, yeh bloody cop . . ."

She plopped aggressively onto the bottom step of the ramp. As if neutral territory would give her leverage to bend Dak's ear. "Aye'll bay tellen yeh who Aye am, strayttt away."

He reluctantly squatted at her feet, to hear how she managed prostitutes' health in the old days. Her tone mean. Her actions bold. She seemed proud that she kept the ladies of the night clean from disease. Cleansed their wounds. Listened to their troubles. Delivered their babies. Lent them money.

"I'm sorry a disloyal, crazy hooker turned on you, and ran you out of town," he sympathized, hoping he could get her to move. He was already headed for a long night. "Let me help you stand." He had a sudden blinding urge to pass her off to whoever was meeting her. He lifted her to her feet. "You have people at the airport?"

"Get away froom may, now." She was as desensitized to the cool evening air on her hot face, as she was to trusting Dak. She wound the strap of her purse around her hand and looked around. "Farty years." A slight breeze rustled past her frowning face. "Et's eh bet quieter, Aye thenk."

The noise of copper mines clanking machinery and cages—the belching of brown air to the surface—as she remembered—had been silenced long ago. No more loud mine whistles to clock time against. She was ninety years old. She'd lost a large space of time being away from Butte.

She took off long before smelters stopped churning. Gone was ashen-gray smoke, and brown shrubbery. The grass had changed from crispy yellow straw, back to deep green blades. Fragrant summer flowers blossomed along the pathway.

However, none of these changes meant a thing to her.

Revenge was tattooed on her forehead.

An agenda that mysteriously bound her to Jeep's urgent need for her help.

"Ma'am . . . can I call for a wheel chair?" Dak asked, tipping his hat. Thick, caramel blonde hair framed his face. The face of Gregory Peck and Robert Redford, brought together into a handsome mogul that women lusted for.

"Yeh thenk Aye'd bay a re-tare-ded crepple, do yeh now?"

"Not much light out here on the runway. Please, at least lean on me for a minute."

"Speak oop . . . end moove yur flunken airss!" she bellowed, adjusting her purse. She straightened up to walk, as best she could.

I stood on the top step wondering who this woman was? Why'd she leave Butte in the first place? Why'd she come back? Aunt Rose will surely know. She knew everyone's life's history. One footprint in Butte. That's all it took.

Dak moved closer to her hearing aid. "I insist on helping you—"

He stopped suddenly to see why a group of people were cheering. His face flushed red upon seeing four snickering female groupies standing by an illegally parked car. Eight adoring eyes were locked onto his every move—as if he held the secret to their happiness.

I saw his Superman muscles bulge with annoyance. He wasn't looking for another whirl on the dating trail. "Look at Dak," I hailed Zoonawme, talking to the pilot.

"Paleface hates being followed around like a rock star," he replied. "Or stalked by women that favored the way he filled out his uniform. Even worse, you can see his anger flame that civilians broke through his deputies' holding line." He cocked his ear. "Can you hear what he's saying?"

We listened intently.

"Get off the premise," Dak shouted. "How'd you get in?"

"We drove straight on in," they snickered.

"You'll be arrested if you don't leave immediately."

"We'll leave our phone numbers."

"Out! . . . Now!" The handsome public servant wrenched at his phone in frustration. "Security detail? Hah! You're all like women with no potty training."

The three Amigos, we called ourselves. Zoonawme, Dak, and I, grew up as close friends in the old neighborhood. He had good reasons for disliking women. His mother, Mrs. Sullivan was a good looking, meek woman, that kept her family troubles to herself. Her heart had been hollowed out by marrying a drunk. In her mousy way, she did nothing to protect her son from his dad's tyranny.

If Dak became a cop, nobody could hurt him, he thought.

Mr. Sullivan was a boisterous, unreformed alcoholic that hammered the daylights out of his little boy, Dak. He played tic-tack-toe on his son's innocent body with strong adult fists. During those abusive, drunken rages, Mrs. Sullivan whimpered in fear, and ran away by herself, to hide. No wonder Dak never wanted children.

"It's an Irish stand-off between two extremely stubborn people," I told Zoonawme. He let the captain pass us. She saluted Dak as she zipped by, and ran inside the terminal. We listened again, but couldn't quite hear everything.

"Get away weth yursalf," Dr. Freida ordered. She despised men—especially cops. She stood on her tiptoes to get in his face, but only reached his chest. Her breath smelled like a brewery. "Yeh flunken cops ere all theh same . . . theh Divil yeh ere. Yeh're all brain dead en every flunken plaice but one."

He backed up slowly—both hands raised high—as if she were friendly bacterium. "Ma'am, I'm leaving. You need anything, ask for me, Dak Sullivan."

"Aye know who yeh ere. Black Dak's kid. Crossbred froom theh O'Mearah-Clare-Sullivan clans." She knew his pathetic Dad. He frequented her workplace. A disgusting town drunk, that reigned terror on prostitutes, his wife and his only kid.

"How'd you know who I am?"

"Yeh look jest lake him. 'Twas a good day when thet mean piece oov rag manure—flunken woman baytter, died. He quit batten up on yur moother, only when he settled her down six feet under, now dedn't hay!"

"Mom died at thirty-nine," he added. "Do I know you?" His face screwed in surprise trying to recognize her. "Have we met before?" He searched her cold eyes trying to distinguish her as someone's mother. Someone he knew. But then, all women past twenty-five looked alike to him. "Your name, Ma'am?"

"Theh whoole flunken town knows may," she answered, wobbling like a broken doll towards the gate. Her hands on her hips.

Dak snailed behind her. Uncharacteristically wagging and swaying his rear end in friendly jest. He helped her navigate through the gate. Glanced over his shoulder at me, and Zoonawme, inching towards the second top step of the ramp.

He spread his feet apart, slapped his hip pocket, and pointed to a newspaper. "Read it," he lipped, turning around to embrace Captain O'Donovan at the mouth of the terminal.

Zoonawme reached in his jacket. Wrenched out a rolled newspaper and handed it to me. The headline read:

Judge Ava Foil
Car Bombing Victim at State Capitol

I could hardly breathe, let alone think. Ava, a Harry S. Truman on steroids, was my roommate in college and a good friend, although I hadn't seen her in years.

"Did they kill her?"

"She was out of the car when it blew."

"Who did it?"

"Just happened yesterday. No one's claimed responsibility."

"You think it was because of her stubborn stand on timber and land use?" I asked.

"No, I don't. Ava's a true country lawyer of the people. She's experienced in all aspects of land issues and water rights. A brilliant woman of the law—to the letter of the law. Montanas need her." He guided my hand to the rail.

"She's logged enough death threats to paper the Court House rotunda, since she became a judge," I said. "Remember? She hired me to analyze them."

"You mean, assess empty threats," he finished my sentence. "Remember how the same-sex issue made headlines just before you went to Europe?"

"Of course," I answered. "Scientists claimed they pinpointed some kind of chemicals that cause same-sex inconsistencies . . . umm . . . differences from the norm . . . in people. Endocrine disrupters that mimic hormones. Especially estrogen."

"Your friend Ava finally came out of the closet."

"Oh . . that," I laughed. "It's about time. Haven't seen her since my house burned. Her papers—legal documents that were stored in my basement—had been incinerated. I didn't want to face her. I was—"

We heard the clack of approaching footsteps behind us. Narrowed sideways to let LB punch his bountiful self by, and hand Zoonawme a couple of pictures. He quickly shook hands with him, touched me on the shoulder, and bustled down the ramp—Dacsu in hot pursuit.

"Caitlin, I'll call you after the funeral," he shouted over his shoulder. "There's a definite, weird connection between Judge Ava Foil, and the robbery." He climbed inside a Duggan-Dolan hearse, rolled down the window, and waved good-bye.

Zoonawme tucked the pictures in his pocket. Scooped me up shoeless, and set me down at the bottom of the stair ramp. "Your getting lighter," he lied.

The sun was down. Montana's endless blue sky had been put to bed for the day. Leaving a vast expanse of dark space overhead. A darkness that blanketed a trio of excited, tired sisters. Stomachs tied in knots. Waiting impatiently near the arrival gate.

"Oover hare, Caitlin," they chimed, standing locked in a ridiculous embrace.

I ran awkwardly over cool, rough pavement that snapped hard against my tender tootsies, to greet them. Hurdled the turn-style like a running-back going for a touchdown—almost breaking my legs. "Hey, dear family, I'm—"

A tingle crept up my spine. It was a strange gut-feeling I couldn't explain. Was I about to taste danger once again?

Chapter Sixteen

"Thar shay es!" Aunt Nell bawled, twitching at a hairnet. She clumsily bunched her gray hair, and cropped it in a bun. Wrapped in a warm jacket, blue cotton dress, and a relieved look, she balanced a portable oxygen tank at her side. Although her doctor said she didn't need it. "Yu'll bay geven yur Ahnt eh kess, now."

I punched through the gate. "Dear Aunt Nell . . ."

She wore latex, medical gloves as we embraced.

Seventy two. The youngest of the three sisters, had been obsessed with a Howard Hughes, cleanliness fetish since her husband died. She couldn't forget. He could have survived injuries incurred at the bottom of a mine shaft. But, he had no defense, when metallic poison crawled into open sores on his leg. The hotness of a torrid heat—hot enough to hard boil a raw egg in 13 seconds—bubbled copper dust into his system. Quickly cooking deadly bacteria to a rolling boil. Racing it through his wounds, and, infecting his young body with a horrible death.

While hugging her, I caught a glimpse of Hummy's face, colorless from worry. She withdrew in the shadows, permitting Aunt Rose, the oldest of the three, to power forward.

My hero—Irish warts and all. Her trademark was a flashy pair of super-sized earrings, and a nosey nature. She appeared fifteen years younger than seventy-eight, as she strutted forward like a chic model in red, three inch, high-heeled stilettos, and an upbeat smile.

"Coom . . . lat me taake eh look et yeh," the special high priestess of fashion said, hogging the entrance. She wrapped her strong arms around me. Pressed hard on my backbone, like a concerned mother replenishing fresh life to an exhausted daughter. "Yeh need sleep."

"We were almost killed." My voice weakened. I wanted to say everything at once. To recite the apology speech I practiced over and over again. "Came very close a few tim—"

"Plenntay oov time later, child." Her wide-eyed stare tingled my spine. Soft crimson slacks, poked through the bottom of a full length mink coat. She swung her bluish-green eyes at my bargain polyester, bell bottom britches. "Aye'm speechless gurl, Aye em."

"I can't think straight. I'm so happy to see you three."

"Tes home way'll bay goen, now won't way, sesters."

I've been decoding Irish brogue long enough to consider it a second language. Almost everything that sounded like a question, was actually a command.

"Caitlin, me gurl." Aunt Nell covered for her son's absence. "Yur cousen Mike coodn't coom, now could hay."

Mike lived as a recluse. Of course, he'd be holed up tight in the Rocky Mountain Springs Hotel he bought a few years back.

"I understand."

"Hay's been worried, yeh know."

I didn't expect my busy cousin to meet me. He stayed home, but not because he was up to his neck in maintenance. Or, overwhelmed by general operations of the two story building, until he could afford to hire help. He strangled himself in work as a convenient vice to keep clear of people. "I'll visit him tomorrow."

"Oov coourse, yeh'd bay veseten," she replied. She stubbed her pigeon-toes on a corner of the fence, as she moved aside to make room for Hummy hanging in the dark background.

Hummy tiptoed. Her neutral colored, flat shoes, matched her jacket—her personality—and the drab curb. "Do yeh—"

A horn honked loudly to startle us. We twisted our heads to the field. A guy driving a pickup was making room for a second Duggan-Dolan's hearse to head uptown.

Aunt Rose massaged her jaw, and pointed to the hearse. "Now . . . whose ryden en thet meat wagon?"

"Slippery McDoon—for one," I answered. "And Gunner."

"Meldred's old man? Never liked hem anyway," she deliberated. "Whose en theh ambulances?"

"Mr. J.P. Palagretti. Met him on the plane," I explained. "The copilot. One of the flight attendants."

"All thengs happen fur a raysun. Now, don't they child?"

"Caitlin," Hummy whispered.

Beneath the glare of a bright overhead light, I saw her thin face lined with relief. It was as if I'd seen her for a first time. She looked amazingly beautiful wearing a pale blue hat she crocheted. She stretched it close over charcoal-gray hair, curled tightly in a classic Butte-do that older ladies love to wear.

"Hummy . . ." Dread and misgivings burned my throat. How could I have treated her with such pure disdain after Sam left? How could I have searched for my birth mother, when she disapproved?

Her head tilted slightly as she plodded slowly towards me.

Then came the sweat. My guts shook with apprehension. Eyes swelled with shame. "Blessed Mother, give me a way to crawl inside her heart, and find forgiveness."

"Now, me Darlen, Caitlin." Her soft voice put me at ease. Blue, loving eyes, and easy manner could soothe a cougar. She drew near. Reached out. Carefully placed one of St. Therese's world class calling cards—a heavenly scented, long stemmed, red rose—in my hand. She'd always been timid to display affection to me. Especially, when anyone was around. Yet, she cleverly found a way to show me how much she loved me, without having to hug in public.

"It's beautiful . . . *Mother,* " I mumbled. I'd gotten my sign from the Blessed Mother. I brushed the rose's therapeutic fragrance of miracles over my face to gather more courage, and saw Hummy's jaw drop.

Obviously stunned at being called Mother, she scratched her head and frowned. Her eyes drifted to her sisters—both in shock. Both silent. Hummy was cool. She remained poised. Although, I could see her chest beat like a wild drummer.

"Aye bayged St. Therese oov Liseux, patroon saint oov pilots, teh kape yeh safe . . . now dedn't Aye!"

So . . . St. Therese was the patron saint of pilots.

"That's very sweet . . . and loving of you . . . *Mother*!" I repeated. I love you, too." I said it twice. Then, out came fear of the unknown.

She heard it twice. Clutched her chest, and dropped back. She kept her eyes down. Nervously adjusted the shoulder pads on a brown and red plaid, Pendleton wool, 49er jacket, beneath her warm coat, and backed into Aunt Nell.

"Tes theh day oov moor then one miracle, now esn't et!" Aunt Nell mouthed.

We walked inside the terminal. Dak was huddled with the pilot a few feet away. Talking heatedly about what took place in the sky. He caught my eye. "Hey . . . over here . . . Caitlin . . . it's Dak. Don't leave. I'll come over soon as Mary's finished her story."

From the sound of Mary O'Donovan's voice over the intercom, I expected her to look sleek and athletic, not short and heavy like Bette Midler. She was medium height. Had mousy brown, straight hair, cut short like a man. Wore ill-fitting, baggy slacks, and a blazer much too small to cover her healthy sized breasts.

I expected the fashion police to arrest her any minute.

Predictably, Aunt Rose strode over to them, to eavesdrop.

We'd learn later, that she overheard Dak joke with his long time friend. "Mary, were you waiting for headwinds at five to ten knots before you set her down?" They laughed. A ha-ha chuckle of relief between good friends. Before she laid a terrifying story on him on what happened in Montana's big sky.

"Butte's no longer exclusively shielded from wild weather by vaulting Rocky Mountains," she told him. "It might have been calm weather on ground level, but circling the city in weird wind drafts was a nightmare."

"How'd you get in a position to have to circle?"

"You see," she said in a hushed tone.

Rose came in closer.

"I don't know why my copilot, Patrick, suffered fits of hysteria. But, he damaged implements before we could tie him down. We flew off course. In the middle of my *May Day*, contact with Butte dried up. Shortly after, I underwent the worst sudden turbulence drop in my career." She paused to drink water. "Jesus, Dak . . . two passengers died under my watch."

"Let's sit down," he suggested. He led her to a bench, and noticed a flight attendant hailing them. "She's looking for you, Mary."

"I'll get to that in a minute," she continued. She raised her arm and gave Dacsu a five fingered halt. "In reality, I was lost up there. I'd tell you I attributed finding Butte, to divine intervention, but I know you don't believe in God."

"Bunch of hooey," he admitted. "I believe in your skills." He scratched a five-o'clock shadow that gave his masculine, square jaw, and white teeth, sex appeal. "So, you took in the educational route . . . please go on."

"Stumbled onto a route. Then, landing gear froze. I had to burn fuel away from the population. Catch 22—fly low to burn petrel—at the same time, ride that plane like a wild stallion in horrific wind pattern—"

The noise level rose to a deafening pitch before she could finish. Cigarette smoke billowed in the no smoking zone. Passengers just learned they couldn't pick up their luggage, until everything in the plane had been sorted out. The lobby was in a state of confusion.

Jake and Bill stood in the hallway toasting, with two large water glasses filled with Jameson Whiskey and ice cubes. Several reporters from Helena and Anaconda, broke the Security line to bother everyone. An opportunity for Aunt Rose to step in closer to hear Dak and Mary talk.

"Flying over your city . . . looked as if you could'a used me for evacuation," Captain O'Donovan said, lighting up a Camel.

"For what?"

"During the bombing of Butte." She forced herself to keep a straight face. "Your town's craters are larger than the abyss the Atomic bomb left at Hiroshima."

"Hey . . . cut that out," he shot back in fun. "Here, I've been telling my friends that you're a real doll, the finest flyer I ever knew, and a sensible woman."

"Bite me! You have friends?" she warbled, peeling off her jacket. A white sweat-soaked shirt stuck to puffy love handles circling her middle. "Serious side . . . where *did* you hide the richest hill on earth? You bragged, and bragged, and bragged, how the copper mines on that hill supplied enough copper to build military tanks, make artillery, and manufacture ammunition for our side to claim victory in WWII. Where's the hill?"

"We relocated our famous *Hill* in your honor," he chuckled. "Replaced it with a deep lake."

"Believe me," she said. "I was grateful for that lake. Passengers owe their lives to that cesspool of poisonous, thick sludge standing in the hill's place."

"I don't understand?"

"Without navigation charts, or contact with the airport, I didn't have one clue where to look for Butte in these treacherous mountains."

"Ah, come on. What happened to the charts?"

"Ask Patrick."

"He didn't bring them?"

"Looks more like the dog ate them," she said.

"Go on. You said you didn't have a clue where Butte was."

"Until that slimy stuff, that surfed on the top of the lake, glared at me. Damnest thing I ever saw. The water looked like an oil spill on a greasy driveway that squiggled in the rain."

"Shoot from the hip, Mary!"

"Shiny sledge bounced off a fading sun. Reflected colors throughout the sky, and illuminated my search for Butte. The sight of silver, green, purple, and black—that collided together—almost blinded me. I followed the slimy beacon to the source."

"You're amazing." He lifted her off her feet with his strong arms, and hugged her hard. Meaningful. "You were bringing me something?"

"Oh, no, you don't," she said, grabbing his collar. "First, how'd you haul that watery crap into the hole?"

"Easy. Copper prices died. Mining stopped. Tons and tons of dead water rose to the top when the pumps that kept the tunnels dry, were turned off." He paused without noticing aunt Rose acting as if it were her first day at school. "Our Super Fund's got a couple of glitches, but Butte's cleaning up the lake. You'll have to come back. Go water skiing with me . . . now . . . what'd you bring me?'"

"Dak, you listen to me now . . . with your heart . . . not your tough, obstinate head!" she commanded. Her voice was serious.

"Last week you phoned me about a special package you were bringing. What's this is all about?"

"This isn't going to be easy. And, I leave early in the morning for Denver. I'm only going to say this once. You may want to have some privacy for this one."

"Lesten teh thes," Aunt Rose puffed. With an urgent burst of speed, she ran in her stilettos over to our group. We were seated on a bench drinking bottled beer. Talking to Zoonawme about how Dak was so proud of his new car. And, curbing my impatience to hug Dak. It'd been three months. I'm really bad at waiting. "Are yeh oop fur theh tellen?"

Of course we were curious.

We pretended to protest her eavesdropping. Truth is, we were glad she owned the biggest set of ears in town.

"Slow down," Hummy said. She uncrossed her legs.

"Theh pilatt, Amelia Earhart oover there's gevin out cegars," she reported, smoothing the collar of her mink coat.

"All that fuss just for bringing Dak cigars?" I said. I reached down to snug the broken pant-zipper on my pants into my waistband. "She have something ugly packed in those stogies she's handing out?"

"Dak's eh Papa," she insisted. "Aye'm tellen yeh, Dak's eh Papa!"

"What'd you mean?" I blurted. I couldn't believe my ears. She's known for her brash honesty, yet, she made no sense.

"Et's true."

"Don't tell me you inhaled one of those cigars? He doesn't even like kids . . . not possible!" I craned my neck to where he was engaged in an animated, three-way conversation with Mary and Dacsu. "Dak couldn't have masterminded a miracle child during the three months I've been gone."

Zoonawme looked on silently. Patiently.

"Et's true," Aunt Rose repeated. Her grin was sly. Her hands on her hips. "Plenty moore teh tell. . . theh convare-sation went lake thes."

Her mouth stretched wide with a tell-all attitude.

I hated what she told.

I hated how her news affected my life.

Chapter Seventeen

"Et went lake thes," Aunt Rose continued.

"As to your surprise," O'Donovan said, bracing her stance. "I wrote you that I volunteered as a medical records helper for the nuns, at a hospital back east last year."

"You did," Dak said, twisting his head. He was distracted by his phone ringing. Emergencies were popping up faster than a past due tax bill. He tugged at the waist of his pants. "Can this wait?"

"Not on your life! It has to be now."

He held up his hand, and answered a call. "There in a couple minutes." He tapped his foot repeatedly on the seat of the bench. "Look, Mary, I've got some bumbling deputies out there that need a swift kick in the groin . . . surprise me tomorrow." He started to walk away.

"We do it now!" She gripped his arm. "I'll skip the prelude. There's no easy way to say this. No safety net. You've handled a lot worse." She slapped him hard enough on the shoulder to jar him off balance. "You must meet someone immediately!"

"You've got to be kidding?" He threw his head. "Mary! Never knew you to be the match-maker type . . . not interested!"

She motioned for Dacsu. The young flight attendant waited patiently by the counter. Reluctantly, she stepped forward.

"Now isn't the time for a set up," Dak ordered. She was beautiful, he thought. But, he never went for blondes. Especially one still in the cradle. Besides, he surely wouldn't be interested in someone that dropped in and out of Butte like the mail. He could barely look at the inexperienced, young woman. His eyes blinked with impatience. "You know I'm done with relationships."

Up 'til now, the young flight attendant thought Caitlin was teasing her, that he was deep in his forties, and counting. She believed it now, when she saw that Dak was at least twice her age, handsome, and well built. She drew nearer, blushing. "Sheriff's right, Mary. An intro can definitely wait!"

Dak muttered to himself how embarrassed he felt. He squinted at Zoonawme standing close by, to follow him. Then, he turned sharply to leave.

Mary headed him off.

She held him motionless with her powerful biceps. "Dak Sullivan, you want the whole place to hear this?"

"Mary, you're overtired. After a good night's rest you'll—"

"I'm leaving tomorrow, friend!" She forced him to look her in the eye. Pointed to the flight attendant. "Dammit! I'd like to introduce you to your daughter, Dacsu!"

"Not in the mood for a practical joke."

"Me neither," the young woman chimed in. "What's going on here?"

All three stared at each other amid a moment of silence.

The whispers came. That's when Aunt Rose meandered to our group, anxious to spill more beans.

"He would have told me he had a child," I said in disbelief. "We—all three amigos—tell each other everything."

"Hay dedn't know . . . now ded hay," Aunt Rose replied.

The O'Shaughnessy women all spoke at once.

Zoonawme weighed in to referee. "Ladies." His husky pitch commanded silence. "Until his friend sprung this on him, Dak didn't know he had a child. He would have told me and Caitlin." He paused. "His . . . umm . . . daughter was blindsided, too."

No wonder Dacsu reminded me of someone.

"I just didn't connect the dots." Both arms raised while my mouth dropped.

"Dots?" he quizzed.

"I'm a trained observer of human behavior. An investigator of facts. I never run on assumption. I screwed up this time. She reminded me of . . . Dak. I see it, now. Besides, I missed the most important dot of all. Dacsu had been named after her father, Dak Sullivan, and it got by me."

"You've had a rough trip," he said, walking towards the front door, and signaling us to follow. "Ladies, time to call it a day. My truck's outside."

The shackles of female curiosity jumped up.

"Wait." I couldn't put a feeling to how my heart should react. Dak was my blood brother. I'd welcome Dacsu as my niece. But, how would he feel? If, in fact the story was true. I folded my arms. "Dacsu told me she's an orphan. If Dak's really her father—who's her mother? This doesn't add up."

"Ahemm," Aunt Nell sneezed, snapping disposable latex gloves onto her hands. She'd never touch dead animal fur. Expired carcasses carried diseases, she believed.

"You all right?" I asked her.

She tugged at Aunt Rose's mink coat. "Thet Banshee yoo haired howlen last night. Es Dak's baying eh father, theh bad news, now es et?"

"Banshee means eh death omen," she straightened her out. Old world, Irish superstition. Banshee. "When yoo hare oone oov them shriek en theh night, et's tame teh get oonder theh coovers end stay there," she explained.

"Death?" I itemized. "Two passengers died. Should be it."

"13th oov June esn't over, now es et?" Hummy's shoulders drooped. It was a full day of double superstitions. "Es et?" She'd adjust to Dak's child. Welcome her into the family. However, being called *Mother* for a first time by me, had taken a burdensome toll. She didn't know if she could handle any more surprises.

"Now, may Caitlin, way've felled yur fredge weth food," Aunt Nell explained. "Way'll all bay leaven strayttt away." She waited for me to move, then edged behind Zoonawme.

I threw my voice at Dak, and waved. "We're going home."

He lifted his neck. His face looked sour. He rushed over to press his warm lips to my cheek. "Missed you paying for my morning coffee, Doll Brat."

Expressionless, the group waited while he took me aside.

"You know, my deputies dropped the ball . . . again," he told me. "If it weren't for LB, Needlepoint, and Costello, I'd order a mass firing of the lot of them . . . maybe I'll just shoot them all myself. Why when you think—"

"I missed you, right back. We'll catch up tomorrow," I jumped in, giving him silent permission to leave.

He made no mention of a daughter.

Zoonawme turned to Dak. "Luggage?"

"No one gets luggage until the mess on the plane was taken care of. Got a full night. Details with respect to corpses. Airline documentation. Follow up on all injuries." He tilted his head at me.

I squared my shoulders. "I'm fine. Shaken up, but fine."

"Right, then," he continued. "Keno Savvy, I'll need your help after you've taken the girls home—"

"Hey, Sheriff." Jake came running over. "FAA reps are on the phone. When can you help chronicle plane damage? I'll need guidelines for airport costs. Already been asked where to send requisitions from fire department, the hospital, and Duggan-Dolan Mortuary." He hesitated. "Can someone take care of that dammed, nosey media?"

"I'll call you, Caitlin." Dak whizzed off in the direction of Mary again.

"I'll get the girls moving." Zoonawme herded us to the exit door, where Aunt Rose spied Dr. Freida winding unsteadily behind us.

"Does shay need a rade? Who es shay?" She narrowed her eyes.

"You must know her." The town encyclopedia on residents' lives recognizes everyone.

"Aye don't, now do Aye."

Nobody stumps our expert busybody.

If you left one footprint in Butte, Aunt Rose knows you. She knows all registered voters by name. Including those buried in our five cemeteries—many of their names, still, invariably show up during election day to vote.

"Doctor . . . something or other . . . my mind's a blank," I said. "She resided in Butte a long time ago."

She jetted her jaw forward, and squinted. "Doctor . . . whoo ded yeh say?"

"From what I gathered, she worked at Mike's Rocky Mountain Springs Hotel in the 40's . . . around the time you were a waitress there."

She glanced at her sisters uneasily. "Shay's all dried oop lake eh prune."

"She's probably older than you. I met her. Want me to introduce yo—"

Before I could finish, the doctor's shrill voice prickled the hair on the back of our necks.

We turned to see what happened.

"Aye'll take yeh all down . . . now won't Aye?" she cussed, throwing her voice all the way uptown—seven miles away. She threatened to kill a tramp named Riv Etter for spreading rumors that got her kicked out of town. "Aye'll bay getten me eh gun, Aye well. Yeh hare me, do yeh?"

All of a sudden, Aunt Rose backed into a flag pole.

She threw up her hands. "Holy saints prar-zerve oos." She put on a pair of distance glasses, and inspected the doctor like a science project.

"Aunt Rose, what is it?" I asked.

She wrenched her grip away from my hand, and beckoned her sisters for a caucus.

"Who is this woman?" I watched the color drain from all three faces.

She directed her command to her sisters. "Coom hare . . . theh two oov yeh . . . Aye'll not bay waiten eny longer . . . coom now!"

They wedged into a secret summit.

Necks collared so tight together—the Boston strangler couldn't have pried them apart.

Zoonawme stopped their mysterious meeting.

"You come with me now, or hike home. Caitlin needs rest." He ushered us outside. The air was fresh. Calming. He pointed to a walkway across the street, leading to the parking lot.

Then, he stopped, and gave me the *look*.

I knew what it meant. "You've been visiting Zakhooa?"

"I camped at her burial ground on the mountain this week."

"She give you a message this year?"

He thinks in modern terms, but he clings to Blackfoot Indian tradition. Much like Irish Catholics cling to centuries old Scripture, and superstitions. Once a year, he follows a native custom. Roams the Indian spirit-world at Medicine Water Soaking Pool near Whitehall. Through campfire smoke, he talks to his dear wife Zakhooa.

"She warned of bad omen—like Rose's Banshee sighting. The shadow spirits see a strong negative presence this summer."

"Murphy's Law probably does, too. After all, I'm back home. When someone asks me what my *sign* is. I tell them, *Murphy*." How do I keep losing hair bands? I cropped my hair in the back with a rubber band I found on a counter. I was grateful, that no one commented on my ragged, blood stained blouse. Broken front zipper. Slacks that barely stayed up on my hips. And, hair that looked like a hurricane hit it.

My family really does love me.

I had one foot off the curb when Dr. Freida screeched again. Like she was howling to the moon. She swore like the captain of a hockey team. Some of the words I've never heard before. That's a mouthful, since I grew up in a copper mining town.

She stumbled her meanness to half a block away.

The three sisters glued their eyes to her movements.

She staggered in front of a taxi stand. Pointed an arthritic, crooked middle finger at one of the few cabs operating in town, as it passed her by.

We all bent our necks to listen.

"Flunken cabbies . . . those checkered soons oov—"

All of a sudden, we whirled around at the sound of Dak, screaming wildly.

He darted out of the building to warn her. "Look out! There's a car speeding towards the front of the sidewalk where you're standing." He yelled like a fog horn. "Lady . . . hey, lady. Step back in here at once. Move. Now!"

"Aye got me rights, yeh know," she snorted hate. The sisters were riveted to her words. "Yeh flunken cops doon't own me enymoore."

I looked up to see Dak anxiously race towards her. He forcefully pushed an empty luggage carrier, blocking his way, to his left. Accidentally butted an elderly man, hard to the ground in the process. "Please Ma'am . . . run over here to me. . . . look out!"

The man screamed in pain.

Dak reached down to help him to his feet.

The belligerent woman held up her hand. Gave him her crooked bird. "Lave me illone."

Zoonawme and I darted our heads like tennis balls, between the car and the ornery old woman, fiddling with her hearing aid.

Aunt Rose acted quickly.

She disappeared faster than that turncoat contractor, that let my sink overflow. Then vacated the house, while his handiwork flooded my new hardwood floors into shriveled splinters.

Hummy scrambled in discord. Dak chased her into the lobby. He kept yelling to the woman. So did Zoonawme.

I seized Aunt Nell's oxygen apparatus. Shoved her behind a lonely trash container near the curb. A kaleidoscopic of pain whacked the smarts out of my injured shoulder, as I dove for cover between my frightened aunt—and a smelly garbage can, that'd been ripe since the Christmas of 1880.

Her trembling fingers dug into my arm. "Way'll die froom theh methane cooking en theh garbage." She covered her mouth and sneezed into a hanky. I thought her heart would beat out of her chest. She was more frightened of germs than of being hit by a car.

Dak was busy chasing pedestrians away. All the while, throwing his voice at the doctor.

Zoonawme was closest to Dr. Freida.

He leaped forward. "Ma'am! This way . . . quick!"

"Sweet Blessed Mother." I howled in disbelief, seeing his dexterous feet hurdle high into the air. "No! Please!" I knew he'd give up his honorable life, to save a hard of hearing, disorderly, intoxicated crank. He always seemed to do the right thing. I screamed again. "Somebody help them."

Aunt Nell and I, crouched low, as the former all-star, high school running back coursed like a young athlete. He was attempting to outrun a souped-up, green, Chevy sedan, accelerating straight for Dr. Freida.

He's Superman to me. Mid-forties. Fit as a bull rider—but, could he pull it off? I feared not. Notre Dame's entire football team—Knute Rockney's famous band of fresh-legged tacklers—wouldn't stand a chance against an oncoming speeding missile.

Bad things happened fast.

A set of loud, squealing brakes pierced my sore ears. Drummed the nerves of my teeth. I gyrated my head.

My friend leaped high. Swerved to one side. My sick stomach pulled me down. I ducked lower. Closed my eyes.

What happened next, took twenty years off my life.

I heard an awkward, unnatural noise. Tires skidded across the sidewalk. The night air was filled with a clangorous sound track. A James Bond, 007, flick.

The next horrible sequence reeled in slow motion.

Played out like a Chuck Norris demolition scene for anyone brave enough to watch.

Screech!

Slam!

Thud!

Splotch!

I cradled Aunt Nell's ears, to dull the splattering racket of a human body being hit by a moving transport.

Followed by an unwitting silence.

"You all right, Auntie?" I asked, squeezing her shoulders.

"Aye thenk so," she weeped.

"Stay down."

"Stay down?"

"Just until I see what happened."

Slowly, I craned my head up over the can. Squinted to find out what happened to my friend, the elderly doctor, and the car.

"How bed es et?"

"Bad," I murmured. "Real bad!"

Chapter Eighteen

I peered through a cloud of black-gray smoke, straining to see Zoonawme. Dr.Freida's battered body lay twisted like a pretzel on the sidewalk. Puddles of red blood surrounded the corpse. The sight of a dark pool of crime shocked me. I leaned over and emptied my queasy Irish stomach.

Aunt Nell clung to my arm. "Great ghost oov Banshees, es may sesters all rate?" she probed, handing me a clean cloth to wipe my mouth. "Yur stomach. Et was thet smelly can, now wasn't et?"

"No!" There's no easy way to sugar coat what I saw. "That poor woman's pint-size frame must've rocketed upward," I described. "On her way down, she slammed violently against a front barrier near the wall. Maybe . . . I'm guessing, she bounced ten feet high before she landed several yards from where the car rammed her."

Aunt Nell's eyes hollowed into a trance. "Whar'es our Zoonawme?"

I slowly looked again, afraid of what I might find.

He was lumped in a ball near the wrecked car, high centered on the curb. Smoke and confusion all around him.

"Zoonawme! . . . Zoonawme!" I screamed over and over in the direction of the crash. My shoulders ached from the weight of steadying Aunt Nell.

"Es hay dead?"

"Don't know." I couldn't move.

"Ooh, God halp oos, now."

As the mist evaporated, I made out Dak's silhouette. He dropped to his knees next to Zoonawme.

"Wake up Keno Savvy, you lazy Indian," he urged. He lifted his heavy head, and placed two fingers on his neck. "Good pulse."

I untangled myself from Aunt Nell's clutches. Sat her on a curb, and galloped over to my friends. Just in time to see Dak throw a hard slap to Zoonawme's face.

He moaned. Another moan.

Dak slapped him again and again.

There was a slight twitch of his lips.

Dak jiggled his scarred, right wrist and pulled him up by his shoulders. "Come out of it!"

"Can we get him to stand?" I asked.

"Not without a crane."

He hit him harder and harder.

"You open your eyes . . . I don't have time to put up with make-believe. We've got work to do. I need you!"

"Zoonawme, it's Caitlin . . . do you hear me?" Life without either one of them would be hell.

At last he grunted to consciousness. Painfully stretched his head. And strained his muscles to stand.

"The elderly woman?" he cleared his throat. "She make it?" He reached up. Gripped Dak's arm from swatting him again. "Hey . . . hey, Paleface . . . stop!"

"A horse doesn't pull a wagon without a goal," Dak voiced. We both helped him to stand. A sticky trail of warm blood on the palms of Zoonawme's huge hands, smeared the side of my face as I helped Dak boost him to his feet.

"You all right, friend?" I asked.

"Who made that tackle?" he muttered, twisting his neck side to side.

Suddenly, Dak bucked to his feet. He scrambled to the victim. Threw his jacket over her. Then, examined the driver of the vehicle. He stomped back. "How much of you is hurt?"

"A little dizzy . . . that's all." He looked down at both scraped knees protruding through his tattered pants. Swiveled his head to me. "Your cheek's bleeding, Cat Woman."

I stood on the balls of my feet to position his ten-gallon hat on his head.

"What just happened here?" Zoonawme queried, dusting off his favorite western jacket that hung cockeyed, and torn, as he surveyed the scene.

"That crazy teenager," Dak roared, pointing to the wreckage. "Mayor's son . . . got liquored up. Rammed through a roadblock at the mouth of Airport Road, and came back for seconds. That's what happened!"

Moonbeams spilled over a city in shock as we edged to the damaged vehicle.

"We can't move the kid until the medics show up," Dak decided. The medical team had their hands full. They've heard a crash, but can't respond. "God knows what shape he's in."

Zoonawme limped slightly to reach the car. He poked his nose inside the vehicle. "Agreed, he shouldn't be moved. I see the blood on his neck, too." He asked for yellow tape to cordon off the area. Advanced slowly to Dr. Freida's body. Realigned Dak's jacket, spread over her.

"Aunt Nell O.K.?" Dak asked. He assumed so, and walked over to his car a few yards away. Wrestled a roll of tape from the front seat. Called a deputy. And, left the door swung open, as he listened to a lame excuse from one of his staff.

"We're getting to the problem of the Security breach," the deputy told him. "We could use more help."

"More brains," he hissed. Hung up. Dr. Megan Pat called.

"What's going on over there? We heard a loud crash," she asked.

"Body count's climbing . . . Megan Pat . . . this connection's bad, can you hear me?" He tossed tape to Zoonawme.

"Yes, Dak . . . I hear you," she answered, working across the field with her rescue team. "What'd you need?"

"Send help over here to the mayor's kid. He's been in an accident. Cut up pretty bad," he ordered. "Better keep this line open. What? . . . yes, I already checked, but, . . . hold on." He reached through a broken window and felt for a pulse. "He's alive. Blood's dripping from his face." He paused. "No, we won't move him."

"On my way," she answered. "Anything else?"

"Advise Duggan-Dolan Mortuary to dust off one more slab!"

"Will do," she obliged, hoping the slab was for Caitlin.

Mortuary! It wasn't long ago, the funeral home doubled as a sports' medicine chamber, for high school athletes.

"Zoonawme, you remember how football . . . basketball . . . and baseball players laid on—"

"After a game, us boys laid on a table upstairs of the mortuary," he recalled. "Trainers massaged tight muscles to condition our overworked brawn. Taped injuries, too. We'd lay there holding ice packs on our swollen limbs, and discussing the game." He frowned, then added, "The facility today, will be crammed with victims no one can repair."

Dak hung up. Sprinted to the other side of the terminal, ready to string his men on a post.

Zoonawme dusted my face with his long black ponytail as he swung around. He favored his back as he limped behind Dak.

I trailed back to check on Aunt Nell.

"Caitlin, me legs won't wark," she wept, having rolled her oxygen tank to a different edge of the sidewalk. She sprayed a spot on the curb using a bottle of disinfectant stored in her bag, and stared into the night. Blackness reminded her of the shaft her husband fell down. Darkness was her enemy as much as germs and bacteria. "May sesters?"

"Hang on, Sweetheart." I propped an emergency flashlight—that a deputy laid down—in the palm of her unsteady hand. "I'll see about the family." I slithered slowly past Dr. Freida's body, and stopped short. What did I hear?

A grinding crank of a key repeatedly twisted in the ignition of the wrecked car. I listened to a series of quick jabs without turning the motor over. Then I saw the mayor's son wobble from the wreckage. His car wouldn't start. Dazed, drunk, and determined, he searched for a way to flee.

Before I could reach him, he managed to beeline into Dak's car. Close the door. And, roll up the window.

"Get out of that car!" I yelled, banging on the window. Why did Dak leave the door wide open? "Get out, kid!"

A half turn of the key primed the three-month-old, special built, super engine. It started instantly. The second the kid ground the gearshift to low, I backed off. He burned rubber as he sped from zero to seventy in six seconds, towards the exit lane.

Even from so far away, Dak heard his engine, and came running. He'd memorized every ping of his car. Every squeak. Every sound it made. It was his baby. He gaped in horror at seeing the back end of his expensive, state of the art, special equipped, Ford sedan, racing to freedom.

I mumbled to the wind. "This is awful. Dak'd lobbied at length to purchase a classy Sheriff's car. Specially equipped with latest crime fighting technology. Months to make. The department's once in a lifetime purchase. No one else drove it."

"He's getting away," Dak yelled.

"On it." Zoonawme drew his 38 revolver from his holster. Feet spread apart, he stood like a drugstore wooden statue, training his farsighted eyes on the back tires of Dak's new Sheriff's car.

I scrambled inside the terminal, and heard a moan. "Halp me," Hummy whimpered. She was corkscrewed underneath a low counter. Her face was as white as her new teeth. I leaned over her. "*Mother*?" I clumsily groped her around the waist, to help her stand.

"Ah . . . me Caitlin," she said, sweating beneath her warm coat. "Air may sesters all rate?" Her struggle to get up was miniscule compared to her struggle to absorb, *Mother.*

I felt ashamed I hadn't treated her kindly since I was twenty-one. "You all right?"

"Aye can't ghet me knees teh straiten oop, now!"

In the middle of my tug, I apologized. "I'm apologizing for everything I ever did to hurt you." Try blunders, ignorance, ingratitude, self-pity, I thought to myself. Not one of them came out. I straightened her coat and helped her to a chair. "Everything . . . please forgive me?"

"Furgev yeh?" she winced. A shadow in her eyes stretched way beyond nostalgia. She shook out the hem of her floral housedress. Sat down slowly. Her knees made a crackling sound. "Thar's noothen teh furgev, now es thar! Aye love yeh, me swate Caitlin . . . love yeh 'til Aye die!"

Embarrassment ruled. Before we could bond, Dak rushed over, his nostrils flared in anger. He shouted into his communicator at someone Uptown. "There's a stupid, drunk kid driving away with my car!"

"Take it easy, Dak, the men depend on your skills," I cautioned.

"Ha! Caitlin . . . my fancy Security barriers . . . deteriorated . . . like the Berlin Wall, you just saw," he shrieked pointing to more people that surrounded the accident perimeter.

"Murphy's law!" I rubbed gravel from my bare feet.

"I'm dealing with deputies . . . good men laced with excitement. So much, they forget to follow orders," he barked. "Otherwise, we wouldn't be up to our elected necks, coping with a mettlesome public clamoring to help."

"How can I hel—"

He pivoted his head to Zoonawme's gun. Saw him release his thumb from the hammer. Take his finger off the trigger.

"Too many people milling about," he complained. "Couldn't get a clear shot at the tires."

More people raced to help.

That wasn't all that was racing.

Dak's car streaked past an historic, two-seater monument. An airplane—USAF 30997 jet fighter—flown in the Korean War. Mounted high on a cement block at Airport Road entrance. He about passed out when his car disappeared north on Harrison Avenue, the main road that led to Uptown.

"The kid would have to follow it for awhile until he could turn off," I figured. "You have somebody patrolling up there?"

"Incompetents," Dak roared. The thought of whitewashing their careless actions raised his anger, as much as the humiliation of losing his car. He knew he'd make excuses for his deputies' ineptness, he thought, holstering his weapon. He put Mr. Smith and Mr. Wesson down for a nap.

I ached to nap with them. This day had seventy-two hours in it. I hobbled Hummy to the lavatory. We pushed through a blur of discontent to get inside. Phones rang. Disgruntled people shouted for luggage.

"Keystone Cops," Dak muttered, eating the bottom of the receiver. He tore into deputies parked on the far side of the runway. "Where the hell are you? No! I told you to secure . . . ah, never mind. Get your sorry, rear appendages over here to police these rambunctious folks. They're acting like Greyhounds dogging a rabbit. I don't want anyone else hurt!"

What he wants, is to box their ears off.

Deputies' screw-ups made him look like a weak leader.

Yet, he'd record his men's misnomers as unintentional.

His pride wounded, I kept my distance.

Zoonawme gently massaged our friend's angry heart with kindness. "I need more yellow emergency tape . . . and a bottle of beer." He pointed to a partially roped-off crime scene.

"Cattle prods, too!" Dak said amusingly, punching numbers into his phone. "I'm trying to catch that female rookie before she gets down here."

What I saw happen next made my heart beat like a tom-tom.

I thought I was watching a mystery movie.

Sweet, retiring Hummy plodded over to Aunt Nell on a dimly lit sidewalk. Snatched her flashlight. Ambled next to Aunt Rose, leaning over the doctor's body, her knees glued in blood.

Hummy steadied her arm to make the flashlight dance on Rose's strong hands—clenched around the victim's throat—attempting to kill Dr. Freida twice.

Aunt Rose silently, deliberately, squeezed harder.

The flashlight beam slowly raised. Streamed over Aunt Rose's thumping chest. Her head sprang in four directions, to see if anybody was looking, while she scooped up the victim's purse.

"Jest look queck," Hummy advocated, without budging. Aunt Rose focused her eyes on the contents. Looted a document. Tucked it into her blouse. Stood. She helped Hummy up. They retreated a couple of feet back to Aunt Nell—nodding yes.

"Sweet Blessed Mother," I called out to them. "What did the three of you just do?"

Chapter Nineteen

Dak wiped sweat from his brow. He concentrated on the phone. Waited impatiently for verbal acknowledgement from his rookie. He didn't notice what Aunt Rose just did. "One more Broad that's anxious to flex her beefy biceps," he said.

"She passed your rigid qualifications, didn't she?" I prompted. "Next to me, she's a slim, going on slimmer."

His peppery, male attitude got in the way. "She's nothing like you. Probably's putting on lipstick before she gets back—"

His phone rang.

"I'm on it, boss," said the perceived outsider to his team. She snapped her voice into the phone. "How come you're using a cell instead of your car communic—"

He told her what happened.

"I don't think I heard you correctly, boss," she played innocent. "Could you repeat that?"

He threw his weight into the receiver at the only deputy near the getaway car. "A hit and run . . . you do know what that is?" Pause. "You heard me. The mayor's kid is strutting around in my new car. Coming your way . . . and fast."

Like some of his men, he didn't believe a woman should be on the street enforcing law or keeping the peace.

"Sir, my phone's breaking up. Umm . . . you did say *your* car's been stolen?" He could see a sly smile lighting up her face, through the phone. "What'd you want me to do, boss?"

"Do not apprehend without backup," he shouted into the mouthpiece. He squared his jaw to adjust to her feminine pitches as they came over the plate.

"Is the driver a suspect in that hit and run down your way?"

"Follow your orders."

"Yes, Sir," she copied. "What is it . . . exactly . . . that you want me to do?"

"Tail the car and report to me." He slapped his phone on his hip. Shook his head my way. "Newcomer. She's all I got in the vicinity."

Meanwhile, Zoonawme quieted the crowd. Cleared them out without incident. Shopped for a dry spot, to kneel next to the O'Shaughnessy sisters—squeezing shoulder to shoulder.

He balanced over the body. "You know this woman?

Hovering over the victim again, like three black hawks, they cemented their lips shut.

King Kong did a better acting job.

Whenever these three women of the Apocalypse closed ranks, a live cannon ball on their tails couldn't get them to talk.

I'd let them have their secrets for now.

But, just wait until I get them home!

I burrowed next to Zoonawme. My bare feet slide on a pool of blood, running wild like a broken water main over the sidewalk. "Her name's Dr. Freida!"

"Anyone meeting her?" he quizzed.

"She muttered something about getting in touch with a woman named Riv Etter," I explained. "Jeep, the fellow that was rushed to the hospital with head injuries, knows her."

Just then, the driver of a hearse propelled himself forward. Pushed at our shoulders to move away from the body.

Zoonawme angled sideways, and saw the victim's purse sprawled wide open, next to Aunt Rose.

"Et esn't mine, now es et?"

He'd been friends with them all his life. He knew from their eyes something was wrong. "You rifle through this woman's personal effects?"

Silence.

The sisters were among the most honest people he knew. The O'Shaughnessy clan was his family. He'd die for them . . . but, he wouldn't lie or steal if his own life depended on it.

"Put back whatever you took!"

"Ware jest helpen . . . now waren't way!" Aunt Rose explained, taking charge of the lie.

Helping themselves was more to the point.

They got caught with their fingers in the cookie jar. A cookie jar that spelled intrigue. Had they all gone mad?

What was the link between these four women?

"We'll get to the bottom of things tomorrow," I glossed over, as Dak pulsed by and helped us to our feet.

"Zoonawme," he said, taking a deep breath. "Get these girls home."

Through a smell of fresh pine gently breezing from the trees, the five of us muddled to the parking lot, blinded by high wattage street lights fencing a wide and empty trail. Climbed into his red pickup truck. Squeezed together on the bench seat.

I crimped my neck over my shoulder. Stared out the back window at the crime scene, as we drove away. Tire skids behind me that stretched across the sidewalk like giant pen marks, shrunk smaller and smaller with each roll of the wheels. While an air of silent tension inside grew bigger and bigger.

Aunt Rose broke the silence. She strained her neck to see the top of the mountain. The Blessed Mother's white frame stood against a dark sky. "There's a—"

"The cemetarry," Aunt Nell shrieked loudly. She pointed to a short row of gray headstones near the edge of a tall, spooky fence that bordered Airport Road. "Way'd bay waven et Sam, himself, now woodn't way?"

"Nell!" Hummy scolded. "Mind yur bezness."

I closed my eyes as I always did whenever I passed the unsightly gravestones that marked the O'Toole family plot.

There lies my dear Sam, one headstone was inscribed.

The love of my life had been buried next to his mother for twenty-five years, and was still driving me crazy with passion.

Predictably, Hummy's hatred for Sam surfaced. She cupped Nell on the chin. "Doon't yeh bay utterin hez neyum . . . yeh hare me!"

"Bay quiet," she snorted back.

"Theh lot oov yeh shut oop," Rose butted in. "Yur both trooble maykers." She waved an authoritative hand in front of them, hitting the dash board with a loud snap. "Stop fighten, Aye'm tellen yeh."

Whenever Sam's name drifted into a family conversation, plenty of rude bickering dominated the trio.

"After all this time, why can't you just leave it alone?" I begged.

Zoonawme waved his arm to quiet us down. He didn't want to talk about Sam, anymore than I wanted them to know I found Sam's dad, Private First Class Erin O'Toole. I intended to keep Erin missing-in-action until I've had a few nights of sleep.

"The sisters are distraught over the airplane scare. Seeing that woman killed in cold blood," he said, reaching down to turn on the radio.

"Theses ladies aren't edgy because there was death in the air this night," I whispered. "Seventy-year-old women around here talked about death, like virgin teenagers talked about sex. They perceive to know a lot about a subject they've never experienced."

"Hush, ladies," said the peace maker, cranking the radio up to his favorite country and western station.

Marty Robbins was singing.

A bullet hit him while riding his horse, on his way to Rose's Cantina, the woman he loved. Wounded, half out of his saddle, and writhing on a bumpy mountain trail, he sees the Cantina and keeps going.

Just before he reached his darling Rose, he died.

The song was appropriate.

I never reached happiness with my Sam. My heart died.

I knew just how sad and weak Marty felt at the finish line.

Silver Bow County covered a large territory, and Dak had most of his men at the airport. However, after deputies, Needle Point and Costello finished settling a drunken brawl at the M & M Saloon, Uptown, they called in to Dak.

"Back up rookie, Cindy. Then drive to the airport," he ordered.

"Been one pithy night," Costello reported on the phone. He set aside a bad habit of swearing. Cussing was a personality trait Dak insisted his men leave at home. They did a fairly good job of it. "Miner's Union Day sure does bring out . . . umm these sons of . . . umm . . . orders understood."

Costello was a stout little man that looked more like a short order chef than an officer of the law. Yet, he was a good person, and one of the best deputies the department ever trained.

Half an hour later, he jumped out of the car before it stopped, and sputtered to his boss. "Lost the new kid while she was in pursuit of the hit and run."

"No! You didn't say that," Dak gasped. "You telling me you lost the rookie . . . and . . . you also lost my car?"

Needle Point fumbled out through the driver's seat, his light skin flushed scarlet. "Yah, you betcha, we did!"

The Finlander was a good match for his partner. Honorable. Reliable. A square shooter. He scratched his bald head and wondered. How could he support his partner's report without looking incompetent? Not even the black of night could hide that he was uniquely different in the way he looked—unparalleled in appearance, compared to every other man in town—in the entire state of Montana, for sure.

His body resembled a road map of the world.

As the story goes, he was a young guy despondent at being prematurely bald. One fateful night the deputy walked into a tattoo parlor in Anaconda on a dare. He asked them to burn a picture of blonde hair on his head.

Except, the poor fellow forgot to say when.

Not one inch of this tall, slim, Finlander's, fair-skinned body had escaped the needle. Right down to black and white argyle socks incinerated on his feet—up to his ankles—stopping at the top of his thighs. They say he has yellow and orange shorts tattooed on his skinny behind. Regardless, he's resigned to his fate.

"We were driving south bound," he said kindly. "Whipping fast on the lower side of the curve by the old Eddy's Bakery. We saw your car going the opposite direction from us. It sped by, stopped on a dime, and ducked in an alley past Eddy's."

Costello added, "Just as we swerved to turn around, the new kid—hot in pursuit—stamped a led foot to the peddle and almost rammed us. We spun out just as the rookie turned up that back street to follow the perp."

"I knew she'd screw up," Dak said. "I'll never understand why personnel has to rob the cradle to fill these positions. She started the job with three strikes against her. Female. Under thirty. No street experience . . . not right a woman should tote a gun."

"She's related to fu . . . I mean, freaking Joey Chitwood," Costello huffed.

"What'd you mean?"

"More like a high speed car chaser. She drives like she's the Dufus of Hazard."

"Ah! She did screw up! . . . I knew it!"

"That damn . . . I mean that darn kid drove with all four tires nailed on the road," he reported.

Costello was a year older than the rookie he called a kid. More experienced on the force. Yet, he'd been bested at his driving skills. "For a lightweight, small shouldered, five-foot-five woman, with no as . . .er . . . that sits hipless on 110 pounds, she puts tough, smart shoulders to the wheel with—"

Needle Point turned his head to answer his cell phone. "Come in . . ." Pause. He held the receiver close to his mouth. "Say that again." His hand waved for silence. "One more time . . . O.K. . . . understood. Yes, Sheriff's standing next to me . . . I'll tell him."

It was a call from Dr. Megan Pat.

She'd been standing alongside another surgeon, outside intensive care at the hospital. Waiting to talk to Jeep before he went into surgery for his head wounds. She needed to question him about his heart history, and secure the name of a relative they could contact.

"That Italian guy is still unconscious. She wants to know if you found Mr. Palagretti's wallet?"

"Eagle Eye's trying to resurrect what's left of the contents on the plane," Dak pledged. He outlined the workload of Zoonawme's cousin. "She say anything else?"

"She called me because your private phone was busy," he told Dak. "It's about the rookie, Cindy. Said your new deputy's waiting in the lobby of the hospital. She needs to report to you—but your phone is ka-fooey."

"Don't tell me Cindy's been in an accident?" he wiped his brow.

"Not at all."

"She had a heart attack?"

"Not that I know of."

"What's Megan Pat got to do with all this?"

"Said she's the only one in town that could reach you . . . anytime she wanted to. That she's got a direct line to you."

"Yeah? You don't say!"

"Your female deputy bravely apprehended the assailant," MP reported to Needle Point. "Single handed." He waited a few seconds. "Also said the kid that stole your car, had enough booze in him to sink a battleship. They brought the drunken thug to the emergency room for observation."

"And . . . what about my Sheriff's car?"

"Cindy wanted to report to you in person, of course," he paraphrased. "She's following procedure—tied up supervising the tow truck that'll haul your car to the garage."

"Tow truck? Go ahead and drive it."

"Cindy's monitoring closely what's left of the vehicle—as evidence involving a crime."

"What's *left* of the vehicle?" Dak's face drained from deep red to ghost white. "Could this night get any worse?"

Chapter Twenty

Zoonawme gripped the steering wheel as we approached Harrison Avenue. We turned right. Rode twenty minutes uphill. Past a shopping area. Residences. And, several landmark buildings that disappeared by fire.

"There goes the Rialto Theater." He pointed to an empty lot.

"No more American Theater, either. Medical Arts Building was—"

The game stopped short. Before someone blurted out how my home was mysteriously incinerated. Or painfully reminded me that one of my twin dogs, Whiskey, died in the blaze.

Silently, we channeled over deep potholes, anchored in front of hundred year old gabled houses on the west side. Toured north past four-story, brick mansions erected when the city mushroomed with wealth.

At the top of North Excelsior, we turned left onto an unpaved street that led to O'Shaughnessy Road. Dodged a few boulders for quarter of a mile, and pulled up to a six room log house covered with an A frame.

The brakes set in place, Aunt Rose opened the door to cool, crisp mountain air that bathed her lungs. She bounced to the ground. "Yeh can see et froom hare," she announced, managing Aunt Nell's oxygen tank to the ground. She hobbled up fourteen, wide, wooden steps to the front door. Pointed down the mountain where old Shanty Town once thrived.

Her sisters spilled out of the truck.

The three women gaped. As if they actually could see a rambled shack they shared when they arrived in Butte. Their first home sat empty. Silent against a backdrop of a gallows frame gone haywire.

"Et warr eh long tame ago, now wasn't et?" Nell confirmed, squinting through wire-rimmed glasses.

"Aye, thet et was," Hummy joined in. She imagined her long-gone youth, living next to an abandoned mine yard. Covered by cobwebs, and bittersweet memories.

Rose looked at her watch, thinking how she'd set her timepiece back then, to the mine's noon whistle. "Ware all tired. 'Tes late, now esn't e—"

Bark! Bark! Bark!

My frisky roommate, and companion, a Silver Fox Mountain Kodiak—special breed of Samoyed dog—lunged from the long porch that stretched around the front of the house. She raced towards me wagging her long, full-haired tail.

"Pen Doodle," I cried out, bracing myself against forty pounds, that made me forget everything, but my lonely dog.

"Good companion to my dog, Spirit," Zoonawme piped up. She smothered me under her fluffy white coat. "They get along like brother and sister . . . same as us." He pointed to her belly, nearly healed. Four years, daily, he rubbed on cocoa butter, and deer salve, to soften burn scars from my house fire.

She swept my deserter face with pink-tongued kisses, and sniffed for a treat.

"Sorry, old girl," I apologized. Her dark, oblique eyes whined with disappointment. Like me, she was born with impatience. "Your treats are at the airport being sorted out by Eagle Eye." Zoonawme's cousin worked as Jack of all trades at the airport. He handled a job at a snail's pace. That sod buster's oil . . . I'm water when it comes to quickness. I've told Pen Doodle before. He's as slow as the coming of Spring. Of course, she's reasoned out, by the time he sorts out the mess on the airplane, her treats will be as stale as my feelings for the elder Blackfoot Indian.

"Bater go on en," Nell said, shying away from dog germs.

Zoonawme checked the windows.

Satisfied the tricky seals installed hadn't been tampered with, he lobbed over to a small box nailed near the door. Rigged to flash on flood lights, and ring loudly, if the right code wasn't punched in. Labeled meticulously in tiny handwriting. "Eagle Eye's idea to protect you from a possible set-fire . . . or a break-in . . . is holding up just fine."

"I'm sure the nuns are jealous of his faultless handwriting," I educated. I waited for him to open the door. "Nuns are big on that perfection stuff. Like, dotting every small "i" so close to the letter, you need a microscope to verify a smidgen of space between."

"My cousin's a good man . . ." He paused. "He doesn't care that you don't like him, he still has your best interests in his heart."

"I'm sorry, Zoonawme. I think he's an Indian reincarnation of nuns. Flawless attention to detail in the written word. In all his actions. Sorry, but he drives me nuts. It'll take him forever to separate, sort, label, and identify six toothpicks."

"You ever see him separate tooth picks?"

"Silly."

"How'd you know so much about his penmanship?"

"I screened his handwriting for employment at the airport."

"Why?"

"Job compatibility."

"He's been working out there a long time." He punched code numbers on the alarm pad, opened the door, visually searched the front room, and stepped back. "Come on in."

We shuffled inside to the smell of pine-sol, and deep cleaning agents. "Your fingerprints are all over the freshness, Aunt Nell."

"Finesh aboot Eagle Eye!" She gave me the *look*.

"I wanted to report he'd be perfect for painting quarter-inch mosaic pieces. Organizing a chess tournament for blind seniors. But, employers were only interested in security factors, and he was as honest, and reliable a man I'd ever analyzed."

"Slow poke?" Aunt Rose assessed, without taking a breath. "Et's no secret hes mindfulness es eh dynamite specialist, saved Shannon's and McLeary's lives, when they ware trapped et theh 2,000 level oov theh Travonia mine, now es et?"

Rose felt the same adoration for Eagle Eye, that I did for Zoonawme. Either, something between them in their past, or his neatness habits turned her on. I hoped she didn't start with how he lined up canned food labels in his cupboard. Like soldiers standing at attention. How he color coded his sock drawer. Matching each pair next to a corresponding tab, stamped with date of purchase.

How she knew all of this was one mystery I didn't care to solve.

Hummy came from the kitchen. She threw her dollar into the pot. Gossiped about Eagle Eye shoveling snow. Freezing it into square ice blocks, that bordered the sidewalk on both sides. Like two perfectly constructed, five-foot igloo walls. "Aye made eh pot oov coffee en thet new pot yeh got fare eh house warmen."

Aunt Rose ambled to the kitchen. Grabbed two beers, and came back with a Dagwood sandwich for Zoonawme. A five decker roast beef, and Swiss cheese creation—cold fried onions, spicy pickles, thin cucumber slices. Durkee's spicy mayo sauce. All stacked between homemade, whole wheat bread.

"Theh lettuce died." She handed him the acid burner, and a beer.

I put on a pair of socks from the hall closet floor. Sat on the bottom step of my stairs. Stared blankly while he inhaled his snack.

He asked. "What time're you going—"

"To the hospital tomorrow to check on Jeep?"

"Yes. You want me to—"

"Of course."

"Maybe we can—"

"No. I'll grab a bite to eat here, instead." I nodded to the fridge bursting with food.

"See you around 1:00 o'clo—"

"Hellup . . . hellup!" Aunt Nell bellowed, unable to stop my dignified dog from shellacking her white face, to a creamy purple. "Get hare off oov me. Shay's carrien garems, now esn't shay."

Zoonawme waved goodbye. I gave what I had left.

I ran to the couch. Swatted Pen Doodle's flat paws off my aunt's throbbing chest. "You know licking is forbidden," I reprimanded, wondering if I'm ever going to bed.

She jumped to the floor. Looked at me with disappointment. Playfully clamped her teeth on the toe of my sock.

"Improper chewing is a no-no. Please lay down." I aimed my finger at her bed in the kitchen. She owned more furniture than I did. Six plush doggie beds. One in each room of the house.

Hummy swabbed her sister's face with disinfectant as they walked to the door. "Way'll bay layven now."

Of course, Aunt Rose shot the last round from her hip. "Yur dog end yoo ere both vary highly intelligent. Boot willfully resistant teh obedience trainen."

I waved goodbye. They piled into her vintage Chrysler. Rode off into the black of night, that swallowed up the mountains. I finally exhaled. Skated to the kitchen on shiny hardwood floors.

Nixed the coffee, and opened the cupboard.

I poured six fingers of the good stuff, Paddy's Whiskey from Ireland, into a thick rimmed cup. A souvenir from the old Chequamegan on Main Street—a long gone café. It was a sacred cup to me. One that piped caffeine into both Sam's, and my study veins, during our senior year of high school. I gulped the resilient relic dry, and re-loaded, as Pen Doodle brushed lovingly against me, wagging her tail. I felt thankful to be alive.

Thankful that my dog and the cup were rescued from the ashes of my house.

Too tired to crawl upstairs to my bedroom, I sat cross legged in front of a red brick fireplace. My eyes felt heavy, hollow. They drifted to an original oil painting, that hung above the mantel. Glassy eyed, I watched cowboys wearing guns, sitting at a campfire in the wild west, being stalked by Indians carrying bows and arrows.

I heard Pen Doodle toot a few.

She didn't care one raspberry about looking at an expensive house warming gift, funded by Aunt Rose's successful stock dealings. Her narrow rump squatted near the window to watch the moon pass out of sight, while my eyelids dropped.

I don't know how long I gaped at my favorite artist's work. A huge Charlie Russell, depicting life in the old west—without seeing a thing.

No more than I remembered, at what time I fell into a deep sleep.

Chapter Twenty-one

"Pen Doodle . . . stop that!" She pulled at the covers, torturing me to wake up. My mouth tasted sour. Every muscle on my body ached with tension. I don't remember coming to bed, but I wanted to stay under the warm covers. Tell myself I dreamed up a phone call that brought me to Berlin. That I never answered an ad in the *New York Times* for a forensic handwriting scientist. That my life was still humdrum. Uninteresting. Safe.

Things were simpler when I settled for shallow.

Until last December. Shivering in bed at 40° below. In high country, the morning mist sometimes lasted 'til noon. I laid around waiting for the day to clear. No enthusiasm for facing life, or going to work. The phone rang. A man sounding like Zoonawme, faking a German accent, asked me to interview—over the phone—for a job with the Geneva Historical Council. What happened next thrust me into an adventure overseas . . . ending with a harrowing ride on Flight 411.

I smart-mouthed back, in five different languages. "No legitimate expert would trust a voice on the phone, when it came to important work that might alter history."

Zoonawme knew I answered the ad on a lark. That I see me as a little squirt in a big field of experts—never expecting a bite.

All I wanted was bragging rights, that I was considered for an international job. "What'd you need with all those languages in such a small town?" Zoonawme, I thought, goaded me into a feisty encounter.

"Like you didn't know," I charged in Hungarian.

"Educate me."

I told myself he must really need me down at the office. Toying with my thought process before I've had coffee. Out came my feistiness. "I'm trained to analyze writing in other languages. Copper Dust Forensics is full service. We investigate personality like the FBI investigates terrorists! Give me a break. Quit pretending. You know Butte's a unique city. Different ethnic backgrounds. A kaleidoscope of handwriting that's challenged me . . . but never has beaten me."

Zoonawme persisted. Or, so I thought!

"We decided to call," he said in broken English. "Butte's famous for copper production. Not for an investigative expert of human behavior with experience in legal proceedings."

Out came my cockiness. Partly in Italian, German, and the rest in Russian. "You couldn't afford me anyway." I hung up and turned on the answering machine. Tooled off to meet Zoonawme at the office, to face his lame denial that he called. Next thing I knew, an executive from Geneva group left a message on my machine. He was impressed with forthright, snappy answers. Language know-how. Confidence. He came to Butte. We sealed the deal on a fluke. Out came my guilt.

I robbed some other expert of 15 minutes of fame.

Of bending over a lighted forensic table, to analyze madmen's script for authenticity and motive.

Pen Doodle pulled a pillow to the floor. She kept after me. "Thirsty?" I squinted at the alarm clock's hazy green numbers, and jumped out of bed. Did it ding off during the night when I was in a deep dream sequence? And, what a dream! Just when I found my birth mother, Ella Fitzgerald, whipping up Irish stew in the White House kitchen, I heard a bothersome phone ringing in the pantry.

That's when Pen Doodle nuzzled my aching legs to help me swim out of a deep sleep. To answer the phone. It rang again.

I rubbed sleep crystals from my eyes as I picked up the phone. "What the? Hello . . . hello?" I heard the door bell ring. Slapped the receiver down. Stumbled to the hall, clung to the stairwell railing, and stopped at a harmonious glockenspiel, crafted in Galway Bay, Ireland, chiming "*Danny Boy.*"

The door bell persisted.

"Keep your shorts on," I yelled, slowly descending each stair, trying to shake off a troublesome hangover. I stepped warily to a crisp peal of slow, well-timed bells, coming from amusing Gaelic chimes that welcomed me home. The Grandfather clock Aunt Nell gifted me, signaled 3:00 p.m. Reminding me I was two hours late to meet Zoonawme.

I twisted the front door knob.

Zoonawme raised his high cheek bones, full lips drawn wide into an appealing grin. "Everything all right, Cat Woman?"

"I think so. Those extra couple of hours felt refreshing."

He watched me stretch an over worked, elastic waistband, on my flannel pajamas, into a safety pin. I drew the britches up higher to cover my German cake calories. *Evil jammies!*

"Why'd you ring the bell? You always let yourself in."

"Came in when I carried you upstairs." His deep, chocolate brown eyes lit up the room as he talked. "Sorry. I left my keys on your dresser." He handed me black coffee in a Styrofoam cup, and placed a box on the floor labeled, *Mr. Coffee.*

"What time was that?" I asked, guzzling the brew.

"Yesterday noon." He patted Pen Doodle's head. Rubbed her belly to calm her down. Ushered her outside to play with his dog. Shut the door. "You've been asleep for two days. Your cousin's been anxious to see you. Said he's got something very important to talk to you about."

"Two days? Mike? Oh, God."

"Yup!"

"I'm so sorry." I sipped coffee. "Mike's probably antsy to get the bottle of holy water I promised him I'd bring back from Berlin."

Then out comes the snide.

"Your cousin Eagle Eye will never—"

"That's your answering machine whining," he interrupted, ignoring my crankiness.

It recorded a fresh call next to a dozen other calls to return.

"You think they're all from Mike?" I flipped the switch to turn it on. "Why a new coffee pot? Just received a new one for a house warming gift, shortly before I left for Europe."

"Yours blew up, almost started a fire while you were asleep."

"You kidding me?" I gasped. "You can't be serious?"

"Several hours after the pot automatically turned off, it started up on its own. Lucky I came by when I did, or we'd be sifting through ashes right now."

I read his mind. "The pot didn't come with a card."

"I gave the remains to Dak. He'll run it through his lab. I'm tracking down sales receipts."

I listened to my calls. Three came from an agitated Mike telling me to get over to his place, pronto. Hospital called—Jeep underwent surgery for serious head injuries. Copilot's appendix burst while we were in the air—he didn't make it. Judge Ava Foil. Hummy. Dak . . . asking me to meet him concerning his daughter.

LB called, but the tape ran out before he left a message.

"I listened to them yesterday," he informed. "Told Dak we'd meet early tomorrow."

I drank from Styrofoam, raced upstairs, and jumped into a hot shower. Wedged my hostile thighs into a pair of blue jeans, pulled on a sweatshirt, slipped into a comfortable pair of old running shoes, and sped downstairs.

"Ready," I sighed, angling my backpack over my shoulder.

Zoonawme had taken Pen Doodle for a walk, and was in the kitchen washing his hands. He smiled. Handed me a briefcase.

"No way! . . . Eagle Eye? . . . no way!"

He held up a dry towel for my wet hair. "So far, you're the only one that got stuff back."

"Divine providence," I admitted, rummaging for a bottle of holy water labeled with Mike's name.

"You saying, divine?" He bumped up against the kitchen counter. Listened without interruption. Just as he did at the airport, when I spilled my guts. How a handwriting job, World War II, trapped me in a dimension of time I didn't belong in. Led me to find myself.

I told him again. "Millions of families were destroyed. Entire blood lines were erased completely because of Hitler's madness."

"You've had a religious experience, all right!"

I turned on the faucet. Drew a glass of ice cold water, and cradled it in my hands. "That coffee pot incident gives me the shivers."

He wiped his mouth from the sting of ice water, flowing straight from underground, to the tap. Filled Pen Doodle's water bowl. Opened a kitchen window, and surprised me. "Let go of the past . . . let go of Sam! You can't move forward until you've left the past."

"A tough request I already planned to do," I promised, taking in a deep breath.

There's something special about Butte's air. It swirls my life in front of my nose. Like recalling the day I stood at the altar of St. Pat's Church. Wearing a long white gown. Zoonawme, dressed in a tux, smiled at his wife, Zakhooa. She looked beautiful in her traditional Blackfoot garb. Fussing with my long train, like an experienced Maid-of-honor. LB and I stood in the back. He wore the role of a substitute father with pride.

We took a few steps forward.

Then, Dak sprinted up the aisle, screaming.

Horrified and out of breath, he yelled to the congregation. "Sam'd been killed earlier. His truck overturned on a winding curve, high on Roosevelt Drive."

"Earth to Cat Woman?" He shut the window.

"I don't even care why Hummy hated Sam, and—"

Zoonawme answered the phone. "She'll be glad to hear that." He looked at his watch. "Jeep's asking for you."

I hastily fed Pen Doodle a handful of German dog yummies. Told her to mind the house, set the alarm, closed the door behind us, and dangled my keys. "Your car or mine?"

"I'll be working at the office later on," he said, closing the door to my forty-something laundry truck. I bonded with the old, two door, faded-red, Chevy panel truck, Paumie Dye House discarded when their business folded. Partly because we were the same age. Partly because we both needed a fresh coat of paint. Mostly—because my insurance never covered the full extent of my losses, when the house was destroyed by fire.

His dog, Spirit, barked wildly to be with Pen Doodle. Last year on a fishing trip in the Bitter Root Valley, he fought off a cougar, that wanted to eat my non-aggressive, Sweetie. A match made in heaven.

"Follow me to the hospital," he waved.

I gave the high sign to his hundred pound, almost extinct, Native American Indian dog, quivering with recognition from the back of the truck. A cross between an albino wolf, and a Siberian Husky. His long white fur splattered with a broken pattern of silver and black markings. Like his Indian ancestors, Spirit Dog was trained to pull large, heavy loads—protect children—hunt everything from quail to rabbits—bear to beaver—elk to moose—and to fish.

I mumbled to myself, *Dr. Freida dead! Gunner Dead! Copilot dead! Jeep hospitalized! Oh, man!*

I navigated through winding roads past a high school outdoor stadium. Looking more like a stately mansion in desperate need of some loving restoration, than an arena where football history was made. It was named after Zoonawme's brother, Avalanche, that once dominated the state of Montana as a brilliant quarterback.

Now, he was a deceased war hero.

Zoonawme honked the infamous Indian code, utilized in the second World War to signal alert. Beep . . . pause . . . beep, beep, beep, quickly in succession.

Saluted his brother.

I signaled the same beep code back to him. We drove off. He followed me into the hospital parking lot, where I cringed, seeing *Megan Pat the Terrible's* Mercedes, grinning at me.

We eased out of the elevator. Bristled past a female candy striper, wearing a high school letterman sweater that smelled like after shave. "Afternoon," she nodded. She was wheeling a cart of candy bars, and Catholic pre-surgery books, on how-to-save your soul—if a medical procedure should fail.

We stopped at intensive care ward, at the Nurse's station. MP rushed out of Jeep's room, bumped into me, and snarled. No doubt, hoping to see the first signs of my rigor mortis. "Oops." Her voice took a razor's edge. Until she spied Zoonawme standing behind me. "Sorry, honey," she smiled sweetly. "Caitlin, you here about your shoulder?" She flipped over a sheet of paper on her clip board, and began to write.

Her penmanship looked like a poster child for Palmer's Handwriting Method.

Smooth lines, just right strokes—not too light, not too dark. Written output of an intelligent, accomplished, and brilliant mind. I knew it would change. Drastically.

A multiple personality could fool everyone.

"We came to see Mr. Palagretti," I choked.

She pointed to the waiting room lounge. "You just missed his wife. You did know he was married?"

Zoonawme had visited Jeep before, and was making his way to the room.

Before I could follow, MP grabbed me under the arm, pulled me aside, and spoke softly. "Wait a minute, dear."

"What for?" I quivered. We were alone. I was aging at mock speed.

Chapter Twenty-two

"That should do it." Costello rubbed his hands together, and walked away from the railroad loading platform. He hiked his pants close to his waist, allowing for belly overhang, and reached for his wallet. "LB's real upset about his friend. What an awful way to go!"

Dak nodded, and waved goodbye to Slippery's body stored on a train travelling to Helena, where his family waited in sorrow to bury him. He shook hands with the station attendant and bent over a box to sign paperwork.

"You hungry?" Costello asked him, separating his paper money apart.

"Hmm?" Dak's stomach churned. He was hungry to learn more about his newfound daughter. He looked at his watch. "Lunch time. Have to follow up on something before I know if I have time to stop."

"You bet, boss." He angled behind a cart and checked to make sure Dak wasn't listening. Dialed his partner. Kept his voice low. "Needle Point, what time will you be there? We need to . . . umm . . . you know what I'm talking about." He listened. "No, he can't hear me." Paused. "Yes, tell LB we took good care of Slippery. Did you guys square Mildred around with Gunner's funeral?"

"All set for tomorrow morning," Needle Point said. "Ten o'clock. St. Pat's. Going to be a real doozy. His being one of the more popular editors of the Miners' union paper back in *the day*. Lots of friends. Fellow miners. Family."

"His enemies will want to be there, too," Costello advised, stepping into his car.

"Of course . . . to gloat."

"Rose O'Shaughnessy will be first in that line!"

"Right you are. Hope she doesn't make trouble."

Costello frowned. "Nah. Caitlin just got back from Europe. But, bank on Bridget and Nell to be at Duggan-Dolan Mortuary tonight at seven o'clock sharp. Rosary's in hand."

Needle Point cradled the phone under his chin, and opened a sack lunch. "Even in nice weather, I dread fighting for a parking space on the steepest part of North Montana Street. You need magnets on your shoes to walk on that sucker—slopes straight down like the top of a ski run."

Costello hung up. Hopped out of his car in front of Nancy's Pasties. An icon in Butte of a delicious, affordable lunch, and friendly conversation. The tasty Cornish, brown crusted, tender meat and potato pie, was as much a part of the town culture as mining. Folks ate pasty, cold in one hand, or at the counter drowning in thick, hot gravy—with a side of sweet, tangy Cole Slaw.

Meanwhile, Dak received a call to quiet down a bad-tempered scuffle at the C.O.D. Saloon, located in a rough part of town.

He drove off grumbling, at how slow his rented car climbed a steep hill to Uptown.

"I'd lay bet, grown men in the saloon were in a fight over where to buy their lunch pasties." He shot daggers of disgust at a broken clock on the dash.

It was a bright, sunny day. The weather felt calm. Too calm, he thought, as he arrived to see the bartender, a gangly man with a seventy-two-hour, blonde shadow, work the crowd to keep peace.

"Come on fellas . . . keep it straight." He pointed at the Sheriff, and shouted. "Hey, friend . . . heard you increased your family recently?" He snatched a hard boiled egg from a cooler, wiped it with a napkin, and held it out to Dak as he swaggered across a creaky floor.

"Heard right," he admitted, stuffing the car key in his pant pocket. He cranked his neck at a clock on the wall. It'd taken him forty minutes in his rented junker, to travel an area that should use up twenty. "Need help here?"

"A while ago, yes. Took you a long time to get . . . oh, yeah! You're hauling tail on a different set of wheels."

The rowdies looked down, laughing, and shaking their heads. Then went back to pounding their fists on the bar. Stomping their feet over a difference of opinion concerning Rose O'Shaughnessy, and Gunner.

More to the point, they were trying Aunt Rose in a court of public opinion, before they lynched her . . . or crowned her with jewels.

"Slut!"

"Damn good woman pioneer!"

"Brazen Hussy!"

"A real Irish beauty!"

"Too smart for her own good . . . stealing Gunner's property in a poker game," one patron said.

"Looking to make a buck . . . foolish Gunner lost it fair and square," defended a scraggy, retired lawyer parked on a high stool. He stroked his long beard. Swiveled around to greet Dak. "Gambling isn't for timid. Like you, man, you get the job done right . . . or you lose. No defense."

"What'll you have?" the bartender asked Dak, setting up a free round before he repeated *the* St. Patrick's Day story of the century, based on truth. The tale carved Rose O'Shaughnessy's name in Butte infamy, and grew bigger with each telling.

"On duty."

"Set a spell."

"You sure you don't have trouble here?"

"Nah! These guys know how to follow orders to the lett—"

"Go on," Dak encouraged, expecting him to criticize his over zealous deputies. Butte's grapevine was faster than the speed of light. By now, the whole town knew Dak's car had been stolen and totaled. He wouldn't blame his men for lack of security. But he blamed himself for leaving the door open, and the key in the ignition. "My men and I were overwhelmed with the tremendous crises at the airport. Enough said. Tell your story."

He dove in. "Picture a young, beautiful Rosie with long shapely legs. An exciting smile like Rita Hayworth." He tilted his head up. "Flowing red hair. Tiny waistline a man with large hands could easily go around twice. Ah . . . and a face like an angel . . ." He stopped to adjust his bifocals.

"You forgot the hooters," the lawyer scolded, spitting into a brass spittoon by his feet.

Loud round of applause.

"Her hooters may have been loaded, but, even at twenty, she was smarter than any man in Butte. That's why she applied to Montana School of Mines. She'd of made one helluva engineer if they'd accepted her," he continued.

"We're all better off it didn't happen." A large man with a black goatee, and a ring of hair on his head, said. He snapped his suspenders.

A middle age, ex-butcher, bottomed his beer. Wiped his face with his shirt sleeve. "They don't dare turn down an applicant these days . . . just because she's a woman."

"Long time ago," a voice came out from the men's room open door. "You get to the good part? The mother of all mothers part, at the St. Patty's Day parade, yet?" He climbed on a barstool.

"Shush . . . shush!" The group prompted.

Dak smiled as the bartender animated his story. Arms outstretched, hips wiggling.

"Pretend you're there when she rides high atop a float decked out like Ireland. All covered in fresh, green carnations. She sets up the driver to stop in front of a viewing stand for mining engineers' Board of Directors. And, their uppity wives. Women she approached for help, that refused to bend the ears of their men for Rosie's intellectual future. They basked in sun drenched bleachers wearing wide-brimmed, fancy hats. Modeled fashionable togs brought in from New York for the occasion."

He stopped to draw a draft beer for himself. He poured a second round for fifteen men anxious to hear the familiar ending, when a young girl walked in to buy candy.

Harsh cussing, and slanderous jokes ceased.

Some men coughed and choked, as with all miners. They sipped beer. Snickered. Until the little girl walked out the door, and the bartender continued.

"The women pillars of a phony society, were more interested in catching the eye of the Ladies' page of the newspaper, than in helping a nobody like Rosie."

"Yeah," the lawyer affirmed. "After the blatant turn down, just how did she manage to become the richest woman in town?" Uproarious laughter. Raised eyebrows.

"Hey . . . she's like family to me," Dak protected. "Keep the gossip to yourselves."

"Well . . . well . . . " the bartender stuttered, slapping a cup of Java on the bar. "Hey, what is . . is." He hauled over the sugar.

Dak motioned to his watch. "The point?"

"When Rose began to perform, the Ladies' society editor wasn't looking at custom made frocks. He brushed past colorful summer suiting and pristine hair styles to gaze . . . in awe . . . at Rose—"

Dak answered his phone. "Yeah . . . I'll call you back in ten." He pitched a fistful of small change on the bar, and stood.

"Your money's no good here—"

"You know better."

The bartender stroked his chin. Milked his story as if he was Charlie Chaplain going for an Oscar.

"After bragging on Rosie," slurred a soused man they called Shoot the Moon. "Tell about all women school teachers in Butte forced to sign a contract they'd never get married."

"This isn't a women's libber stint about smart females," he answered. "Rose had the misfortune to be born intelligent. She ached to get formally educated. Take care of her sisters."

Dak shifted his weight at the entrance. "She was the first person ever denied access to the School of Mines." He put on his uniform hat. Saluted the men, all begging him to stay, while the lawyer jumped the gun, and filled in the dotted lines.

"Rose draped her gorgeous body in a bright, Kelly green outfit . . . like square dancers wear . . . all fluffy and lots of petticoat." He paused to cough. "She rides on top of a large float, holding a first prize, blue ribbon for best of show. The band plays loud Irish tunes, as the platform on wheels bellies close to a viewing stand. The city's movers and shakers frolic. Drink champagne. Eat fresh strawberries . . . the status fruit of the wealthy.

The float slows down. Stops squarely in front of the stand.

Big wigs cheer. Clap.

The music ceased abruptly. Rose grips a large megaphone. Yells at them all . . . over and over again. *Denied Access! Denied Access!*" He hesitated. Made sure everyone's got their ears glued to his theatrics.

"Then, at a leisurely pace . . . she turned her back to the money men with power, and their women. Raised her skirt." He grew excited as his voice grew louder. "Then she takes all her clothes off completely. No panties! No underwear! Exposes her firm backside—lovely, pink, naked cheeks—to a crowded viewing stand. The band played on for five minutes while she mooned shocked parade watchers!"

"Geeshus," the ex-butcher said, swallowing hard. Silence filled the dingy, smoke filled room waiting for a finish they've all heard before. "The hooters, now."

"No one watching wanted to stop her," the lawyer emphasized, sticking out his jaw. "Why stop a good look-see at a tightly sculpted, perfectly proportioned, bare behind on the bottom end? Stacked hooters, pulsating to a frantic Irish rhythm. Lovely hands clutching a megaphone. Who's dumb enough to stop her from broadcasting her special message in that cockeyed position? She megaphoned . . . *Deny access! Deny access!"*

The story ended as usual, with Rose's hooters growing bigger each year. A heated discussion resumed.

"Joan of Arc!"

"Bride of Satan!"

Just then, Dak edged back to the group to find his car key, that dropped out of his pocket when he pulled out some change. "You fellas be good. Unless you want to visit some of your buddies we arrested at the airport for compromising a crime scene?"

"They the ones wearing badges?" the lawyer laughed. It was only noon. He was as drunk as a night time bar fly. "You got them locked in with that *dumb* kid that stole your new car out from under your nose?"

Dak didn't respond. He learned as a child that words never hurt—like his dad's fist, a belt, a wooden chair, a cast iron fry pan, or a locked door holding him in a small, dark closet over night. His phone rang again. He hurried to his car to check on a gas station robbery . . . and to return a call to Dacsu.

LB phoned while he was en route. "Boss, what time you get off tonight?"

"Any more calls . . . it'll be midnight."

"Met your daughter on the plane. Object if I look in on her?" Everyone in town knows Dak registered her two days ago, at the Finlen Hotel—built for dignitaries when Butte was thriving and economy ballooned.

Dak kept the line open, tilted his head to the tallest hotel in the city. Nine stories, towering on a hill in the heart of Uptown business district. A copper-shingled roof reflected light from the sun, across the city. The clerk said he'd put her up, either in the room Charles Lindbergh slept in. Or, where John F. Kennedy, and his wife Jackie were guests. Regardless, from one of its many windows, his daughter'd be enjoying the cycle of a summer season unfolding.

"Check if she needs anything and get back to me."

"How about you agree to let me take her to lunch?" LB asked, sucking on a breath mint. He knew, that after budget cuts, Dak's salary wasn't enough to cover her hotel bill.

More to the point, he couldn't wait to see Dacsu again.

"If her nose isn't too much out of joint," Dak said.

His worn tires sounded as if they were filled with rock chips as he pulled into a Mobile gas station. Clickety-clack. Clickety-clack. Clickety-clack. He had a few dollars left on his credit card, or he'd buy new tires himself. To pay Dacsu's expenses, he planned to live without golfing with the Bishop. Eating restaurant dinners and fishing at the Big Hole River on his only week of vacation in August.

"Fill her up?" the attendant asked.

"Charge it to the department."

Petrel flowed.

His mind wandered to what Mary O'Donovan told him shortly before she left Butte.

"During a hiatus," she said. "I volunteered in medical records division at a Catholic hospital back east. Nosed into a sealed file. Blew my mind when it concerned you . . . of all people."

"I've never been back east," he remembered saying.

"Part of you did."

"No riddles today, Mary. Give it to me right between the eyes."

"A young woman, Megan Pat—"

"She graduated high school with me, and went straight to some eastern college."

"She brought something with her to medical school."

"Money . . . she's got enough to buy Butte. Her dad partnered with ACM stockholders to get rich."

"But . . . you partnered with her, too!"

"Hey . . . cut that out."

"She didn't go directly to college, my friend," Mary told him. "She waited a year."

"I did hear she added an extra year of school to specialize in cardiac surgery."

"Look, Dumbo," Mary said to him, frustrated. "She had your baby . . . named her Dacsu . . . put her up for adoption . . . finished school. Came back to Butte—her secret hidden from everyone. Even your daughter!"

Dak's face drained thinking about the conversation and how he responded to Mary. "Oh, no! My God! There was the night of the Senior prom. Once. That's all it was. Once. I'm not romantically inclined towards her. You sure?"

"Only takes once." She handed him a copy of a file that proved her allegations.

"Mary, did you tell Dacsu about her mother?"

"You know better! I conned her to come to Butte to introduce the two of you. I'm done." Mary O'Donovan left town issuing an order. "Call me with the rest of the story!"

"Yeah," he promised, thinking how tomorrow, he, Zoonawme, and Caitlin—three amigos—would meet for coffee. Caitlin would go ballistic. But, he took comfort knowing they'd never faced a problem together that they couldn't solve.

Chapter Twenty-three

Why're people quiet in a hospital? Patients aren't there to sleep. People mill in the halls. Family's gather. Staff is paid to meddle with the sick. "Time for a shot. Medication. Water. I.V. Temperature. Blood pressure. Blood draw. Change sheets. Bathe. Eat." It's not as if speaking loud would harm them, or interrupt medical care. Or, put you on detention.

My first impulse was to scream when MP held me by my arm. I muffled my fear, knowing no one was looking, when she thumped my ribs with her fist. She just uttered, *Red,* in a hateful voice, when Zoonawme sauntered down the hall to the men's room, glaring at the two of us.

Right then, she adjusted her temperament like a dimmer switch—from mean and hateful, to happy and bright. Relaxed her grip. "Your shoulder will heal over time. Just don't use it for awhile, Caitlin . . . umm . . . please wait here." She raised her voice slightly across the hall at her assistant. "Will you bring me Mr. Palagretti's chart?"

I waited anxiously for Zoonawme while she read the chart.

"Mr. Palagretti's wife learned he's going to fully recover," she told me. "You're going to want to meet this woman!" She twisted her mouth until her nose wrinkled. "Yeah . . . you definitely are going to want to meet his wife!"

She put the file into Nurse Chambers' hands.

Her special assistant, was a good-sized woman with crooked teeth. Born in Walkerville, a suburb of Butte, that grew their women tough, and whoop-butt smart. Saliva drooled from her mouth watching MP strut to the elevator. She shifted her steel gray eyes to me. "Ma'am?"

Her steady stare confirmed. She'd been briefed on my terribleness. Clearly, she worshipped MP, and intended to make mince meat out of me. "What room's Jeep in?" I asked her.

She walked over to her boss with a pronounced stoop. As if she was struggling to transport her thighs from one place to the next. I felt sorry for her. She handed MP a second clip board, and waited. "You have enough information, Doctor?"

"Yes, thank you," she answered. One foot was jamming the elevator door from closing. "Something else?"

She pointed. "That elderly woman's waiting for your signature to release her."

"Oh, yes, that's Mildred," she said, rearing away from the elevator. "Wait, I need to write her a prescription for a Selective Serotonin Reputake inhibitor."

She pulled a porous tip pen from her pocket. Scribbled an RX. Formed heavy, squiggly marks on a release slip. I watched her writing go from small to large. At this moment, she felt overly good about herself. Super proud of her work, as if she expected to be added to Mt. Rushmore.

"Should I get this Prozac filled here?" the nurse asked.

"Yes," she said turning to me with surprise. "Caitlin ... what're you still doing here? You want something?"

"What room's Jeep in?" I hesitated. I knew I was on the wrong end of all of her personalities. I think Zoona—"

"Nurse Chambers will show you to Mr. Palagretti's room. You have eight minutes," she sneered.

Oh, God, no! Eight minutes? She said it on purpose. She knew that was a trigger phrase from the past, for pain. That Sister Agatha gave our fifth grade class, eight minutes to drop Valentines in a brightly colored box, and exchange. That I proudly dropped in a card for everyone.

That it didn't matter.

MP controlled my classmates' minds. The only time they'd speak to me was in her absence. *Sheep!* Each card I received offered evil wishes: Leave school! Die! After class we'll cut off all your hair! *Eight minutes!*

My shoulders felt lighter to see Zoonawme poke his head out from a room down the hall. He motioned me to slide past Nurse Chambers, handing Mildred her release forms. Then she huddled herself in a group of her peers.

I noticed Mildred sobbing buckets. She saw me. "Caitlin O'Shaughnessy. Please wait!"

"How're you doing?" I inquired, hugging her softly. Her face was drawn. Eyes red rimmed, and empty.

"Gunner was my life, you know. I don't want to live."

"Can I do anything for you?"

"He told me something on the plane that you should know."

My heart raced in anticipation. "Go on."

That lady," she motioned. "Down there in that group of nurses." She pointed to where six nurses were being given assignments by MP. And, being instructed not to step on her shadow.

"She was the one that ran from your house the night of the fire."

My God! Nurse Chambers was at the center of the group!

I wanted to run up to her. Grill her under hot lights.

I thought better of it, when I noticed her standing sideways. Hefty bulges hung on her hips. Was she packing a pair of forty-four magnums, loaded with hydro-shocks?

I assisted Mildred's daughter, to help her mother to the elevator and figured Zoonawme must have slipped past me, into Jeep's room. I entered just as he was showing Jeep the photos LB fumbled into his pocket during airport crisis.

"Hi friend," I whispered to Jeep. His expression was hard to read under heavy bandages around his head.

"Caitlin, thank you for what you did for me on the plane!" His voice lucid. Dark eyes lingered on the tubes in his arm, as I straightened his pillows.

"I didn't do anything."

"We're old friends now. You saved my life . . . it'd belong to you if I wasn't married to Orla," he joked. He applied humor as a defense against pain. "They told me you did not get hurt?"

"I did not," I told him, wriggling my shoulder.

"It is apodictic I fell from the ceiling," he murmured. "Inanition would have deluged my recovery. However, I make a panegyric, for the concinnity of the medical staff."

"English, please!"

"Being injured happened for a reason. My wife being here saved me from emptiness. And, hooray for the doctors."

I shuffled my feet to the end of the bed, where Zoonawme held pictures in his hand, and looked at them. "This some kind of joke?"

"These belong to your new friend," he said.

I gasped. My brow furrowed. I darted my eyes from the pictures to Jeep. Then back and forth again until my neck hurt. "Where'd you get these?" It was like looking into a mirror.

"Out of my camera."

Just like a lawyer . . . throw words at me. Wait until I come up with an answer he can charge me for. I sat in a chair and waited for Zoonawme to clear things up.

He remained silent, stiff, confused.

A poem I wrote for high school graduation, rolled around in my head like a steel bullet:

I THOUGHT I KNEW I KNEW IT ALL,
BUT NOW I MUST CONFESS,
THE MORE I KNOW I KNOW,
I KNOW I KNOW THE LESS.

BY CAITLIN O'SHAUGHNESSY, SOON TO BE MRS. SAM O'TOOLE.

I gripped the foot rail of his bed with one hand and held the evidence in the other. My gut tied in a knot. "How'd you make these? What's the catch? These photos are of me."

"I took the pictures myself. They're photos of my wife, Orla."

Murphy's Law came to mind, but it didn't fit here.

"I don't understand." Again, I turned to Zoonawme.

"Dead ringer for you!" he agreed. "I can't explain."

"I've never worn my hair that short," I retaliated. "What's going on? Besides, it'd take a steam roller to sculpt my thighs into that svelte body—"

"Calm down, Cat Woman, " he said, kicking a stool over to me. Put your feet up. "Our business is to solve mysteries."

"Handwriting mysteries. Forensic mysteries. You're right. We can analyze the photos for authenticity. We'll get to a motive later."

I drank Jeep's water to clear my head.

First dot. The pictures explained his odd behavior towards me on the airplane. "You did insist . . . I . . . her . . . played a practical joke on you," I said to Jeep. "Claimed a disguised appearance. Long haired wig. Rudeness."

"It's like looking into a highly reflective glass, that actively reproduces someone else," he added.

"I knew that."

"Told you I had something to show you."

"Why'd you back off when you saw the heart shaped mole on my neck?"

"Didn't match Orla's," he explained. "*That* shocked me."

"She has the same birthmark?"

"Yes, located on the other side of her neck. You'll meet her in a minute. She's talking to the doctor."

"I saw her from the back," I replied nervously. "That is, if she was the slim redhead, tastefully decked out in a bright blue, linen pant suit. Carried a brown canvas handbag, adorned with a colorful jeweled owl?"

Zoonawme slid his hands on my shoulders, and forced me to sit down. "And you find fault with Eagle Eye's preciseness?"

Silently, we did a double take on the pictures.

"Maybe I'll think different when I see her face?" I whispered. "Lately, my track record for reading people has been as bad as Liz Taylor reading calories."

"You mean reading an assembly of her husbands?" Jeep weighed in.

"No . . . you seen Liz lately?"

"Here comes Orla, she's—"

I panted when Orla walked in briskly.

Filtered light from the window fell across her shiny, red hair. She'd been more prepared for the meeting than I was. Even so, she stopped suddenly in her tracks to stare at me. Greenish-blue eyes fixed on my nose . . . eyes . . . mouth . . . forehead.

"Hi," she said softly.

Her voice sounded a lot like mine. This was freaky. I knew that most people have mirror images in the world. They just don't ever meet. I waved.

Orla's turn.

Silence.

My turn. We should be shaking hands, or something. "Jeep told me you two would be in deep trouble without Dr. Freida's help?" I was afraid to touch her. I changed the subject. Neither of us could handle this one.

"That's right," she said in a Chicago twang. Her manner soft. She reached over, and took my hand. Gently squeezed. "He didn't hear about Dr. Freida's death until he came out of surgery."

"So sorry about her accident," I sighed, pulling myself a bit more together.

"Yes," she said, staring intently. She came closer.

I stood next to my double. Same height, same hair. Different weight. Any conversation about the two of us at this time would be ridiculous. We'd get it sorted out—sooner or later. "Can we help . . . whatever your problem is? We know everyone in town," I asked her.

"Not unless you know where Dr. Freida stored her records from the past."

"What kind of records?"

"We're not sure," she said. "She claimed she had a reliable lead to a family member. Has a document to prove it."

"That where Riv Etter comes in?"

"We're pretty sure she's a connection."

"I don't get it. Neither of you has been to Butte before?"

"Correct."

Jeep mumbled. "Bronco Billie from Butte, sued the doctor for stealing a large sum of money from her, a long time ago."

"That's how we met Dr. Freida, " Orla said. "Jeep worked on the case in Chicago."

"Too much information. Even if I knew what you were talking about. I haven't recovered from my first trip overseas."

"We think God put us with the doctor to find out who my mother was," Orla said. "Or, if she was from Butte. If not, I'll die sooner than I'm ready to. I need a blood match in the near future . . ." She hesitated. "Although we don't consider Dr. Freida a reliable source at ninety. We need to follow up on all leads."

Last time I saw Jeep, he was frightened for his life. Now I learn, he's frightened for his wife's life. I desperately wanted to help. Not because Orla looked like me—because I truly felt committed to family again, after all these lost years.

"I thought Dr. Freida was coming back to Butte to settle a score with someone?" I questioned Jeep.

"That, too," he slurred.

"If you've never been to Butte—"

"It's not complicated," Orla countered. "I'm adopted."

"But . . . Jeep talked about your great relationship with your mother—"

"Right. I adore my adoptive mother," she said convincingly, as Nurse Chambers rushed in. Muscled Zoonawme and me to the door.

Clearly, she didn't like us or the horses we rode in on.

She wanted to take his temperature—the old fashioned way. "This patient needs rest," she barked.

No sense arguing with someone exhaling buffalo breath. "Yes Ma'am," I cow-towed. Zoonawme and I left her, and her stagnant breath, that hung in the air like cigar smoke.

"Cousin Mike's now?" he asked, standing in the hall.

"Hate to admit this," I told him. "Seeing those pictures . . . meeting Orla . . . has sucked the life out of me. And . . . that damn coffee pot almost burning up while I slept. So much has happened in such a short time. I need to go home and rest."

He held the door open to the parking lot. "Tomorrow mor—"

"You . . . me . . . Dak . . . a giant Montana headache . . . and a brown sugar addiction."

I climbed into my car. Started the engine.

Listened to Spirit dog bark goodbye as they drove away from the hospital.

Raced to O'Shaughnessy Road.

After I replenish my nerves, Hummy gets a call, first thing. What'd they steal from Dr. Freida's purse? How can Jeep and Orla actually be connected to her? How're the three sisters involved with her? Who is Riv Etter?

Pen Doodle met me at the steps.

We both had a snack.

Then camped out in the front room until we fell asleep.

Chapter Twenty-four

LB's an easy going kind of guy, deeply satisfied with Butte the way it stands. Now, he thought, sitting at lunch in a dated restaurant—duct tape patches on booth seats. Worn foot paths on linoleum leading to a bank of slot machines. And, cigarette smoke mixed with Shorty's non-stop steak grill, fried onion smell permeating the walls—he wondered if a furnished, two room apartment, down the street from a vacant Hennessey's Department Store, would embarrass him in front of Dacsu.

"Our town's great," LB informed her. He attempted to let her see Butte from his eyes. He didn't dare hope she'd see it from his apartment. "Summer—outdoors. Perfect country. Great snow in the winter. Ski-mobiles. Ice skating."

"That's real nice," she replied, staring at a chicken club sandwich the size of a loaf of bread. "I used to have time to ice skate. Nothing fancy."

"Around here, we brag about our ice rink, where Olympic skaters come to train. When you come back in the winter, would you go skating with me?"

She blushed. "I'm not coming back."

"Oh . . . I see."

Her blonde hair glistened in the sun, standing next to him at the cashier's station. She carried a to-go bag of French fries, and one-half of a sandwich. "I don't know who set me and Dak up," she frowned. "I intend to get to the bottom of things. My job doesn't pay much, but I'll reimburse your Sheriff for my lodging . . . and any expenses he's coughed up."

"He's an admirable man." He handed the cashier a twenty.

She thanked him for lunch, and asked to be taken back to the hotel. "I think Captain O'Donovan played a joke on her old friend, and I got caught in the cross-fire. No harm done."

"You sure you don't want to do some sight seeing?"

"I'm sure," she replied, short of breath. "I'm not quite used to high altitude . . . this sharp, clear air sort of stings when I take a deep breath. Besides, there's an uneasy calmness in the atmosphere. Don't you feel it?"

"Oh . . . are you into astrology?" he asked, walking to the parking meter. He kicked himself for saying something so stupid. He felt light-hearted in her presence. Short of breath, too, but not from a mile high altitude. He didn't want to hurt her by revealing Dak's paternity was validated with legal documents. She'd find out soon enough from him. Unless Butte's gossip grapevine, gets to her first.

"I see lots of different weather," she said, kindly. "There's not as much movement in the air like when we first arrived in Butte. Something doesn't feel right."

"I see," he lied, twisting his head to a deep blue sky with dark clouds approaching. "If you don't mind a question?"

"Not at all. You're very easy to talk to."

"Did you ever wonder who your real parents were?"

"Yes, when I was young. My adoptive parents fell on hard times. I don't come from wealth. They applied for welfare," she said, brushing crumbs from her bright pink jacket. "Doesn't really matter now."

He scribbled his phone number on a napkin. Slipped it into her hand before he dropped her off at the hotel. "Think of me as your contact while you're in town."

Later on, LB dialed Dak. He shouted into the phone. "Big trouble, Boss! Can't contain this wild bunch at Lydia's by myself. This ugly crowd would make Custer's last stand seem like a picnic. How soon can you get here?"

It was six-thirty in the evening.

Dak was on his way to Duggan-Dolan's to ride rough-shod on Rose. If she showed up at Gunner's Rosary, there'd be a skirmish for sure. She was a master at holding a grudge against him. He'd published the infamous St. Patrick Parade story about her, on the front page of his Miners' Union paper.

Complete with explicit, X-rated photos that shamed her two sisters. His death ended a vendetta she's held for many years.

The Union didn't want her working in the mines. Educators didn't want her earning a mining engineer's degree. Winning the deed to Gunner's acreage, complete with log cabin, near the reservoir grounds behind Roosevelt Way helped—in part. A pound of flesh won in a poker game, helped the stalwart Irishwoman to tolerate consequences of being an independent woman.

Dak thought for a minute. "I'd say to call rookie Cindy but, from what you're describing, you're going to need muscle."

"I'm sure I'll need *your* muscles."

"I'll call Costello and Needle Point," he countered. He feared Rose the warrior, could easily slap the corpse around during the Rosary.

"Called them already."

"Oh, yeah?" he pondered. "Right. They're off duty tonight."

"Gotta go, now!" LB's firm tone urged compliance. "People are really heated up. Looks bad. You coming?"

"I'm up here near the mortuary. Hang in there." Directions in Butte are easy. Uphill is north. Downhill is south. Dak turned his car around, and headed downhill to Harrison Avenue.

"He's coming!" LB, senior officer, reported to a group of apprehensive law enforcers. They sat at a table, in a softly lit, posh dining room at Lydia's, waiting for their boss to show up. "He's seven miles away."

They planned to butter him up—Butte style. Kiss and make up. Food, booze, sincere apologies, and plans to do better.

"Let's go over our story again," a voice rang out. Certain Dak'd lower the boom for *missed-communication* at the airport.

"Remember," Needle Point said, rocking back in his chair at the front end of the table. "This surprise party wasn't my idea. You know how he hates surprises! No guarantee he'll bury the hatchet."

"We know where'll he bury it if this goes haywire," another voice piped up.

Costello had been drinking heavily for an hour, and was enjoying the buzz. He wasn't a drinker and it showed. "Well, he sure got one helluva surprise at the airport!"

Crafty looks at each other, roved around the table.

Needlepoint worried. "Forget about his daughter." He looked at LB. "Say . . . you're on his preferred list. You doing the talking when he gets here? Right?"

"After all, you pack the most weight," a waitress joked, carrying in a plate of sweet potato appetizers.

Uproarious laughter.

Sandwiched between beer and joviality, the deputies knew things could sour. Dak had every reason to fire the lot of them.

"He's not going to fire me?" Costello playfully hailed a waitress. Ordered another round for the group. "No way in hell . . . oh, damn . . . no way he'd do that . . . I been real good about not cussing . . damn it to Geeshus. . . real good, damn it!"

"Give the boss some credit," rookie Cindy spoke up in his defense. She surprised them with her attitude. "The guy's got class. If you screwed up on airport duty during crisis, you'll just have to scrape egg off your face. Accept consequences. Then, get on with your life."

Silence overtook the group.

"You'll be the first to get axed," one deputy alarmed. His speech slurred. She knew that most of the men didn't want to serve with her. "A woman deputy. Ha! What a joke!"

"Here's what we say," Costello pounded on the table. "*Listen up Sheriff of Nuttyham*, you want our badges? . . . Or, or was it our shields? . . . Cindy's dress shields? Geeshusss Chr— oh no. Dak says I gotta keep my mouth clean . . . umm . . ."

When contagious laughter exploded again, every customer in the joint joined in.

Fun was on the menu, but at whose expense?

Cindy appeared confused. She set her beer down. Stood up, smoothing her short skirt. Her long, shapely legs were tan. "Thought you guys liked our boss?"

"You bet we do," LB confirmed. He motioned her to take a load off her feet. He was poised on the edge of a seat, near the lower end of the table. Counting money he collected from the guys to hand to a waitress. "We're just letting off steam . . . the Nutty—and ham—described us. You, included." He bent over at the waist to pick up a $10.00 bill he dropped, and cut off his air.

More entertainment.

As he started to rise, his pants ripped in the back. A loud tearing sound magnified his predicament a hundred fold. The seam easily spread apart.

Costello roared. No one had ever seen him three sheets to the wind. He clumsily backed his chair from the table. Held up a beer, as if to toast something, and tripped over his tongue. "I don't think that noise came from faulty restaurant pipes. You see guys and doll . . . Dolly . . . hmmm. Goofy stuff happens . . . even when you're trying to do things right."

Meanwhile, Dak, a few blocks away from Lydia's, yanked his phone off his belt to answer another call from LB.

"Sheriff here . . . I'm minutes away." He turned into the lot. Adjusted his gun. Rushed through the front door, cautiously patrolling his eyes around the dining room.

"Surprise . . . surprise!" His wet-nosed, half-tanked staff thundered. Drawing in other customers to clap, and cheer loudly. "Surprise . . . surprise!"

Dak froze. A deer caught in headlights. He sucked in his cheeks when he caught on that he was a victim of a surprise party.

"Why?" He fired a firm tone. Stared at each man separately, cataloging their befuddled expressions. "What's all this crazy stuff about?"

Instantly, his staff shut up.

Customers turned their heads away.

Dak snarled at being the center of attention. "If I thought, for one minute, this was an illegitimate call—"

"Boss," Needle Point said, pushing a tray of hot peppers to one side. "We want to show appreciation for the forgiving way you handled our slight bungles at the airport."

"Forgiving?" Dak's nostrils flared. "And what makes you *bunglers* think that I've finished handling the situation?"

He started for the door.

Chapter Twenty-five

The owner of Lydia's walked briskly from the bar, over to Dak standing near the exit door. He muscled a large complimentary tray of beer, mixed peanuts, hand made bread sticks, and scrumptious salty things he imported from Rome. He tossed thick, dark hair from his charismatic, Italian eyes. "Please, Dak. Calm your people down a couple notches."

"You're absolutely right. This is my problem."

"I just mean . . . while I welcome free advertising—we don't want to read in the newspaper tomorrow, that Butte's finest tore the joint apart?"

"This is an unusual circumstance. They've been through a terrible ordeal, like they've never seen before. I'll handle it."

Cindy watched Dak strut forcefully to the table. She felt a hand on her shoulder. Snapped her head around to Needle Point's yellow tattooed, bald head, sweating bright orange beads as he patted her on the back.

"You startled me," she said, squirming in her seat at his soft touch. Kind and supportive.

"We're not always like this." He had an interesting face, she thought. Mouth like a poet. Straight nose that fit his elongated chin.

"I'm going to do something that may screw up my career," she said standing. She fluffed shoulder length, warm auburn hair from her neck, and moved an overloaded snack tray to the middle of the table—knocking over a glass of water. She waved Dak to step closer.

Needle Point's eyes welled with compassion. His nod sent support to her for whatever she was about to do. He kneeled on one leg, next to her chair. Elbowed his hand beneath his chin and waited.

"Sir," she said to Dak, measuring her words carefully. "You have disciplinary action to hand out? Do it!"

"Oh, God . . . she didn't say that?" a shrill voice admonished. "Where'd this stupid woman come from?"

Costello cackled. He grew braver with each beer. "My partner . . . Needle Nose . . . er . . . Point . . . and me . . . will work harder, Suh . . . yah, Suh! We'll do dat all right." His hair needed trimming as much as his playful mouth needed a scrub. He took Cindy by surprise. "How'd you get enough balls, anyway, to—"

Dak stared disapproval. "We've got a lady on board!"

"You sound just like my wife," Costello cajoled. His eyes bagged like poached eggs, endorsing the obvious. He was a tea totaler, deep within an excessive alcohol level. He tried to apologize to Cindy. "Sorry, ma'am . . .or is it . . . officer . . . ma'am . . . ma mama?"

"You going to cut your staff, Sir?" She forced a show down. She expected to be fired for chasing Dak's state-of-the-art vehicle, that was totaled.

Everyone wanted to know.

Maybe not this way.

Lydia's owner stood in a doorway to a larger dining area. He cocked his ears in silence. A waitress stopped serving. She stepped back to face a group of patrons holding a free drink while waiting in a long line for a table. "What'd you think?" she whispered impishly. "Ten spot says it's gonna be a bumpy ride."

Patrons at tables surrounding the deputies, clanked their forks down—a hard thing to do in Lydia's restaurant. They glared, knowing Dak's public answer affected the entire Butte-Silver Bow county.

Coals of confusion burned for Dak, too.

For a man that didn't attend church, vehemently claimed there was no God, his high-minded morals were priestly. He was frustrated. Ashamed that Dr. Freida'd been killed . . . whether or not the accident could have been avoided by better security. He was more angry that his new car had been stolen under his nose, than coping with it's demise.

"I have made a decision," he summoned, taking a sip of water.

"That would be?" Cindy pressed anxiously.

Needle Point stood. "She's right. This surprise party was a farce. She asked what we all wanted to know in the first place." He polled the deputies with his eyes.

"Lay it out, Dak," LB said embarrassingly. "Cindy's right. Nobody here wants to dance around a pink elephant, worrying when the ax will fall."

"Please sit down," Dak directed. His own mental well being hinged on being fair.

She sat. The sound of beer flowing into glasses, ice cubes rattling, and hushed comments between each other, sort of broke the edge from thinking the worst. Unemployment. Family debt. Future.

Dak took a moment to sip from a gray pewter beer stein. One the owner provided for Butte's dignitaries. Foamy suds ran down the cup, covering his name inscribed on the side. Froth formed a wide moustache on his upper lip, easing tension, that flooded the room like a broken dam.

LB quickly covered Costello's giggling mouth with his napkin. "Get hold of yourself, man."

"You all know the rules about suspensions," he began, realizing he'd be feeding the gossip grapevine. He looked around the room.

People turned their heads down, pretending to be invisible. The cavities of their ears were opened wide.

"Suspension isn't in our vocabulary tonight. Why should it be? Our department doesn't have any dirty linen to air out. As for my car . . . I take full responsibility!" He scratched his head. "Considering the magnitude of the crisis, staff, you acted responsible. I'm sure the city of Butte is proud of the way you responded to an awkward, frightening situation. None of us knew whether the plane would crash at the airport. We could have all been blown to bits."

"Tell me he's serious!" a male voice murmured, crouching behind a server.

A hard of hearing customer asked the waitress. "What's the bottom line, here?"

"It's a guy thing, for bravery. He let them off the hook."

"Huh?"

"Responsibility," another piped up. "Let's talk about Cindy."

"Oh, God!" The embarrassed rookie jumped up, tipping her chair backward to the floor. "Sir, I don't expect discipline favors because I'm female. I acted wrong. Do whatever you'd do to one of your men."

"Man or woman. I work on facts. I don't do favors."

She stuck her chin out. "Well, I do."

"What'd you mean?"

"There's already a resignation letter from me on your desk. I'm deeply sorry about your car being totaled. That kid was three sheets to the wind. I adapted to the situation, as I saw it." She paused to look at Needle Point. "The kid could have killed someone else."

"Go on," the sheriff sternly prodded.

"It's in the report. He aimed your car as a weapon against Costello and Needle Point, during the chase. He'd already hit someone at the airport. No choice, I headed him off, pronto."

"You saying you followed procedure?"

She didn't flinch. "I'd do it the same way again. Go ahead, accept my resignation."

The men were stunned by her spunk. Her strong nerves. Outright courage for any rookie. They all stood. Applauded wildly as a show of support for her.

Amazingly, Dak clapped the loudest.

"You think I'm not aware of what you did?" he responded. "Didn't these guys point out the eyes centered on the back of my head? You'll learn, deputy, everyone on my watch pulls his own weight."

"Yes, Sir," she corrected. "Her weight."

Costello's mouth opened wide, again. Before he could grind out an obnoxious response, he turned to fend off a waitress, that'd clipped him on the head with a heavy saucer. "I've called your wife to come get you, Costy," she said.

Dak came around the table, to go nose to nose with the neophyte. So close, the smell of her strawberry perfume made him sneeze. "Cindy, you . . . like these guys . . . are solely responsible for your own actions . . . on and off duty."

She sat down in her chair to get away from him.

"Hold on," he said. "Stand up again, please?"

In comes one of those high school, principal authority, moments.

She vaulted up so fast, her chair fell sideways onto Needle Point's legs. "It's your deal. I can handle anything you have to complain about."

"Handle this, Cindy," he quipped. "Earlier, I stuck a document on your desk."

"Where are you going with this?" she stopped him.

Sweat and amazement created a deafening silence.

"I recommended you for departmental reward."

"Is this a joke?"

"You decide," he answered. "Your bravery, quick action. Exemplary driving skills during a crisis. Most likely saved Costello's, and Needle Point's lives. They attested to your superb driving."

"I don't know what to say," she blushed.

"Besides that, Dr. Megan Pat told me your professional actions at the hospital were beyond reproach."

Every man at the table knew that Costello tied one on because he faced a sudden death. He told them the kid was out to ram him and his partner. Plain and simple.

"Was going to schedule a formal ceremony, but this crowd will do," Dak proclaimed. He motioned to the room. When the ovation stopped, he continued. "Why. . . even the way you handled the cleanup of the totaled car—"

"Um, I don't know what to say," she answered.

"Doesn't seem to me you lack originality. Tell me . . . where'd you learn to drive like that? Nothing short of genius! Your car didn't have a scratch." He twisted his mouth into a pucker.

"My dad was a cop in Texas," she said. "Killed in a high speed chase when a perp rammed his car. My brothers discouraged me from becoming a cop. Gave in. Trained me on an obstacle course that Chuck Norris, ala Walker, filmed high-speed car chases—for his television show. Barbed wire traps, blocks of wood bunched together. I dodged four brothers behind separate wheels, chasing me through narrow alleyways, winding streets, and horrendous obstacles."

Cindy sat down. For now, speechless.

The bartender served Costello a final drink. "Your wife's on her way."

He slurped a brandy and seven, like he was drinking a chocolate malt. "And . . . us guys bet money you were . . . pretty . . .umm . . . skinny . . .umm, oh, yeah . . . just another pretty face."

Dak sighed. "You interested in pulling some overtime?"

"Sure am," she said, pushing her salad aside to make room on the table for a hefty New York steak. The men began to pass around a huge spaghetti platter, laced with meatballs, and heavy red sauce.

"Will you teach my boys to drive with the same skill?" He looked at his chicken dinner. He hadn't eaten all day. His mouth watered. "I'll provide hazards. I'll even do the chasing." He lit up a cigarette. Foreplay, before gorging himself.

"Ah, come on, Boss." Costello called his attention to a No-smoking sign.

"What's with this *Boss* stuff?" he asked, reaching for meat stuffed raviolis, and French fries. "I'm aware you fellows call me *Sheriff of Nuttyham* behind my back."

"Busted," they agreed.

"Gentlemen . . . and Lady . . . raise your glasses," Dak ordered. Again, with the chairs. They all stood, hands curled around a glass, or bottle. "As your *Sheriff of Nuttyham*, I knight each one of you peasants, a *Knight of Nuttyham.*" He lowered Cindy's arm, and smiled. "Sorry, Cindy. Knighthood is for men. Unless you want to be called, Lady of the Knight?"

She leaned over to Needle Point. Winked. "Discrimination? That kind of talk from our boss cause for a law suit?"

"Nah," he snickered. "We're off duty. Besides, I don't think you can sue an elected official?"

Costello overheard them. "You'd get as far suing an elected offish . . . official in Butte . . . as suing Nabisco for . . . umm . . . for shredding wheat." He dropped his beer on the floor.

"Oh . . . no!" A waitress warned, watching Costello's wife push through the crowd. "Look out! Sheeeees here."

"Elected official's joke, again, huh?" She smelled his breath. "Save the rest of the boring quips you stole from Letterman.

Come home. Now!" She dragged him out of the room by his ear.

"Speaking of elected officials." LB raised his head. "Isn't that our mayor coming this way from the Ladies room?"

"She's wobbling over to us," Cindy punctuated.

Mayor Lois Fitzgereld was a handsome woman, disciplined and self-restrained. Tonight she was tipsy, and relaxed at her birthday celebration. Making her entrance with toilet paper stuck to the bottoms of her conservative shoes. Curly brown hair with a hint of red, glistened under the many mood lights. Parted in the middle, her long locks fell across a half Irish, half Italian, beautiful face.

She swung her purse in front of Dak's nose. "Sheriff."

"Ma'am."

"Sheriff!"

"Mayor!"

"S . . . O . . . B!"

She straightened the front of her black and white, feathery cocktail dress. Hailed her group she'd be right there. Then she bent over to scratch her ankle. "Got a moldy bone to pick with you, Mr. Sheriff."

Dak looked down. His face burned with embarrassment, staring at the back of her skirt, caught up in her panties. "Keep your eyes off her." He challenged the men with his eyes to turn their heads.

Nobody did.

Not one of them looked away from her cheek bottoms—covered, all right. But, winking aggressively as she moved.

Cindy rushed over and pulled her dress down.

The mayor sputtered. "Dak, you out to . . . out to get me through my punk son?"

"We should discuss this tomorrow."

"You think?" She tugged at her stocking seams to straighten them. Except, she wasn't wearing hosiery.

A stripper couldn't provide better entertainment.

"I want him out of jail, or you'll never see a new patrol car! Or . . . is that a sheriff's vehicle?" She burped. " . . . well . . . you get the drift."

"You'll see it different tomorrow," Dak said, shelving his dislike for women momentarily, thinking how her curved body excited him. Then, he thought about his failed marriages. The entanglement of dealing with his child, Dacsu. And, how Caitlin would react to Megan Pat being the kid's mother.

"Sheriff?" she queried, looking at his stein. "You drinking out of my special cup?"

He was lost in a trance. Staring intensely at one of the artfully crafted, stained glass windows.

It was cracked like his three marriages.

One of the mayor's friends came over to rescue her. "Your beer stein is at our table. Please, come back."

LB poked Dak in the ribs to jar him to the present.

"Oh . . . yeah, mayor," he choked. "Yes. Tomorrow. Not too early, I have an important breakfast meeting."

Chapter Twenty-six

I woke up telling myself it's too late to go to Gunner's funeral Mass. Walk over to the reception after church to eat a free meal, and ride to Holy Cross Cemetery to say goodbye. Truthfully, I dreaded driving by Sam's plot again, where I'd break down. Do something ridiculous.

The phone rang as I was unraveling a few strands of gray hair from my brush, and looking out at an early morning mist. Thankful that last night's sudden heavy burst of rain, drained down Big Butte's mountain without muddying my unpaved driveway.

"Morning, Zoonawme." I cleared a frog from my throat.

"Meet us for coffee. Forty-five minutes," he bargained, and hung up. I got there in thirty, to see every stool at the counter in Bruce's small donut shop, empty.

"Morning, Caitlin," Elsie yawned, drinking coffee by herself, a newspaper strewn over the counter. "Paper's as bad as TV. Nothing in it." She wore the same black skirt, and white blouse, she's worn for years. Today's large fabric flower was pink. Loyal customers knew that June was her pink month.

"Hey, Elsie. How's your mom?" Today's stain on her yellow apron, however, was maple frosting.

"The Lord took her six weeks ago."

"I'm sorry, honey. I know how much you loved her."

"Yeah, we weren't nothing like you and Bridget."

"This assignment's turned me around. I'm going to make up for lost time in the happy-heart department," I replied, dabbing lipstick over dry lips. "Before I was left at the altar, I was pretty tight with her."

She handed me a pocket mirror. "Can't take your lips for granted. They start to disappear at your age . . . welcome home." She slid a cup of coffee in front of me. "When you going to just admit it? Sam was killed in a car accident on your wedding day. Sounds crazy for you to say you were left standing at the altar."

I sniffed sweet bakery smells. "A couple now, and a dozen caramel glazed to go."

"You betcha." She reached under the counter and pulled up a stale article. "Now this was news!"

I skimmed the page of where I was interviewed for cornering culprits. College kids, that drew phallic artwork on the bathroom stalls in the nun's private quarters.

"You own a bird cage?"

"Nonsense. The case was the talk of the town."

"No one's here to talk this morning. Where's the customers that usually fill these stools?"

"My regulars are all at the cemetery saluting Gunner." She packaged a unique, standard dozen—fourteen count—in a commemorative, copper-colored pastry box. "Sorry to hear about your awful airplane experience. I never go on those things. Whenever my kids want to see me, they'll have to come here."

"I'm not planning on a re-match anytime soon," I confessed. I saw Dak and Zoonawme outside near the window reading something, and looking rather studious. "Gunner died right in front of me on the plane."

"Yup . . . Mildred's kids spread the word." She pointed to a bowl of high cholesterol potato salad, the size of the Titanic, that she made for his family. "Why don't those two handsome blood brothers of yours come on in?"

"They will." I patted the coppery donut box. Stared at a picture of a black gallows frame hovering over the Leonard mine, and fished for my wallet. She refused to take my money. Handed me a box of potato salad to go, and headed for the coffee pot, when the door opened.

I looked up to see Dak and Zoonawme ignore a *Closed for Funeral* sign. They plunked down on a stool on both sides of me, and order powdered sugar pastry, and hot Java.

We nodded in silence.

Quietly sipped hot brew for a minute or two.

Finally, Dak wiped his chin and spoke. "Boys gave me a surprise party last night."

"Yeah, I heard," I said, straightening up. "And some mystery woman gave you a daughter."

"No one gave me . . ."

"Cranky."

"It's only seven in the morning . . . and, you heard about last night?" he commented.

"Paper boy told me."

"He tell you who my daughter's mother was?" He handed me an envelope that Zoonawme read outside.

"What's this?"

"Mary presented me with this before she left town," Dak said. "If it weren't for her accidentally finding my name on the records, when she volunteered at—"

"Aunt Rose says there are no accidents, that everything happens for a reason. Is the paper a proof of your paternity?"

He buried his head in his coffee cup, realizing, of course, that the town had funneled its collective consciousness, into a lightning speed dagger before he even got out of bed this morning. Elsie came closer to listen. "You know I hate father authority. My father, the role model. A cruel drunk that beat me and my mom. I don't want the title."

Out comes my lower lip. "Kid at the gas station this morning, said Megan Pat was the mother! Tell me that's a lie!" I waited half-a millisecond for a denial. "That *you* didn't do it with—"

Zoonawme silently sipped his smooth morning wake-up, and waited for Dak to stretch enough rope to hang himself.

"The night of our Senior prom," he managed a tight smile. "Once! That's all there's been to it. Once! She's not my type. You know it. Caught up in a moment of youth. Warm, spring evening. Intoxicating fresh cut grass smells. Stars out—"

"That's not all that was out." I rubbed lipstick off the rim of the cup with my thumb, wishing I could rub away the sting of Megan Pat's motherhood.

"Dacsu doesn't believe I'm her father. You think she'll believe the identity of her mother?"

"That's a load. I know it well," I gasped. "In reverse, of course." I recalled the anguish I felt when I learned I was adopted.

I wiped tears from the corners of my eyes. I'd never escape Megan Pat, now.

Zoonawme read my mind. "Patience, Cat Woman." Elsie stood close by, primping. She'd had her eye on Zoonawme for a long time. He swiveled to Dak. "How can we help?"

"Never made it as a husband—three times. Now, a father?"

"None of us ever had children, but we all used to be kids," Zoonawme reasoned. "The three of us can do this." His deep brown, sensitive eyes telegraphed me: *Keep quiet about the Pink Elephant.*

We all thought it. What we can't change is that Dak never wanted children. He had no toleration for kids. Up to yesterday, he insisted all kids were lame brains. Useless. Now, he owns one.

"Does MP know what's going on?" I asked.

"She might know that Dacsu's here. Maybe she kept tabs on her. If she thought I wasn't aware of a child, she wouldn't expect me to call her about it. After all, Mary's the one that let that cat out of the bag."

"Right, Sherlock," I countered. "Like the grapevine hasn't strangled MP with news that—"

Dak threw his donut on the floor. "That witch actually gave our kid away. Without letting anyone know she had a baby. She's despicable."

"Take it easy." I raised my brow, but kept my tone soft.

Even Elsie joined a moment of absolute silence. She fussed with her near white hair, that grew bluer with each rinse, then filled our cups, staring Dak square in the eye. "Men cause such crapy messes!" she huffed, while moving to the other end of the counter.

I swirled off the stool. Stood behind them. Put an arm around each of their shoulders. “Our good news . . .how events on my trip changed my life. I’m a different—”

“You look different,” Zoonawme interjected. He’d heard my story about coming to my senses before, and already passed it along to Dak. “New hair style?”

“Clown.”

“Critic.”

“Story teller.”

“Night Swamper—”

“You two stop it!” Dak said. “Tickles me you found your spiritual self. Maybe we’ll see less of hissy PMS fits, and more of your smiles? You hook up with your church again?”

He didn’t believe in miracles anymore than he believed in God. “I’ll pray for you,” I promised.

Elsie elbowed to the counter with information for me. “Heard you went to Berlin to work, but when you learned countless families were totally destroyed, you crawled back to the folks that took you in!”

“Where did you hear that?”

“Stella at the grocery store. She heard you decided to quit searching for your momma.” The phone rang. She ignored it. “No more calls ‘til after the funeral. Stella says you decided these here two mugs, and the O’Shaughnessy clan was real enou—”

“Elsie, you change your brand of coffee?” Dak broke in. “My spoon’s standing straight up.”

“Coffee!” Zoonawme exclaimed, twisting sideways, and aggravating his back. “You get news on the coffee pot?”

"You better get your back looked at," Dak urged. "Lab reports it was tampered with. Timed to turn back on by itself. You track down a receipt?"

"Nurse Chambers from the hospital," he answered.

I swallowed hard. "You mean I'm her target?" It was hot in the donut shop, yet, I broke out in a cold sweat. "I don't even know her."

"We're hauling her in for questioning later on." Dak's tone was edged with disgust. "There's more."

Elsie cocked her ears while she filled our cups.

Right now, all I wanted, was to mount that potato salad, and eat maple bars.

"LB's been trying to tell you what Slippery told him on the plane. It was about why they tried to rob your place," Dak said.

"What did he say?"

'They were hired."

"My God! Who would do that? So, they did set the fire?"

"No," he confirmed. "They did not."

"You both know I felt guilty for Judge Ava Foil's stuff stored in the basement—being incinerated at my house. LB mentioned she was involved?"

"Did Nurse Chambers hire them?" Zoonawme's high cheekbones glowed hot crimson, shades brighter than his brownish-red skin.

"Not according to LB," Dak answered. He sifted extra sugar into his coffee. "Boys were hunting for Ava's papers. I showed up. Fired a warning shot." Pause. "Shot startled Slippery to lodge his leg in that faulty step to your basement. I still feel guilty for not having fixed that step for you, Caitlin."

"There's enough guilt to go around," I said, glancing at a clock on the wall. "For openers, I need to return Ava's phone call." I kissed their cheeks. Juggled my to-go food, and tread to the door. "Mike's shorts are in a wad. Promised him I'd get over there this morning. You know how he is—he'll bust wide open, and call the newspaper if I'm not there by noon."

Both men threw money on the counter, and swiveled to their feet.

A wave of seriousness swept over our faces, as we stepped out into mid-morning, fresh air, offering a lighter attitude.

"Later on we tell Dacsu about her mother?" I asked, motioning to the envelope Dak slipped into his jacket.

"Right," he replied. "She comes into Butte as an adopted young lady, and now she has to deal with two parents."

I nodded good-bye to Elsie through the window. She was busy gabbing on the phone, all the while she glared disapproval at Dak.

We did a three-way hug, and walked to our cars.

Zoonawme hurled the door open on his truck. Parked across the street in front of a store stocking skis, ice skates, and 225 horsepower snowmobiles.

Dak's car was parked in front of a store that stocked enough saddles and bridles to fill an entire floor. It handled everything for the horse and rider. He drove away with smoke puffing from his exhaust pipe.

My sallow red, Paumie Dry Cleaner's, prototype for real Vans, hugged a parking meter in front of a shop, that sold swim suits and tanning lotion.

Humiliation season had arrived.

Chapter Twenty-seven

I parked two blocks from Mike's hotel, to walk in the sun's warmth after a torrid rainstorm late last night. Stepped gingerly from the car onto a city sidewalk, destined for new cement. Not merely from vehicle to pavement—but, to my cousin's area in the middle of Uptown. Congested with new construction.

All at once, a shudder tingled my spine. Like I'd been goosed. Except, there wasn't a hint of a breeze. No workers in the area on Saturday. No young entrepreneurs tearing down vacant buildings, to build condos. A soft violet cast fell over the skyline, as I slouched on a wall of a building being sanded for paint. I stared at my reflection in a bank of windows. An extra plump figure was eating a maple bar, wishing her skinny double—Jeep's wife, Orla—would stare back at her. Birds began to chirp again. I liked noise. Made me feel alive. From a corner of my eye, I caught a glimpse of the O'Malley twin brothers. A couple of roguish, Irishmen, moving furniture from their second floor flat to the street.

One of the men called to me from up there. "You'd be wise to move away . . . unless you're carrying a Shamrock."

The Shamrock. A leaf of shimmering green. Symbol of good luck for the Irish, that gave me sneezes. "Don't even own a horseshoe," I joked.

Jet lag? Donut hangover? Again, I felt a different calm in the atmosphere that I've never experienced before. I paced to one side, watching the second O'Malley back up a rusted, 50's truck onto the sidewalk. He motioned to his brother looking out a window.

"Be right up. This the last load?"

I was wiping maple crumbs off my mouth, when a queen sized bed mattress whizzed by my head, thrown out of a second story window. Both brothers were crowding a window sill. Disappointed eyes glued to their handiwork.

"It should've worked," one said, extending his head towards the ledge.

The other pointed his finger. "I told you it was stupid to think we could aim that mattress for the bed of the truck."

"It hit the target," I yelled up. "Bed to bed."

"What?"

"Broke the bed of your truck. Broke your axle. Blew two back tires into rubber bands, before it overturned onto the street."

A good laugh was just what I needed.

That, and a diet that worked.

I adjusted my backpack. Walked briskly toward the Rocky Mountain Springs Hotel. Where the family hermit rarely left his two-story, defunct house of ill repute. Mike purchased the gray brick building, needing repairs, after the owners left town years ago without paying their bills. Not only because it belonged to Butte's past. If he couldn't preserve himself, or his career, he'd preserve architecture.

I thought of my cousin as a protector. The keeper of history carved in the granite of another time. I glanced up at the sole guardian of one of the last box roofs in town. Heavyset chimneys conversed with peaceful skylines, while Mike looked at me from an attic window. The charmer smiled.

"Hey, Mike," I waved. Jealous of his slender physique that resembled a sleek Joan Rivers. Except, she wouldn't be caught dead dressed in a short sleeved, green-plaid work shirt, and tight fitting blue jeans.

"Be right down," he said, flipping his strawberry-red hair, that stood out like the portrait he was adjusting. A painting of a round chested, ornately dressed, deceased Madam—ironically had been nailed to the wall.

I walked into his empty lobby lifting a box of donuts for my daily exercise. "Morning, cuz . . . keeping busy?"

"You'd think people actually lived in this hotel," he quipped, sprinting down the stairs.

"You're a people. You live here."

He set a hammer on a dusty, decrepit wooden chair, complaining the walls seemed to have danced while he slept. "All the paintings needed to be straightened . . . third time this week." He pulled up the shades in the waiting room, to let in the late morning sun. Pointed to a kerosene lamp. A stack of candles. A box of wooden matches. "No electricity this week."

I admired my cousin for his intelligence, and carpentry. Electricity was his downfall. When a light refused to go on and off at the switch, he'd save up to hire an electrician.

"Ah, sweet Caitlin." He swung loving arms around me and squeezed. "I missed you terribly."

"That why you left me a thousand phone messages?"

He tenderly drew a small, Roman Catholic, sign of the cross on my forehead, with his thumb—as only an ex-priest can do. "What I've got to show you is exciting!"

"What'd you have?"

"First, a drink."

"Works for me."

We sauntered past his gym. He shrugged at me, nodding to a washer filled with his dirty exercise clothes. "Waiting for electricity." We strolled two rooms down the hall to the bar. Mike drank more often than he used to. Having felt he fell to the lowest level of his incompetence when he flunked priesthood. He bellied up to a hand carved, mahogany bar. Poured himself a beer, and squinted. "Your usual?"

Frank Sinatra was in the next room crooning a simple ballad on the radio. All his songs sounded the same to me—I'd never be able to name that tune. "Runs on batteries?"

"Running out of them, too."

"Cold coffee, please." I swung my hips over a stool. Slid the donut box to one side. "Hold the cream. I'm starting a diet today."

"You sure do seem different."

"I am."

"Elsie from Bruce's called me earlier."

"What'd she say?"

"That she wanted to kick Dak in the rear. And, that you'd been re-born into the Catholic faith."

"Did she mention my hips disappeared in a blaze of chocolate cheese cakes, and beef tamales during the trip?"

He scaled my backside with his large blue eyes. "There's room for her potato salad."

"You were anxious to see me?"

"Yeah . . . I almost called the newspaper." He couldn't wait to empty his thoughts to me. The only downfall Mike had, was that he couldn't keep anything to himself.

The very reason he left the priesthood.

He'd agonize—recognizing voices in the confessional—telling him their deepest secrets. Keeping a lid on such private treasures, became explosive data, that tormented him to quit the biz.

Here comes the ritual.

A beer toast to humanity, John Barleycorn, and Ireland. He handed me coffee, with a beer chaser.

I held up my cup in one hand, raised a beer in the other.

He hiked his glass high:

"Long live the Irish! Long live our cheer!
May the saints protect you year after year.
Long live the Holy Spirits in bottles of beer.
May you land in heaven before the Devil
gets near."

I drank the beer.

He guzzled down the hops, thumped his glass on the bar, and strode to the hall. "Come with me to the basement."

"You know I'm like Aunt Nell . . . afraid of dark places."

"Well, you're not my mom, and you don't have a choice."

"Why?"

"It's about the woman that was killed in front of the airport. She's connected to your ex-fiancé's dad, Erin O'Toole."

"Do you already know what happened to Erin?" He'd have to be psychic to know I found his whereabouts.

"WWII . . . missing-in action . . . this a test?"

Call in the Feds. I've stumped the grapevine. Erin's secret was intact.

"You say Sam's family's involved? They're all dead! How does Dr. Freida factor in? My God, this woman got around!"

"I saw her obit write-up in the paper. She used to work at this hotel in *the days.* Got me thinking about some artifacts I recently found down in the basement."

I hate cellars. Dark places. Rooms covered in old memories, cobwebs, and dust. "Why can't you just bring . . . whatever . . . up here?"

"Next, you'll be asking me to turn water into wine."Suddenly, I felt my chair move. I dove to his side.

"What was that?" Jet lag would be my option.

"This relic of a building is so old, it's going to shake itself loose before I can restore it."

"Thanks for not calling me crazy." We angled from the bar through clutter, and dusty sheets draped over prize Victorian furnishings. Marched down a long corridor flooded by rays of light streaming from a towering skylight. "You hear about the woman that looks like me? She's a couple years younger, though."

"I figure she's related in some way, to whoever your real mother was."

"That's what Zoonawme, Dak, and I think."

"Sister Mary Margaret told me this is your double's first time on Butte soil."

"Well, if the nuns said she's not from around here, do they say my birth mother lived in Chic—"

I slapped my hand over my mouth. *No more searching*!

By now, he was ten feet in front of me, urging me to keep up. Electricity off line, the farther we inched, the darker it grew. I tripped over a bottom step of a grand staircase. A marvelous, Gone With The Wind, staircase, that led to Mike's living quarters upstairs. Where he looked at scenic mountains in the distance. Visualizing God's impenetrable wilderness, rushing waterfalls, and bottomless lakes, as he prayed for other people's salvation.

"Hang in there," he encouraged, brushing in front of me. He pulled a key from his pocket and opened a rickety door to the basement.

"Why lock it? I can blow it down."

"Don't want anyone to go down there."

"And . . . you want me to go down there?"

"For whatever reason, the building foundation's been acting up. One of Eagle Eye's friends is coming next week to take a look at it," he contemplated. "Shoring this baby up will be costly."

"So what? I don't want to go down there." My baggy sweatshirt seemed to strangle me. Insoles of my tennis shoes felt wet.

"I know, sweetheart," he counseled. "All that ugly business about Megan Pat terrorizing you in grade school."

"Sorry I'm such a baby."

"Look who you're talking to, cousin," he laughed. "A guy on permanent retreat."

"Retreat! Now we're talking."

He smoothed my hair with his long fingers. "Listen up. Last month weak timbers caused a wall down there to cave-in. Out pops a trunk containing a box of—"

"I don't think I wanna hear this."

"Faith, girl. Relax. Historians, and other collectors, would call them treasures. Written stuff, too. You're the expert in handwriting forensics . . . let's go!"

"What's your stake in this?"

"You'll see soon enough." He fidgeted with a flashlight.

"Hey, look at this." I brushed against an old registration book. Dusty pages echoed signatures of famous guests. Charlie Chaplain. Clark Gable—written next to a Pope's name.

"If a Pope ever visited Butte, the whole area would be enshrined," he laughed. "You get to Mickey Mouse's name yet?" He unscrewed the cap. Monkeyed with the batteries, took them out, thumped them on his arm, and re-inserted them. "Although . . . Butte did produce a saint."

Not from this hotel, I thought.

"Not even Irish . . . Mother Bogetto. Score one for Italy. All Catholic roads lead to Rome." He seemed pleased with his wit. Lonesome for his prior career.

I turned a page of the register, and recognized Howard Hughes' authentic signature—from a case I worked on for the FBI. "Geesh, Mike, did you see—"

"Wait!" After two steps down, he stopped abruptly. "Was the phone ringing?" He waited a few seconds. "Yup. Hear it?" The phone was on a table near the front door.

"Ah, Mike. No phone extension on this side of the hotel, yet?"

"Nope." The phone kept ringing.

"Answer it tomorrow!"

"You go on down and get started," he outlined. "Trunk's at the rear of the basement. You can't miss the caved-in wall." He handed me his flashlight. Arced up two steps. Threw his voice behind him. "Eagle Eye rigged up one bulb to work. Said he'd come back to help restore the wiring, after he sorted out damaged goods on the plane you came in on."

"That's comforting."

He ran to the front of the building before I could negotiate the terms of my safety. And to assure him that Eagle eye would be working on that airplane mess for the next year. I wound cautiously down narrow slats on a steep stairwell. Each dry step creaking under my weight. A putrid smell of century old mildew snarled my nose. Blackness at the bottom of the landing chilled my bones. I was about to turn back, when I bumped my head on a fuse box, and remembered the poor man's copper trick to start up electricity. When the power went gunnysack, Hummy'd open a trap door on the floor of her kitchen. Hold her nose, climb down a ladder deep within a dirt basement, and insert a copper penny in a fuse box to get the lights working.

I dug into my backpack. Scrounged up a penny. Unscrewed the first fuse I touched, and twisted it in the slot. Ah, a lucky penny! I saw a faint light shining down the hall. Eased on over to a dimly lit room where one wall caved in.

"I see the trunk." A crackle in my voice telegraphed my bad feeling about this basement, yet I was drawn to stay. "Mike, you up there giving the Gettysburg address?"

I kneeled in a huge pile of cold earth. Brushed dirt away from the top of an old steamer trunk with my sleeve. Then, with two fingers, lifted a rusted latch, and sneezed my eyes red.

I'd found treasures from a stranger's past that'd connect Sam's dad with Dr. Freida—to the here and now.

I balanced the flashlight on a ledge, and poked around.

A heavy cloth sack of silver dollars.

One red, high heel shoe.

A withered, red boa that disintegrated when I shook it. A journal nestled inside the aged feathers popped out. I looked closely at an inscription. Recognized handwriting scribbled on the inside cover. The same writing I saw on Dr. Freida'a driver's license when her purse spilled at the airport. High letters in a vertical slant. Middles of every main case letter clogged . . . *a, o, d,* and *g* filled in . . . as if she ran a black marker over each stroke. Enough anger, and vengefulness to blow up the Empire State Building.

What was that mournful sound I just heard? Every building has unique groans, I decided. I couldn't put the book down when I saw the last entry:

RX for murder.

I'm running from Rosie the Riveter's six-shooter.
If you find me dead . . . you know she gunned
me down, after finding out about the twins. You'll
see on the birth certificates weighted beneath
Bronco Billie's silver pieces. Legal as hell.
Both babies were born healthy and strong.

My pulse skipped wildly, thinking it might be the O'Malley boys. LB and his brother. Or, the McDoon twins. Then, Butte had more sets of twins born than any other city in Montana. Aunt Rose claimed twin-serum came from the water we drank.

I clawed through a sack loaded with silver, and suddenly remembered Judge Ava Foil stored duplicates of old birth records in my basement. Stuff we were going to record on her computer. We both hated computers. Figured we'd learn to use them when we retired together at the Golden Bypass Retirement Home on the Flats.

These looked to be originals!

I was brimming with more questions, than answers.

Why did Nurse Chambers hire the McDoon's to rob Ava's papers from my house?

How did Dr. Freida expect to help Jeep and Orla?

Who was this Riv Etter that she wanted revenge on?

Hmm . . . say that again, Caitlin.

"Riv Etter, Riv Etter, Riveter," I hummed.

Her Irish brogue threw me off. Riv Etter—decoded—was Riveter. As in Rosie the Riveter, a woman that was after Dr. Freida with a six shooter, during WWII.

The plot thickened. But, my flashlight was fading.

I dug through the trunk with fervor, hoping to find whatever Mike discovered, concerning Erin O'Toole.

Chapter Twenty-eight

"Real money," the sisters would say about silver. They distrusted a paper dollar bill when it was first marketed in Butte. Being stubborn Irish women, they won't change their minds. "If you can't rub it between your fingers or spin it on a table, it ain't real," they'd insist. It's been awhile since I fondled silver. My collection? One silver dollar. An ornament on a belt buckle I haven't been able to get around my waist since the birth of Christ.

"What the—"

I jockeyed against a deep rolling motion. Followed by a thunderous noise.

I felt the trunk change positions, and I knew.

Earthquake!" I warbled, coughing up dust.

I used both hands to muscle the sack of cumbrous, heavy coins into my backpack, and with the speed of Zeus, I flipped the journal in a side pocket. Walloped the lid of the trunk down. While wobbling to stand up, I dropped the flashlight into a large people-size hole beside me.

Top heavy with loot, and my feet rolling, I lost my balance. Landed in the hole next to the flashlight.

"Mike, help!" I howled. My legs, and hands, scraped dirt walls to the bottom. I stripped off the pack. Bounced upright.

Stretched high to see the light bulb dangling from an extra long chain above my head, swaying back and forth. Faster—wider, with each turn, generating uneven shadows, that moved on a lone standing, log wall.

A couple seconds more. The 40-watt bulb burst, trapping me in total darkness.

"What's that unfamiliar pitch," I asked myself. It escalated into a loud echo. Sounding like a hundred cymbals banging noisily through a collapsing tunnel. Except this was no tunnel. And, dirt walls do not echo. Mike's Renaissance hotel—the whole shebang—undulated to the rhythm of an earthquake.

Fear electrified me into a familiar dark terror from my childhood. When MP locked me in the coat closet, overnight. Trapped me in blackness. Frightened. Up tight. I huddled on the floor of a narrow cloak room, afraid of shadowy creatures, and darkness. I still have problems with a stiff neck. Think to the present, I told myself. I drank Mike's holy water, reached for the cell phone, and dialed his Rocky Mountain Springs Hotel. The battery was fully charged.

Except, basement dirt grabs sound and buries it.

I started to pull my eyebrows out and prayed instead. I finagled my sweatshirt over my nose to filter out thick dust. Took off my shoelaces. Tied them together to harness the flashlight around my neck. Stood on my backpack. Clawed my fingers into dirt, and drug myself to the rim. Feet dangling. Out of breath. I barely hung onto the border of the hole with the weight of my arms.

Thirty pounds lighter, I could easily pull myself out this mess. I held back the tears. Managed to flash my light on the one wall standing. Squinted at a front page of a faded, sienna yellow poster nailed to the wall with a railroad spike. "What the?" I gasped, hoping I wouldn't fall back before I could take a second look.

I saw a picture of a young woman dressed in coveralls. A bandanna tied Turban style at the top of her hair. Red bangs hanging out. She was flexing female muscles at a shipyard. Standing next to a welder, and steel rivets. An awkward helmet, and saucer-sized goggles, nearby.

I read the caption, symbolizing a patriotic working woman during WWII:

Rosie the Riveter

Helping World War II Effort.

"We Can Do It!"

Did I recognize the strong jaw? Self-assured smile? Yes! Aunt Rose stared back at me. She'd flown with Charles Lindbergh on his flight to Butte. WWII, she went to Seattle to learn to fly, and transport aircraft parts around the nation. Again denied, because she was sole support of her sisters. She never mentioned working at the shipyards.

Why was she hung here, next to a colony of spiders?

I dug one elbow deep into the ledge. Strained my right arm to muscle over the top. I was gaining ground. Or, so I thought. Until The Second Coming, when earth rumbled furiously, rolling with a seismically active wave. I tumbled back into the hole.

With such severity, the clasps on the back of my bra broke off. Like an over-filled grocery sack, my new, eighteen hour, under wire bra, purchased for the trip, burst apart.

Elephant-sized breasts Bungee jumped to my waist, as I thumped to the ground in silent fear. Fetal position. Hot mud mixed with metal oxide, percolating beneath my feet. I lay cramped in shock.

I never thought it would end in a dark, damp, dirt basement.

Darkness was fickle. It had a way of stopping time. I shifted my weight. Listened helplessly to hundred year old studs groan, and whine. Followed by an eerie noise of wood breaking apart. Gigantic timber snapped and collapsed like a Tinker-Toy set. . . then rumbled my way.

I lowered my neck, attempting to hide my head. Waited for braces, that broke apart like cheap toothpicks, to bury me.

The rumbling stopped.

Creakkkk!

Whoosh!

Thump!

Then, nothing at all.

I opened my eyes.

Spit out a mouthful of grit.

Heavy, dust choked me. Small piles of dirt surrounded me. "Thank You, God!" I panned the flashlight beam upward to see a bank of protection above my hole. Piled in various directions, were parts of wreckage that scattered vertical, other chunks lay horizontal. Commingling with damp dirt, and shifted cement, to form a jumbled, piled-up roof over me . . . like the game of Pick-up Sticks.

A sneezing bout with mucous shows up.

I practically rubbed my eyes out of the sockets. Irish stomach! A sickening smell of hot tar, gagged me to puke out a mouth full of Jalopena-hot dirt.

The nightmare continued.

I ran my tongue over pimply things forming in my mouth. Choked from the stink of aged wood, lacquered with black, liquid creosote, and crusted over with time.

I'd been in earthquakes that shook Butte.

This ain't over!

I nailed my arms over my face. Slumped lower in the hole, waiting for another round. It came quickly. More bulky timbers teetered above me like flagpoles. Again, with the ghastly noise. Dirt raced beside me. Surprisingly . . . not to cover me. But, to form a high mound next to me, resembling the shape of a rocky mountain.

Mountain! Earthquake!

Not now! Thoughts about the O'Shaughnessy clan's ugly 1959 camping trip, flooded my senses.

How we narrowly missed being caught in the deadly '59 shaker—the earthquake of the century in Montana that killed so many people. Destroyed an entire mountain. Created a deep lake called Crater Lake, near Yellowstone Park area.

Aunt Nell is credited for saving our lives. For our escaping the epicenter of the quake.

I recalled, that Hummy chased a bird out of the tent. A bird flying inside an Irishman's dwelling—signaled a bad omen. Death. Same as seeing a Banshee. Aunt Nell fretted constantly about unsanitary conditions by sleeping outdoors. In the dark.

We left the base of a mountain that *Murphy* severed in half the next day. *The mother of all earthquakes!*

Over thirty years ago, and the trio regularly prays Novenas, for the souls of numbers of our friends that camped alongside us. All of them killed, when eighty million tons of dirt, and rock, cut loose. Crushed them.

"Ah! The dirt mound!" I angled on it's top.

Struggled. Climbed up successfully. Wedged through an opening of fallen trusses. Grunted. Crawled.

Drug a heavy backpack behind me.

Searched for steps that led out.

They disappeared—somewhere under tons of debris and dirt.

I prostrated my weary self, uncomfortably, on a section of timber, and cried.

"Dear Blessed Mother, please take care of my Hummy . . ."

Chapter Twenty-nine

Outside Rocky Mountain Springs Hotel, a siren screamed. Warm sun covered a haze of dust over a city drenched with rain the night before. A group of dazed people milled around Mike's place. The hardest hit building in the city. They saw him slumped beneath a door jam in the front. His clothes covered in suet, and whatever else comes out of hundred year old walls. They pulled him from the wreckage, his arm trailing blood. Multiple cuts on his face.

He shook off dizziness. Swallowed a deep breath. "We get hit with 7 or 8?" He ran his shaky fingers through his hair trying to get a grip on what happened. He couldn't stand on his own. Something bothered him. He couldn't remember what.

"Too early for a Richter Scale reading," one of the O'Malley brothers replied, just before Mike fell unconscious on the sidewalk. One of them drug him across giant cracks to the other side of the street, and waited for an ambulance.

The other called Zoonawme on his cell. "We pitched for an ambulance for Mike. Caitlin went into his place just before the quake hit. It got hit real bad. Her car's parked down the street. We don't see her . . .."

He stopped.

The second brother seized the phone. "We don't see the entire south side of the building!"

"You sound as stupid as Mortimer Schnerd," his brother chastised. "The west side of the building collapsed."

"Hey, I'm in love with Candice Bergan . . . you leave her brother alone!" the other replied seriously. "Who cares which side? The place is toast."

"I'm coming," Zoonawme acknowledged from Jeep's hospital room. Except for a few broken windows, an overhead door that mangled shut, and shattered equipment spread on the floors, the hospital had been spared from major damage. He hung up, and immediately speed dialed Dak.

No answer.

Called Caitlin.

No answer.

Called his cousin, Eagle Eye.

No answer.

Called the O'Shaughnessy sisters.

No answer.

LB called him. "My mom's neighborhood's O.K. She said the Racetrack area didn't get it too bad. "Headed to pick up Dacsu. We'll dash over to the O'Shaughnessy's. Dak doesn't answer."

"You see my cousin, Eagle Eye?" Zoonawme ask worriedly. "O'Malleys reported help's needed over at Mike's. They're saying it's pretty bad."

"O'Malleys? You know how those two exaggerate." He pulled up to the Finlen. "Don't see much damage up here, on the outer buildings, anyway."

Dacsu stood on the sidewalk, fumbling with buttons on her sweater. Eagle Eye came out of a restaurant across the street and consoled her. "The worst is over. Keep calm."

"Mike's . . . Zoonawme . . . hurry . . ." LB shouted to him from his car, idling in the street. Cars honked. People filled the streets. A refurbished mine whistle blew the obvious. Disaster. "I'll get the three sisters."

"I've never been so frightened," Dacsu admitted, too shaky to insert a button through a hole. She tucked the outer-sweater in her slacks, and hopped in. "Thank you for coming to get me."

"Where'd Eagle Eye come from?" LB asked.

She squeezed his arm, and sat closer. "He was eating across the street when the quake hit. He came right over. Like he was a guardian angel. Spoke to me as if he knew me, but we've never met."

"He's a great guy. Got a sixth sense about people." He exhaled.

"The clerk at the hotel acted the same way," she said. "He put me up in a three room suite. It's going to take a long time to pay back Dak Sullivan . . . you're family here?"

"My mom's all right. Waiting for electricity to come back on." This wasn't the time to think about introducing the two of them. Most likely never. He headed downhill.

"What's that building?" She raised her back. "Look . . . one entire side collapsed."

"Rocky Mountain Springs Hotel," he said grimly. "Eagle Eyes' on his way down to help."

"He on a rescue squad?"

"Everyone that can, helps during an emergency. We all look out for one another in this town."

"Right." She remembered the crowd at the airport. Congestion. Panic. Caring. Confusion. "Doesn't anyone take charge in a . . . situation?"

"We've been muddling through crises since Butte started. Immigrants learned how to survive, long before they came here. I'll show you the Granite Mine monument when things settle down. Takes out guess work about who's in charge."

"My Master's thesis was about Montana History. I wanted to see the mine accident sight." She'd learned about facts from books. Now, she's soaking in something new. Different. Refreshing. The heart of a people unlike anything she's read about. "I still have vacation time here."

LB gulped. He felt inadequate around her. Tongue-tied. He quit college in his Freshman year to take care of his mom. Money had always been tight for him. He didn't desire to acquire possessions . . . like his close friends, the McDoons.

"It is true then," she commented. "There's one on every corner."

He searched for the right answer. After all, he lived here and she didn't. He thought. Taverns? Churches? Brothels? Then he answered. "Takes a lot of grocery stores to feed this town."

"Uhmm?" He lived here, she didn't, she thought. "Food's always good business." She changed the subject. "Is there a bookstore in Butte? I want to read about the Granite Mine. I'm fascinated with the fact, that the Granite could be called the Hindenberg."

"Giving an ethnic name to a mine around here would be like throwing a Christian to the lions . . . not good!"

"I was speaking about . . .how one of the most sophisticated safety systems on the Butte hill . . . the irony of the best ventilation operation in mining, helped fuel the fire below to kill 168 workers."

"I knew that."

He shushed her. Drove silently. Visually assessing as much as he could, before he pulled up to the girls' family home. The fence had fallen. Sidewalk cracked. But, the house, built in 1890, held together. He ran up the walk, with Dacsu trailing close behind. Banged on the front door at the same time Hummy opened it. Her face drawn deep with anxiety. "Coom en," she said simply. She stooped to set down a mop bucket filled with wet rags, and groped for words. "Air yeh fine . . . now air yeh?"

"You girls all right?" he asked sincerely. His eyes following Aunt Rose, carrying a rubber plunger from the bathroom. They traipsed carefully inside onto a soggy floor. "Rose, your water main burst? Can I help?"

"Way're trien teh raych Caitlin and Mike, now, arn'tt way?" She put car keys in her hand. "Theh phone lines arn'tt wurken. Way ware fexn denner fur theh two oov them."

Caitlin's showdown with them was to happen at supper. The Butte way. Eat plenty of food. A relaxing drink. Then comes the serious conversation. "Most phones need service. Wait awhile, then try dialing." Pause. "Mike's got some broken bones," he shouted down the hall to Aunt Nell in the kitchen, awkwardly climbing up a chair and dragging her oxygen with her.

He heard a loud moan.

"No worries. Your son's just fine," he assured.

She fussed with a good luck horseshoe the quake corkscrewed upside down. In a Butte-Irish home, a horseshoe that hung above an entry door, with the opening positioned upwards, had been considered lucky. The O'Shaughnessy horseshoe hung topsy-turvy.

"Good luck . . . Aye'm tellen yeh teh coom back," she ordered. She explained to Dacsu that when properly hung, it had power to catch good luck, and hold it firmly in the cradle of its band. She straightened it to collect luck. Climbed down, snapping on fresh latex gloves, to throw salt over her shoulder. A deal sealer.

Dacsu felt at ease around the women. Comfortable and safe. She sniffed something baking. "Mmm." She watched Aunt Nell pass the shaker to Hummy.

Who, in turn, threw salt over her shoulder, and caught her sister square in the face. "Aye'm sarry. "

Aunt Nell sneezed. Backed up. Bumped a coffee can off the stove. Dacsu held her hand over her mouth to keep from laughing out loud. A three pound, coffee can, filled with soft, left over bacon grease—used and re-used for frying food—flipped upside down, landing on a water soaked floor.

"Zoonawme's seeing to Caitlin," LB assured. "Best if you stay here and wait for news. He'll call soon. How can I help?"

"How can we help?" Dacsu corrected, to Aunt Rose's delight.

"Bathroom walls ware cracked eh bet," Hummy reported.

"Plummen's shot teh hell,'" Aunt Nell affirmed.

Cleaning the bathroom had never been casual work for them, given the frequency with which the room was used. Aunt Nell worried about seriousness of a disease. Any disease. Some of them she invented. If the health of the family was to be maintained, the room had to be thoroughly cleaned. Often. She filled an iron pot with water. Clanked it on the kitchen stove. A black antique that burned coal and wood. It didn't seem hot.

LB put his arm around Dacsu. "Sorry. Everyone, meet—"

"Yeh look jest lake yur dad . . . handsome en tall," Aunt Rose countered. She opened the door to her microwave oven to see if the electricity still ran. Her full coffee cup from earlier, was still sitting in it. "Me thinks theh two oov yeh air real looky."

She didn't feel lucky. She didn't believe Dak was her dad.

"Coom." They invited her to a kitchen chair. Hummy wasn't much for words. She nodded kindly. Closed the microwave. She thought such instant technology must be bad for their health. She'd never use such hoity-toity. She bent over. Wrapped plastic baggies around Dacsu's wet shoes.

"Gled teh—" Aunt Nell flustered, stuffing a package of cookies in the bread bin. It wouldn't do to give a bad impression that she bought cookies machine wrapped in paper containers.

Aunt Rose tried the phone. No dial tone at Mike's. "Es thet eh new style sweater?" She furrowed her brow at Dacsu's unbuttoned top—out of the norm for Dacsu's fastidious, self reliant, attitude—haphazardly tucked inside her slacks. "Hmm?"

"What do you need immediate help with?" LB asked again. His cell phone worked. He dialed Mike's hotel. "Their phone must be out, too. "We've got to check on Pen Doodle. Soon."

She asked him to carry some heavy wood, bailing wire, and tin sheets, clumped in a burdensome pile behind the rabbit hutches. Picked up a snout nose hammer, and sloshed towards a trap door to the basement.

The sisters had been born in County Cork, Ireland, in a thatched roof, three-room, stone house. It had one window. No running water. No electricity. They handled whatever came without complaint.

"Water's shooten en theh baysment, lake Old Faithful, now esn't et!" Hummy spoke, emptying water from her rubber boots.

LB quickly lifted the trap door. Pushed his heavy thighs down the narrow steps. Twisted a wrench to turn off the water. "That should help for now. You'll need to carry water in, from the neighbors." He trekked to the back yard.

"I'm coming to help, too," Dacsu insisted, angling behind him to a mound of debris blocking the alley. She slung three long pieces of heavy wood over her shoulder. Waited for instructions.

"Please, Dacsu, don't lift the heavy stuff."

"You've got to be kidding?" she said. "Let's roll."

It took them thirty minutes to move the pile to the front, next to the garbage cans, as Aunt Rose asked.

"Was that a shed before the quake?" he puffed, walking inside.

"Thet stuff's been thairr fur months," Aunt Rose grinned.

Hummy scowled at her. She walked over to the stove, chastising her sister for doing a practical joke in such serious times. The phone rang. Relief. Exit the quirky Irish humor.

"Et's Eagle Eye . . . hay's eh block froom Mike's hay says."

"You three stay here. We'll do the running around . . . remember there might be more aftershocks," LB instructed.

"Five menutes, they coom oot oov theh ooven," Hummy blurted. She reached for a handle on the stove that was sticking out of a heavy round grate. Pulled the grate off with it, and drug it aside. "Caitlin's favorites, yeh know." She stoked the fire below shifting coal with a poker, until the flames rose. Closed the grate. Moved a cast iron pot on top of it to boil water. Wiped her callused hands. Stirred a vitamin rich pork rind, slow cooking in the pot.

LB's phone rang. "We must leave," he told them, wiping steam from his glasses. This was mountain country. Even in the summer, a heated kettle fogged up the windows.

"Nice to meet all of you." Dacsu said pleasantly, working her way to the front door. "Caitlin told me such kind things about all of you, on the plane." She glanced at a sea of pictures on the piano of Mike and Caitlin, and paused to fondle a grade school chunk of plaster of Paris, with Caitlin's hand print in it. She set it down, and stroked a bronzed pair of Mike's first shoes, mounted on a stand.

"Out swate cheldren," Aunt Rose said. Her face lit up to acknowledge Dacsu's interest in the family. She hugged her. "Jest lake yur self, lass . . . swate."

Dacsu took a strong liking to Aunt Rose. "I'll lend you my sweater sometime."

"Oone menet! Set down fur a wee menet, lass," she asked.

"We must leave." LB's face turned purple. He knew what was coming next. He looked down. Embarrassed. His face red.

Until he met Dacsu, he felt comfortable with his plenty plus size. Now all he thinks about is strangling Betty Crocker.

"Rose, let the lad bay," Hummy scolded, dropping a dry towel for Dacsu to wipe her wet shoes on.

"My oh, my," Dacsu chortled, trying to help him save face. "Maybe another time. We need to see about Caitlin's dog right away."

"Aye ensest."

"Yes, Ma'am."

Dacsu tread water to the couch. Listened to Aunt Rose tattle on a young, Deputy Lard Butt, that got stuck in the Success Café. Butte's hole in the wall eatery that seated four people at a time.

She told how, after a wedding, LB staggered west on Broadway past a sign, *Capacity 400—Four at a Time*. Ducked into the smallest café in the world that seated four customers at a time. Two each on narrow benches on either side of a small table—both walls at their backs.

Predictably. She labeled LB's weight heavier with each telling. "Oover 390 pounds, theh lad ded clock."

The room was thirteen feet long—half the length taken up by the kitchen. She told how he squeezed into a space three feet wide. Punched the end of the story, with a fireman rescue. Then she opened the door.

"Tell may Caitlin teh coom home, strayttt away," Hummy ordered, handing them an entire batch of freshly baked, sweet tipsy cakes. "Aye poot eh coople extra. God bay weth you."

"Yes Ma'am."

"Yes Ma'am."

The two drove off heading Uptown.

"Come on!" she poked him on his side, moving closer to him on the bench seat of his squad car. "The fire department really spend half the night to pry you out of the Success Café?"

"Maybe." He knew she was unconcerned at what he weighed. More interested in how he acted. "I guess . . . longer." He winked comfortably. "They had to eat, too."

Chapter Thirty

For each of us there is a moment of discovery. Especially when the heart is open. This day was my moment. I woke up thirsty, and with a back ache, resigned to my fate. I slowly rolled over. A red high-heeled shoe—*Rosie* monogrammed on the heel—poked me in the ribs. In a perfect world, where Murphy didn't exist, I imagined stories of a network of tunnels built underneath the mining city were true. That one of them connected Butte's bustling Uptown business district, to the Rocky Mountain Springs Hotel.

Oh, Lord! What did I just hear? Please. Don't let it be another aftershock. "Hello . . . someone else trapped down here?" I paused to listen. "Mike? That you?"

I crawled like a turtle in the direction of a grinding sound. If I wasn't dreaming out loud, the sound came from a pipe, or a railing, or some kind of metal poking through a dirt wall. My throat wrenched into spasms. "I'm here by myself on the other side of a dirt wall!"

A regimented clanking sound answered me back. Was that a Blackfoot code? My heart jumped with hope.

"Zoonawme?" Over here. I'm trapped.

One . . . one, two, three.

One . . . one, two, three.

"Zoonawme?" Every time I moved, my sweatshirt stuck to me like plastic wrap on a casserole dish. I cocked my ear to the tapping of the Indian rescue signal—one long clang, then three short ones. Struggled to take my flashlight from my neck. Hit the pipe with it. One . . . one, two, three.

No answer.

Minutes later, a noisy drill tediously worked its way through thick boulders and unsteady rock. To form a small peephole next to the pipe. "Caitlin? You there?"

Another aftershock. Smaller than before.

"Yes," I answered. I spit out a mouthful of dirt. Hearing a drill motor had raised my hopes to survive.

"You there?" Eagle Eye projected his voice through a narrow cylinder. He'd lost most of his hearing during a dynamite blast he set off. A small price, he thought, to help two miners escape from a tunnel cave-in.

"Thank God! I'm all cramped up. Hard to breathe. Is Zoonawme there?"

He didn't hear me. "You on your back or your belly?"

I remember Aunt Rose touting his knowledge of all tunnels beneath the surface as legendary—and there were hundreds and hundreds of them winding beneath Butte—she'd tell me. She said he named each of them, like he labeled the inventory in his house. Priceless knowledge for when, at various times, he rescued miners that were trapped in a shaft, a tunnel, a stope, and one pinned under a mucking machine. During each rescue, my aunt would brag, he skillfully detonated dynamite.

I'll give him his due. He's an incredible Blackfoot tracker that saved others. But could he save me?

I blinked a weak light through the hole.

One . . . one, two, three.

"Good girl," he exclaimed. "Signal me with two short lights for belly . . . three flashes for back."

I signaled twice.

"Cover yourself with something hard, if you can."

"No! No! . . . don't dynamite!" I buried my face into my backpack. So solid my chin bled. Zoonawme must be with him. Why didn't he stop his cousin? "Please don't, you'll kill us all!"

He drilled another hole alongside the first one. Used a pick and shovel to hollow a space the size of a fifty-cent piece. The job would go more quickly now. He ran an oxygen tube through the first hole, and spoke. "We've got about six more minutes of drilling."

I'll die of dehydration first. His six minutes will be six hours. I'm ashamed to think it. They should have named him Molasses.

"Grab onto this here bottle a water, girl." He forced it through the second hole. I imagined him wearing a dirty brown, miner's safety-hardhat while he drilled continuously. Only he knew about deep lines of hurry etched on his face. He was on a tight time schedule to excavate an opening big enough for me to squeeze my chocolate cheesecake thighs through. Without causing a ton of earth to bury us.

He shined his battery operated lamp—encased on the top of a steel safety helmet on his head—while crouched in a partially collapsed tunnel. The light found my blood shot, puffy red eyes.

"Thank God!" I wheezed. He shouldered his arm through to touch me. It was like being touched by an angel. I paid little attention to sweat pouring like a faucet down my face.

"You all right, girl?"

"I think so," I whimpered, ashamed and excited at the same time. I clutched him. Tears ran down my cheeks. In a fast paced, hurry-up world, that seemed determined to divide us from friendship, his careful, slow, and meticulous work was the miracle I prayed to the Blessed Mother for.

"You hang in, little lady."

"Thank you! Thank you! Thank you!" I said to deaf ears. "Where's Mike? Zoonawme? My famil—"

"Don't try to turn around. Keep facing me."

"Should I try and come through?"

My flashlight batteries gave out at the same time as my energy.

"Not yet!"

"Yes, Sir,"I said sheepishly, mortified about my critical, knife-twisting judgment against him. I was sure Zoonawme was behind him, standing by. Except, I didn't know where "him" was located. Other than down under.

He laid his plastic coat over jagged edges of rocks. Yanked my backpack across the hole with forearms like a blacksmith. For a short man, he was strong as an ox, and ugly as sin. I slid my belly across the uneven escape hatch. Lost a swatch of my gummy, red hair that got caught on a rock.

"Ouch! Ohhh, God!"

"Let me do the work," he commanded.

He bellied his arms beneath my armpits. Drew me cautiously, tenderly forward. He allowed me to straddle long enough to get my wind.

"You think you can walk?"

"Thank you, twenty million times," I whispered. My body was one big Charley Horse. My weakened legs buckled beneath me. Breathless, I lipped Zoonawme's name.

"We came in together," replied Eagle Eye.

I knew that in my heart.

He pulled me upright. Massaged the back of my legs. "When he slumped down low in a tunnel," Eagle Eye said. "His back completely froze in spasms. He was hurt worse than he'd admit at the airport . . ." He hesitated. Tested out my legs by bending them, as if I were a horse. "Zoonawme got hurt bad when he tried to save the doctor lady. Spirit dog and me drug him out of the tunnel."

How could I have demeaned this brave, kind man behind his back? He's risking his life to save me, and he knows how I feel about him. "What about Mike? How long have I been here?"

"You must walk!" he urged. He swore in his native tongue. "Hurry! We've got to climb through a network of passages beneath the city. Many of them have already collapsed."

I threw my flashlight away. Began to move in the dark, painfully bending one knee at a time. My right shoulder rubbed against a craggy, uneven, dirt tunnel wall, as guidance. I muddled onward.

"Mike's good." He stepped in front of me. Being almost deaf, he spoke loudly.

I tugged at the sleeve of a man that didn't have to be down here. He came by choice. "Spirit dog?"

"He's bred to pull an elephant. Your dog, too, is waiting topside with the O'Shaughnessy clan."

He took off his safety hardhat. Acting like a father, he adjusted it on my head. "This is how you turn the lamp on and off," he instructed quickly, and plowed forward. Then branched off into another tunnel. We'd trudged through three different ones already.

We ran into a dusty mist that wallpapered the area and burned my eyes. They felt like sun kissed golf balls. I stood there choking. He cleared away dirt that landed on our path after another aftershock, so that we could trudge on. I felt blinded and stopped to massage my eyes. "Can't see."

He twisted to me. "Copper dust. 'Miner's Wallpaper.' It'll go away." He slipped his safety goggles on me. Placed a small mask over my nose. "We'll come out under a bank building."

"Eagle Eye!" I halted abruptly. "Wait!" My moment of discovery—knowing and feeling how wonderful the human heart could be—had come. I slid off my mask. Swiveled him to me, and stared directly into his eyes. "I need to apologize to you. . . now! I ask your forgiveness from the bottom of my heart. From the depths of my sou—"

All of a sudden, yet, another strong aftershock threw us out of balance. The floor danced. The entire tunnel moved, wallpapering our path with more heavy dust again. I struggled to hold myself upright. Fell. Like a cat, he instantly lifted me to my feet. Parked my backpack over my shoulder, and thumped my rear with heavy, underground loggers. Such force boosted me forward like a rocket, as the ground kept rolling.

"Keep on moving. Draw energy from the earthquake's waves. I'm right behind you!"

"What . . .from what?" Just then, I heard Pen Doodle's friendly bark in the distance, and groped ahead.

Through a glimmer of light at the mouth of the tunnel, I saw her standing on all fours. Impatient. She saw me fall. Sprinted uncomfortably towards me. She comes from Alaska, bred to thrive in our cold winters. On a hot, clammy day like this, her white Silver Fox Samoyed coat, was as much a nuisance to her as rescuing me, even if she knew how.

"Leave the backpack," Eagle Eye shouted. "Dirt's moving too fast. I can hear tunnels behind us collapsing." He balanced his arms on either side of the tunnel. Faltered just as Pen Doodle rushed in barking wildly.

Spirit dog followed. His ears pricked upright, barking and snarling at her to get out of the tunnel. His long white fur, speckled with light gray and black markings, were sticky and wet. He stiffened his loyal ears. Nuzzled against me, eager to help. He growled again, at Pen Doodle. Then sniffed at present danger. Out came tears of relief seeing my dog trot away. I wanted to follow. Exhaustion made it impossible.

I waited for Eagle Eye to catch up. "Caitlin. Get out. Now!" His loud voice shrieked.

Spirit's almond shaped, amber eyes narrowed, to assess my predicament. He nudged me with his nose. Again, and again, but I couldn't move. He pranced on a pool of dirty water in a pothole. Muddying his waterproof undercoat, and wind-proof fur. Slowly moved webbed feet—that helped him from sinking in the snow as he hunted elk, and enabled him to pull large, heavy loads—close to me. He had a plan.

He gripped his powerful mouth over my arm. Backed up. Dragged me, and a heavy backpack—that I'm too stupid to leave—several yards closer to freedom before he stopped. I didn't care about the money. The documents that Dr. Freida wrote about in her journal were stashed under the heavy silver. Not to mention that I was chomping to read the journal.

"Good dog," I kissed him several times. On the mouth. Circled my arms around his neck, almost choking him with love and gratitude. He licked my face. "Marry me?" I asked.

Suddenly, a thunderous roar echoed our way. "Hurry, Eagle Eye," I screamed.

Adrenaline oozed from my muscles, as a seismic aftershock tossed us around like a supreme salad. My feet shifted and I lost my hold on Spirit's wide neck. He barked wildly, just before an angry cloud of dust came belching at our heels.

I twisted my head to look for Eagle Eye, and almost fainted.

"Oh, no! It can't be! No!"

The tunnel collapsed at the same time Spirit dog drug me to the tunnel opening. I turned around to see a shadowy screen of crumbled rock, and coppery dust engulf the space Spirit just drug me from. "Eagle Eye . . . Eagle Eye!"

There's a sick feeling I get when I know something bad happened. I knew the earth laid a burial blanket of copper dust on my guardian angel. That repeating his name over and over wouldn't change truth. Nothing would change what is. He'd been buried alive.

"Eagle Eye . . . Eagle Eye . . . "

Chapter Thirty-one

I sweat through my hospital gown from a fever that'd finally broken. Ambled out of bed to change, and hunt up some fresh sheets. Fr. Riley was on his way. I turned up the sound to hear our local Walter Winchell talk about yesterday's quake.

Sticker Noon babbled on the radio how we lost a town hero, Eagle Eye, in a 6-point quake. Bragging how he saved Caitlin O'Shaughnessy from death—then died in a collapsed tunnel connected to Rocky Mountain Springs Hotel. He doted on Spirit dog's heroics—saving Zoonawme—then Caitlin. I could see Sticker through the radio. He was a harsh looking man from Chicago with formal attire, out of place in our small town. He broadcast his talk show with dry wit, a deep voice, and a Ph.D. in weather.

"Atmospheric conditions in Butte-Silver Bow County did plenty of damage to your tax dollars yesterday . . . several Butte houses were already flooded after the June downpour last week . . . then the underground pipe system erupted when the quake hit . . . Mr. and Mrs. Butte . . . wherever you are . . . don't step on any manhole covers today . . . the quake's force overwhelmed 100 year-old rain gutters, already full from the gully-washer . . . thus, causing several manhole covers to blow off."

Father Riley turned off the radio to hear my confession.

He gave me Holy Communion. Blessed our family, at last, huddled together in one room. Where I stayed overnight for observation in MP's domain—without getting killed. Although, I flinched in fear whenever a nurse inspected my shoulder, tended bruised knees, bandaged cuts, and rubbed ointment on my elbows, scraped raw to the bone.

The temperature raised early to a warm 80 degrees. Not nearly as hot as Dak was under the collar, after he interviewed Chambers about the coffee pot. Yet, he let her off the hook. Went chasing after *Dr. Megan Pat the Terrible.*

MP cleverly avoided him, using *Earthquake aftermath*—multiple heart surgeries—as an excuse to dodge his questions. She'd never seen him act so furious towards her. After all, she reasoned, the girl was her baby. Dak never wanted kids. Why tell him? A substitute answer for truth. That her dominant, manly personality wanted a career, more than her womanly personality wanted a baby.

Jeep stood stiff at the foot of my bed. He was wearing double pleated, black slacks, a silk shirt, and a neck brace. "Your Aunt Rose kindly invited me, and Orla, to lodge at their house," he winked. "However, the bedroom floor was immersed in water. We're residing at the Finlen."

"It's great to see you standing," I said from beneath the covers. I understood every word he spoke. "How're you feeling?"

His surgery went well. He'd need a few weeks to recuperate.

"Where's your wife?"

"She's regrouping . . . um . . ." He stammered. "Orla's bewildered how you two share an almost perfect resemblance. Her mother informed us she's as stymied as we are."

I cleared my throat. "Speaking of stymied . . . I found papers under Mike's hotel that might connect Dr. Freida to you and your wife. But, didn't you say neither of you had ever been to Butte? I'll examine them thoroughly, anyway. Maybe the doctor knew something. Mike suggested I do my forensic work quick, so you can read those papers soon," I quipped.

"Your Aunt Nell explained to me that you retrieved rare gold coins, that were incorporated with many silver dollars consigned in your backpack," Jeep countered. "I have connections to people that deal in such treasures."

Aunt Nell annoyingly juggled a shopping bag filled with fresh clothes for me. Everything annoyed me today. My nerves needed a boost. She finally settled down on a chair off to the side, and waved goodbye to Jeep. Tucked loose hairs inside her hairnet, and started to speak. "Aye want teh—"

"Zoonawme's alone," Aunt Rose blurted. She stood erect. Her annoying habit of fidgeting with her large earring grated on my nerves. "Et theh funeral parlor meking errangements fur Eagle Eye."

I could barely whisper Eagle Eye's name without feeling guilty for his death. I wanted to walk through a door into another consciousness. "What's this?" I dug through the bag. "You search my bedroom for an outfit as if you were shopping at a rummage sale just before closing?" I glared at red slacks that matched my hair. A green blouse that matched my sick stomach. A blue sweater that reflected my guilt over Eagle Eye.

"Et's bayn ruff, theh past coople oov days, now hasn't et!" Hummy said quietly. "Ware meken too mucch noise."

"The four of us have to talk." I gazed at Aunt Rose with a mix of admiration and disgust. I raised my voice. "I saw what you did at the airport!"

"Now whut cood yeh bay talken aboot, me Caitlin?"

"You stole papers from Dr. Freida's belongings," I huffed. "And, what about this?" I held up a red shoe, and pointed to a monogram on the heel. "That your name?"

"Way'll bay kapen our bezzness private, now won't way?" She brushed a dust bunny from her green, pin striped suit, and stalled until a volunteer left the room.

The O'Shaughnessy women slid chairs close to the bed, their faces drawn.

"This shoe belongs to you . . . Rosie the Riveter."

"Whar ded you find theh shoe?"

"Your bedroom."

"Et looks old."

"Your bedroom at the Rocky Mountain Springs Hotel."

She started to argue the point, but stopped and walked over to the door. Hummy raised an eyebrow in silence, watching her sister lock the door, ease closer to me, and unclip one of her huge earrings.

"Souvenir froom Dr. Freida." She rubbed a heavily scarred earlobe between two fingers. "Shay pulled may around a room, clutching both pierced ears, bay a pair oov earrings dangling lake exercise hoops. Almost tore may ears off, shay ded."

"I learned in Mike's basement that Dr. Freida practiced medicine in the same hotel that you rented a room?" I stroked the blisters on the back of my heels. "No more lies."

"Way both worked thair, straytt away," she gritted her teeth.

The silence that followed might as well have been thunder.

Aunt Nell coughed, darting her eyes to both sisters.

Hummy pulled up her white collar. Re-buttoned a cream color sweater she wore for special occasions. Then reared back in her chair, and began to cry.

"Mother?"

"Aunt Rose?"

"I know about the six-shooter," I said, holding up the journal I found. "I know about Dr. Freida bolting town. No one's run out of town because of a single fight. You tell me why . . . now!"

Aunt Rose started to talk. "Caitlin, you—"

It was a bittersweet relief when Nurse Chambers' rough voice shot through a metal door. "It's against the law to lock a patient's room. Open this . . . " She turned sharply to listen to a young nurse tugging at her arm. "Yes, issue discharge papers after lunch."

"There's an emergency," the perplexed nurse uttered. "We're having problems stabilizing old Shoot the Moon. He insists he ate cottage cheese from a milk carton? That he's poisoned?"

"Stupid girl! The guy received three bronze medals with gold oak leaf clusters for meritorious conduct during the war. You think he ate—" Not one lock of her heavily lacquered hair moved as she rushed down the hall.

Meanwhile, Hummy walked to a window, squeezing beads on a single strand, pearl necklace as if it were a rosary. After a minute, she leaned in to hug me. "Et's time! . . . now esn't et!"

"Yes, Mother . . . it's time someone told me what's going on!" Unbelievable! Nurse Chambers used her pass key to unlock the door. She stormed in carrying lunch, and a bad attitude. "Smells better than last night's—"

Aunt Rose seized her arm, threw her out, and shut the door. "Bridget's rate. Et had teh coom out some tame." She braced a chair up against the door knob.

She'd been spokesperson for the trio since I can remember.

By the look in her eyes she was prepared—even relieved—to air our family linen. My stomach curdled hearing the same monotone voice she used when the sisters told me I was adopted. Were they going to tell me I came from outer space? My clean red hair—minus a large clump on one side—draped listlessly around my head. As listless as my heart.

I listened silently.

She told me she was Rosie the Riveter—in the picture. She'd gone to Seattle during the war to be a pilot and was rejected. Worked in a shipyard, sent money home to the family. None of the three had a husband's income to fall back on. When the war ended, women were fired, so men returning would have jobs. She came home to find work.

"I figured that out," I said, sipping a Mocha milkshake through a straw, and dangling my legs over the bed.

Hummy put her arms around her sister, and hushed her. "Aye'll fenesh fur yah." She sat down, staring at the floor and continued. She told how Rose was forced to work in Butte at jobs that didn't pay much. How she was black-balled as a miner, and denied formal education. That a waitress didn't earn enough to provide the O'Shaughnessy's only income. What with two small children, and the three of them.

She was blaming the bad luck on Murphy's law, when Aunt Nell placed her hand gently over Hummy's lips. "May sester, Let Rose tell—"

"Are the rumors true?" I asked. "Does our money come in from Gunner's valuable property you won in a poker game?"

"Not oone sant," they all chimed. She invested all the proceeds from renting the place over the years, into a bank account for Mildred. Aunt Rose found a way to have the last word, and she took it.

"Why not to Gunner, when he was alive?" I knew she hated him for humiliating her in his union paper. That she felt squeezed by the union on one end, and executive big wigs on the other end. Neither group thought a working woman was worth her salt.

"Now thet hez dead, Aye'll sign theh deed teh hez family."

"You always buy me such expensive gifts. Put me, and Mike through school. Where does our family money come from?"

"Et dedn't coom froom hooken," her tone edgy. "Aye liked theh gurls wurken et Springs hotel, where I wuz a bookkeeper. Scheduler. Understood thar predicaments, thar worries, now dedn't Aye!" she exclaimed. She wasn't a woman's libber, like the town labeled her. She was an every person's personal rights activist. She'd have made a great stateswoman. "The owner oov eh Shipyard en Seattle during theh war—en me Rosie theh Riveter days—hey was single, childless—died en laft may hez sizeable fortune bay theh tame you ware ten. Et wuz nobody's bezness."

I sat up straight, wiping cold sweat from my forehead. "Tell me truthfully, Aunt Rose."

"Aye well."

"Are you my mother?"

"No. Aye'm not yur moother."

I fell on the pillow in, what appeared to be, bitter disappointment. "I'm surprised. Really, really surprised!"

Tears streamed down Hummy's waxen face. I've hurt her again. *Bad Caitlin.* I held my head in my hand.

"Since Europe, my roots, and heritage don't matter. *You,* my Hummy, are my only mother. I love you Bridget O'Shaughnessy. I'm ashamed of how I treated you after Sam died. *Please!* Forgive me?"

Aunt Nell was desperate to escape. She jarred the door open and stepped into the hall, claiming a hospital room was filled with mold, bacteria, and germs.

Aunt Rose dug in her heels. "Enythen alse?"

"What did you steal from Dr. Freida at the airport?"

"Jest soom papers froom theh old days." On this point, she took the Fifth Amendment, and they scurried from the room.

Too much went down at the airport for me to believe bloodied earlobes, and a cat fight were the problem.

Why did Dr. Freida skip town?

Why was a six-shooter in Aunt Rose's possession?

I telephoned Dak.

No answer.

Called Zoonawme at the mortuary. They put me on hold. I dressed myself in a mismatch of tight clothes. Opened a box of Shepperd's Candy, popped a brown sugar treat in my mouth, signed insurance forms, and lifted the receiver to learn Zoonawme'd been with Dak earlier.

"Paleface told Dacsu that her mother was Dr. Megan Pat. It didn't go well."

"I'm sorry I wasn't there," I replied. Her parentage was undeniable. She'd have to accept that Dak and Megan Pat were her birth parents. My poor friend. He's one of the most charismatic men I've ever known. In time, he'll win his daughter over, and make her think it was her idea.

"He's hopping mad about how it went with Nurse Chambers."

"Is he going to arrest her?"

"Can't arrest someone who buys a coffee pot. And, he can't prove she tampered with it. We know for sure it'd been programmed to burn your house down."

"She admit to torching my place?"

"Total denial."

"Is Dak coming over there?"

"He's hunting MP down as we speak. He must be somewhere at the hospital. No cell phones allowed. I'll call you later."

I called a cab.

Chapter Thirty-two

I walked inside Duggan-Dolan Mortuary. Hugged Zoonawme, and wept when I saw Eagle Eye's name posted on a room roster. "He's got the large room in front that's reserved for important people. I'm the nobody. I should be in a casket instead of him. Except, I'd be somewhere in back. The small room that doesn't hold many flowers. Nobody likes me, anyway. People don't know I've changed for the better. Why, when you think—"

"A moment, Caitlin. He's not in there yet." He shook hands with the owner. "A Blackfoot Indian accepts his other-world journey with joy," he told him. I knew that. But, I didn't feel it. Shouldn't I feel the same as Zoonawme? The three of us turned sharply, at the same time, distracted by a group of Chinese filing into Eagle Eye's empty room.

"The staff will provide more chairs for you as soon as we bring Eagle Eye's remains in." The owner spoke softly to a large company of friends, and most of the Blackfoot Nation, that'd come to pay respects.

Again with the soft speaking, when it doesn't matter. "Why does everyone wait until you die to get all reverent, and polite," I asked my friend. My hands were shaking with remorse. My nose trembled at the hint of pollen.

Just then, an army of employees paraded past, carrying enough fresh floral bouquets to stop my breathing altogether. I buffered against a series of sneezes.

"Don't beat yourself up for how you treated my cousin. It didn't matter to him. He was one of your supporters. You're just a little edgy right now, my dear friend. You've been through hell."

I went to the Ladies' room. Downed a mild sedative from the hospital . . . at least I hoped that's what they gave me. Just because I never saw MP, didn't mean she wasn't watching over me. I came back to hear an assistant ask the owner a question.

"Anything else?" They looked like twins. Both wore the same kind of dark, blackish, suit. Their shoes polished to a shine that reflected the ceiling. They spoke softly.

"This one's getting bigger by the minute," the owner replied. "Same routine as we do for a Catholic."

"Flowers?"

"Yes."

"Singing?"

"Of course."

"A priest?"

"No . . . not that much Catholic." Zoonawme stopped shaking hands abruptly. With his red skin, it was hard for me to recognize a haggard face. His voice betrayed his exhaustion. "I'll say the proper words. My cousin'd want them said in St. Ann's Church."

"I don't understand," the owner said.

"That's where Caitlin was baptized. He'd want to share the beginning of his journey with her."

"He related to her?" He stroked his chin. He'd heard the rumor long ago. That Rose and Eagle Eye were Caitlin's parents.

"She was with him when he died. Sharing one's last moments on earth is as important to a Blackfoot Indian, as the moment he's born."

"Understood." The owner scratched his head. "Uh . . . does that mean you want a Mass?"

"No," he said, sniffing me. He sniffed again. "Different perfume?"

"They use lemon cleaner at the hospital. It must've rubbed off on me." I felt calmer. Braver. Dropped a newspaper in the wastebasket. "Father Riley forgave me. Will you forgive me? You know his death was my fault!"

"Nonsense, Cat Woman," he comforted, walking towards me with a limp. "Father Riley didn't forgive you."

"You heard from God direct? I knew it. God's gonna wait awhile to ease up on me. Penance. That's it, I'll do some—"

"Caitlin, stop!" He swept his arms gently around me. Squeezed firmly. "Father Riley doesn't have the power to forgive you. Only God does. He's done that already. Now . . . forgive yourself."

I gulped in silence.

"I remind you that Blackfoot believe, unlike the destiny of the one event that changes a life—like a chance meeting with someone, a book, a movie, something you overhear, an event we may not be aware of—our time of death is the one certain destiny decided before we're born. It was his time to journey."

"I read about Eagle Eye in the paper this morning," I told him, looking in a mirror that hung on the wall. "I never knew he entered the service in 1943."

"Three years in Europe. Participated in the battles of Ardennes, Rhineland, and Central Europe," the manager piped up with enthusiasm. Then he strolled to his office.

"He did tell us he was the only ethnic in the 10th Armored Division during the Battle of the Bulge," Zoonawme said proudly.

I traced brown circles under my eyes with my fingers.

"You see that Blackfoot man over there? He's an elder. Believes that Eagle Eye's serving with honor in Company K-333 Infantry, was tied to your destiny."

"Please, no mumbo jumbo today."

"He received the American Theater Service Medal for his specialty as an explosive expert. That meant, he also knew when not to use it." He handed me a quill pen and a guest book.

My fingers were swollen. Hair on the back of my neck raised. Did MP monitor that medicine I just took? I held the pen in my fist to write my name. Instead, I drew *JMJ-envelope,* seven times for spiritual insurance."

He hustled me aside, to avoid hurried activity all around. World War II veterans have a way of focusing on their own experiences at events. They hogged the hallway, talking how Eagle Eye was best friends with Erin O'Toole and Gunner. All veterans."

A funeral is a good time to spill my guts to Zoonawme about where Erin's been for more than forty years.

He shook hands with Father Riley, and a Blackfoot woman wearing traditional Indian garb. She approached him cautiously, carrying an eagle's feather, and a determined look. They talked briefly before he sat down with me on a couch in the hallway.

"Searching for my birth mother in Berlin . . . I had a key to a vault filled with documents provided by both sides of The Wall, after it fell. I randomly rummaged through rusted boxes, unopened since Germany lost the war in 1945. Poured over handwritten documents like I was at Woolworth's Five and Dime, going out of business sale."

"What'd you find?"

"My mother wasn't in that basement. But, I discovered military documents that bread crumbed me to Erin O'Toole."

"How so?"

"Sam's dad hasn't been missing-in-action, like the three sisters talked about quite often. They must have been good friends with Erin, because they hushed to silence whenever I entered the room."

"Sure, they were close neighbors." He coughed. "Where's he now?"

"You aware of the Daughter's of Eve?"

"Groupies of Eva Braun." His eyes grew large. "She's the blonde that hid in an underground bunker with Hitler. She married him on their last day together."

"Guru to the Daughter's of Eve. National German heroine. Women envied her female power over Hitler. As much as they envied Hitler's obsession with Sonja Heine, the blonde, champion ice skater he wooed without success."

"You're not making sense. You know I don't like blondes. MP is blonde. Maybe only madmen liked blondes? That what you concluded?"

"The Daughters, the document stated . . . due to Eva's weird climb to sort of a, behind-the-scenes, national status . . . were umm . . . were treated like royalty and presented with handsome men . . . to father children for the future of the Third Reich."

"I don't like where this is going!"

"Sam's dad led six American soldiers to escape from Eva's private stud farm. All were killed on the run. Except, Erin was captured, tortured, his body disfigured . . ." Having said this out loud, I'm not sure I could ever repeat such an atrocity to Butte people. "He was murdered publicly in a town square. His name's recorded as being justly put to death according to military rules of war for escapees."

"Relax. Eagle Eye will meet him soon. He'll be satisfied his friend was a war hero."

"I know where he's buried, but there's no family left in town for me to tell. Will you help me keep the secre—"

I whipped around to see a Blackfoot woman wearing brown leather garb, turquoise beads sewn in the form of an eagle, and a headband to match, creeping silently over to see me. I shivered when her icy hand touched me. "Does she want me to shake her hand?"

"Stand. Stay still," he advised, jumping up. He looked serious.

The woman stared into my eyes, like she was staring into my soul. She waved an eagle's feather over my head, and said something in her native tongue. Then she handed Zoonawme a pouch filled with bone fragments and mores feathers, before she walked out of the mortuary.

"Ancestor stuff. Don't worry." He led me into the viewing room to place the pouch in the casket. "There's no protocol for mourning."

"I don't get what's happening? Pouch? Eagle feathers? You didn't do that when Zakhooa died."

"Eagle's feathers . . . for Eagle Eye to begin his journey. Zakhooa was given beaded moccasins. You should bring me a bear tooth when it's my turn." He towered over me as we walked to the casket—walking with a hitch in his get-a-long. "She brought you a warning."

"Serious?"

"You're going to endure an ice water bath, unlike any emotions you've ever experienced, regarding your family. Her medicine will help you cope."

"Is she nuts?"

A mourner sitting in the front row of seats, unwrapped a bottle of whiskey. Took a long swig. Passed it to me. Hmm? Booze mixed with whatever I swallowed from the hospital. I declined. No one in the room paid attention when he turned on a radio to listen to Sticker Noon.

We listened to him interview the president of the Silver Bow Saddle Club. The Chicago meteorologist had never ridden a horse. Or, thrown a horseshoe.

But, he hyped up the World Horseshoe Pitching competition in Bozemen, scheduled for the end of summer.

"Chew on this . . . guaranteed to be a sunny day . . . filled with good thoughts . . great food . . . and enough positive energy . . . Mr. and Mrs. Butte . . . to recover from all the funerals that took place these past few weeks . . . get your horseshoe pitching arm buffed up . . . Sheriff Dak Sullivan entered the contest again . . . he's looking to capture, yet, another trophy."

"If he doesn't go to jail after meeting up with MP," Zoonawme responded. "Bad enough she hid the truth about Dacsu. Dak's on her tail, as we speak."

"Wanna rephrase that last part? I think Nurse Chambers is the culprit, here."

"No! Chambers is small change. A freelance parasite shopping for someone to shackle. She's got her eye set on MP. Harry Johnson lived down the street from your place. He saw a woman run from your house the night of the fire."

"Another late witness? Why didn't he come forward?"

"He . . . like everyone in town . . . assumed MP was a good friend of ours. That we knew about her being there."

"MP?" Shock. Surprise. Where's that bottle? I wanted to abuse my liver.

I kissed him quickly. Silently. And, left to go home.

MP's nowhere near being family, but, I knew the ice water bath had begun.

Chapter Thirty-three

Pedal to the metal, I drove like a madwoman to my A-frame on Big Butte. My head reeled in confusion. Eagle Eye's amazing kindness. Why would he give up his life for me? Aunt Rose's astounding revelations. Her secret life at Rocky Mountain Springs Hotel. Her animosity towards Dr. Freida. A woman the O'Shaughnessy's never mentioned during my life. My double appears out of nowhere. Coffee pot. A hit man, or woman, looking to wipe me out by fire. MP's secret baby. Why was she training for the Olympics by my house the night of the fire?

One certainty. It's always comforting to get home where it's safe. My fortress. Nobody can break my heart when I'm here. I parked by the porch where Mike—sour look, chin out—waited, nervously, petting Pen Doodle.

I don't think he came here to give me a blessing.

"You read those papers?" he grilled immediately.

"Umm . . ."

"Do it now."

I punched the alarm code.

He hurried me inside. "This is extremely important."

My hands shook as I dumped the papers on the table.

"Here . . . this one!" he shuffled it in front of me.

It read. Birth Record:
Twins born. Dated on my birthday.
Father: Erin O'Toole.
Mother: Rose O'Shaughnessy.

I dropped the document. "Does this mean what I think it does?"

"What'd you think it means?"

My eyes glazed over. "That Aunt Rose held back some of the truth. She gave birth to the McDoons, or some other twins, the same day my real mother had me. That Sam's dad was their father!"

He pointed to the next line with his finger.

Sex of children: Female.

"Twilight Zone! Was this document a forgery?" I wanted my question to be the right answer. "I researched. No other females, let alone twins, were born in Butte on my birthday."

Mike's priestly voice spoke out. "Read further."

I read further.

Attending Physician: Dr. Freida, House Physician.

"Wait a minute!" I reared back. "You can't mean your hotel?" I wondered if blood rushing to my brain could kill me.

"I'll call the sisters . . . tell them to get over here now," he snorted. "They know what's going on."

"I'll see if Zoonawme wants to take a break from the funeral parlor. Then, I'll find Dak," I said, gathering an army of support.

He found Rose waiting for Nell at a drug store, ordering Lifeboy, and Lava soap bars. A strong disinfectant formula that miners in the old days washed with after a shift.

"Yeh know they heven't made thet soap fur years, now doon't yeh?" Rose chided, understanding that Nell was buying time. Not one of them wanted to face the music.

Thirty minutes later, we heard her loud engine grind to a halt, a couple blocks away. Her car idled like a tank. Rods begged to get out. Spark plugs shuttered. Battery was near death. She'd stopped at an intersection, yanked out a bottle of Jack Daniels. Drank, and passed it to her sisters.

I stood at the window tapping my foot, and glaring at them, as they parked between Dak's rented clunker, and Zoonawme's truck. Marched up fourteen steps, and rang the bell.

"Why so formal?" Mike stomped his foot in the doorway. He scooted Pen Doodle outside by Spirit dog. Sat on the floor by the couch, and twisted his legs in a classic Yoga, stress reduction position. "Caitlin and I found papers that say Aunt Rose bore a set of twins."

"Et's eh lie," she defended instantly. Vehemently. From the pained look on her face I almost believed her. "Et's eh darety lie, strayttt away!"

Dak's cell phone rang. He switched it to text message, a new idea his department was testing. He scowled at Rose. "We're going to run this birth certificate through the lab. Check it against state records."

"You're all so busted," Mike added. He knew that a brutal interrogation would run them off. He'd have to skillfully maneuver them to come clean. He drew his verbal weapon. "You know I can't keep what I already know, to myself."

Rose was smart, and calculating. The story must be told correctly. She slapped the stolen item from the airport on the table. "You read thes!"

Birth Record:

Female child born.	Dated on my birthday.
Father:	Erin O'Toole.
Mother:	Rose O'Shaughnessy.
Attending Physician:	Dr. Freida, House Physician.

Hummy turned whiter than usual. Doubled over with stomach pains. The other two spoke in Gaelic to each other. I never learned that language. Decoding their brogue was difficult enough.

I raised my arm to quiet them down. "You first, Aunt Rose. Did you give birth to a child?"

"No! Aye ded not."

"What's this certificate all about that you stole from Dr. Freida?"

"Et's true. Thar wuz eh child born on thet day."

We sat unbending, hearing that Dr. Freida was the brothel's exclusive physician. That she attended to the girls' health care. Kept them clean from disease. Delivered their unwanted babies, and put them up for adoption, through a secret, lucrative pipeline to outside of Butte.

"JMJ-envelope! . . . you saying I was born to a prostitute?"

Numbness conquered. I've always relied on these women. They bandaged my heartaches. Why couldn't they have just said, I had enough fathers to make up a baseball team? The secret was out. "No wonder you objected to me finding my birth mother."

Hummy's legs slowly crumbled. She wailed like a wounded coyote. Fell. Passed out on the floor. Mike carried water from the kitchen, and splashed her face. He was determined to get answers. "Talk."

Again, we listened. Family business. Dak and Zoonawme sat off to the side, like room monitors. They wouldn't interfere.

"The girl child wuzn't born teh eh prostetute," Hummy wept. She clutched at her heart. "Shay wuzn't born teh may Rosie." Another long pause. More tears. Elephant sized. "Theh papers ware rigged teh bay false . . . Aye wuz theh pregnant oone."

This time, I fainted. I'm not sure why. I didn't understand a thing she said. Other than, I've been lied to . . . all my life.

Twenty minutes later, I wiped ice cold water off my face. Mike stood over me with an empty water glass. My blood brothers sat like statues in the same spot. "I'm sick of fainting every time I don't want to face a bad situation," I said to them.

"Then . . . don't faint. You gave up cigarettes, didn't you? Give up the cheap theatrics," Mike ordered. He expected me to be strong. I'd always prayed to find my birth mother. I'm getting closer. Live with it, he thought. He was also irritated at the sisters. His being a hermit never looked so attractive to him. "My mother has more to say."

Aunt Nell's mouth curled with an outward strength I've never seen from her. She told how the youngest of the three, Bridget, at sixteen, fell wholly in love with a handsome neighbor next door. That he loved her back. Promised to divorce his wife, after his discharge from the military, to marry Bridget.

"What kind of a man would take off knowing he got a girl pregnant?" Mike's priestly heart asked.

"Hay dedn't know," his mother explained.

"Eh good Irish Catholic, unmarried gurl, doosn't gett praygnantt," Rose stated firmly.

Between the three, we learned Rose hid Bridget at the Rocky Mountain Springs Hotel, to live until the baby was born. They told people she went back to Ireland on a visit. Nell, already widowed, stayed alone at their Dublin Gulch shanty with little Mike . . . until her sister supposedly arrived in the States, bringing an orphan girl she adopted.

"Hmm?" Mike frowned, stroking his chin. He remembered they lived between Gunner, and the O'Toole family. He quizzed his Aunt Bridget. "Why didn't you write your troubles to Mr. O'Toole? Surely he'd help."

"Erin's wife wuz pregnant et theh same tame," she admitted.

Right then, a knife sliced through my heart at what I heard.

Dak and Zoonawme jumped up. "No!" They both shrieked.

Sam's family lived next door to the O'Shaughnessy clan. I connected the dots. Hummy and Mrs. O'Toole were pregnant at the same time, by the same man. Sam and I were brother and sister. At last I understood why God sent me to Europe!

Zoonawme gazed into my eyes. We shared a horrible secret about my own father . . . that must never be told. All I could do was gulp air, repeatedly. "Sam? Caitlin's brother!" he raged. Stomped to the door, and disappeared into fresh night air. Away from a distressing pall that hung over the kitchen. Blackfoot woman spoke truth today, he thought.

"Oh, God, help me!" I always imagined a different kind of meeting when I found my birth mother. Music. Peaceful thoughts. Tender beginnings. She'd rush over to me, saying she'd been looking for me all her life, too. A mix up at the hospital. But, that was a corny movie plot. My reality is, God sent me to Europe to find my father. Then, He gave me my mother. Aunts. A cousin. Roots in Ireland. My faith, once again. Plus, a bonus. A bittersweet sickness that I almost married my brother. What kind of a family have I been born into?

I wanted to hug Hummy. Console her. I wanted to hit her. Punish her.

"Yair me dotter," she said, dropping her eyes to the floor. "Aye've looved you sence burth. 'Tis true."

Mike was visibly shaken. His voice rattled at the sisters that were raised in Catholic Ireland, in a time of Victorian philosophy. Trapped by the holy trinity of Amour propre—family honor. "Why didn't one of you tell Caitlin the truth?"

On impulse, Dak opened a kitchen cabinet, pulled down a whiskey bottle, and drank from it, and silently waited for Zoonawme.

He returned, twisting his ponytail like a piece of rope. "A Blackfoot woman carries no such Victorian baggage. She is what she is. She lives whatever happens. Reputation isn't in our vocabulary." He marched to the fridge and clutched a cold beer. "Where's Caitlin?"

"Shay's seck."

A toilet flushed.

Zoonamwe motioned the group to sit at the table. "When she calms down, she'll want to know why you women allowed her to go through with marrying Sam?"

"Et'd never get that far," Rose pledged. "Way were en the bride's room et St. Pat's . . . wurkin oop teh theh tellen, when Dak cooms runnin oop theh aisle about Sam's dyin."

Red-eyed from crying, I stumbled back to the round table. Seven of us. Like knights preparing for battle, we sharpened our swords, and our tongues. "Aunt Rose, you spoke of preserving Hummy's reputation. You think the town labeling you a prostitute didn't destroy your reputation?"

She was squinting at my garden window at a dark night sky, tears blurring her vision. I'd never spoken to her with such disdain. I felt ashamed, yet, I wouldn't take my words back. "Yeh doon't know whut real freedom es untel you've lost yur reputation," she snapped back.

Mike exchanged an anxious glance with me. He appeared calmer. "They protected our family reputation. You were in the family slot you were meant to be. All this happened at a time in Butte, that a woman had no rights that a man need respect. Aunt Rose already lost her reputation during the St. Patrick's Day Parade . . . " As far as Mike was concerned further words weren't necessary. "You heard Aunt Rose. She was our sole support, but she wasn't a prostitute!"

"Let's all . . ." Dak's voice dropped to answer his phone. "You can't hide from me forever," he shouted. "Look, Megan Pat, you meet me tonight, or . . . I'll tear your hospital apart to find you." He agreed to a place and hung up.

"History's written," Mike counseled. "No do-overs. We all start from where we are to mend fences. . . and that's that!" he said, lifting his eyes to his Aunt Rose.

Aunt Rose's voice was harsh with grief. She spoke directly to me. "Aye promised our parents, yur granddparents, when way laft theh old country, thet noothen woold get en theh way oov taken care oov may sesters. Yur moother protected Sam, as well." Aunt Rose's eyes narrowed. "Shay pooshed himself teh lave you alone, shay ded."

Nell added. "When Erin dedn't coom home froom theh war, yeh know, way dedn't know whut to—"

"Did Dr. Freida deliver me?" I asked objectively.

"Aye, lass, shay ded."

All along I felt I was connected to the doctor. Not like this. Zoonawme's puzzled look reflected what I was thinking.

"What about the birth record of the twins?" he asked Aunt Rose. "How does that fit in with this mess?"

She throttled an empty Bourbon bottle. "Dr. Freida dedn't want Bridget teh watch theh delivury. Shay shot her unconscious weth medicine. Promised shay'd not bay feelen eh theng."

"Why is that important to hear?"

Information was coming out like a machine gun.

"Eh few weeks later, eh Chinese chemist thet worked et theh hotel, told may thet may baby sester, Bridget, delivered twins on thet day. Hey said, not one girl . . . two . . . identical female babies, they ware."

I was shocked beyond all feeling.

A strange horror came over Hummy.

"No! Et can't bay true, sester!" Her soft voice trumpeted like Gabriel blowing his horn.

I felt a stinging urge to get drunk, and stay there for the rest of my life. To eat donuts and burritos until I went blind. Somewhere in the depths of my buzzing head, I thought of Berlin. The Geneva Historical Council. That every event I incurred since *The Wall* fell in Germany last November, was an orchestrated step to guide me along my yellow brick road to truth.

Dak gently lifted my chin to arouse me from a trance I was stuck in. "Huh? . . . you . . ah . . . did I . . ."

"We'll deal with consequences like we've dealt with our problems since we were kids," Dak said, jumping to his feet with a start, responding to Bridget's screams.

"Aye have two dotters? Ded yeh say et, Rose. Aye birthed twins?" She crumpled on the chair like a limp sweater. Aunt Nell took deep breaths from her oxygen tube, and held onto the kitchen sink.

"Everyone take a deep breath," Dak ordered. He was having difficulty coping with his own set of betrayals. Now this. He turned to Aunt Rose, and butted in. "Where's the second baby?"

Her story thickened with grief.

She told how Dr. Freida raked in thousands of dollars for each adoption. By chance, after it was too late, Rose learned that Bridget bore twin girls and Dr. Freida adopted one of them out. A fight ensued. The only fight Aunt Rose lost. At that point, she stole a six-shooter from one of the prostitutes. Threatened Dr. Freida's life, unless she returned the second child to the O'Shaughnessy family. Dr. Freida promised to do so, but skipped town forever.

Not without leaving a poison pen letter.

She had powerful connections. Her tentacles ran throughout the state—to high government—church leaders—civic leaders. She had the goods on men that frequented the hotel. She often used that to her advantage—this time to have a false birth certificate made to look legal. Identifying Rose as a whore giving birth to a bastard baby girl. Rose never expected to find Caitlin's twin. She kept the secret. She did expect Freida'd return with the false document. It was up to her to protect her family.

"Dear sester . . . yev'e been carryen to beg oov eh load, knowin aboot twins." Aunt Nell said, hugging her tight.

Hummy sat in a daze.

"Thet theeven crook stole may silver pieces, Bronco Billie's gold pieces, may clothes, en theh proper papers thet'd prove twin gurls ware born. Aye wuz fearen her return," Aunt Rose said.

Mike was dazed, too. He tenderly swept Hummy's gray hair from her face, and helped her to the bathroom. "Someone, please bring us both aspirin."

The three amigos exited silently to the front porch, and sprawled on the steps. We listened to the crickets in the stillness of mountain air. Both dogs barked at a cat across the road. I had no words to express my numbness.

Chapter Thirty-four

I bathed in the clear night air, realizing that I, too, had acted with disdain for years. I was digesting that mistakes were made by all of us, when Dak leaned in and whispered to me.

"MP called earlier." He was absorbed in my grumbling when he looked at his watch. "She agreed to meet in an hour. Wanted you to come with me. Said it was important."

"What'd you think?" I should have known, of course, because of MP's connections, her power within the state, she wouldn't rest until she cleared herself. "I don't have anywhere else to run right now. You promise to stay close by?"

"Tell the family you'll be back in a couple hours." His eyes drifted to the house, every light inside was turned on. All the courage built up in my heart, had so easily broken down at this unlikely diversion. One mention of MP would do that to me.

"It's late." Electricity bill. I'd thrash Montana Power with my bare hands. "My new family will probably leave soon."

"Stop right there!" he admonished, shaking my shoulders. "Your *family* has always been your real family. Shame on you.

You should be thanking your God—your prayers were answered. Sure, a secret came out. Lots of them—"

He stopped abruptly. It was out of character for him to dispense advice about spiritual matters he didn't believe in.

"Cat Woman, you got what you prayed for!" Zoonawme didn't mince words. He pulled off his boots. Stretched his long legs on the steps, and fanned his toes. He was calm. Always strong. Always peaceful. We spun around as a porch light sprang on. Mike laid two dog bowls near potted flowers Bridget planted in ceramic pots. One of the bowls spilled on the landing next to special starters, red Indian Paintbrush, as he backed up towards the door.

"Everything all right out here?" he asked, his voice strengthened with compassion.

"Things are starting to sink in a little," I promised. "How about inside?"

"The girls have lost all their pride, and they're not sure they didn't lose you—or that they'll lose your twin sister."

"The only place I'm going, is with Dak for a couple hours right now. Tell them . . . um . . . I'll talk with them tomorrow."

"Grab a sweater, Caitlin," Dak advised. "Night air is chilly." He turned to Zoonawme. "You mind the store for awhile?"

"I'll ask Rose to whip me up another Dagwood. That is, if Cat Woman's got any crocked pickles, horseradish, and sauerkraut, left in her fridge."

A Blackfoot Indian understands that food is the universal language of love, I thought. Like Eagle Eye, he loved unconditionally. Other than for MP, Zoonawme never judged people's actions.But her many personalities confused him. They only seemed to appear when either one of us was around her. That's what worried me, I pondered, as I slipped back into the house for a sweater before meeting my nemesis.

I looked in a mirror to hastily dab on lipstick. Powdered my reddened nose, and chapped face. Opened the hall closet. Threw Hummy's old brown sweater over my shoulders and laced up my shoes. I hailed the group commiserating in the kitchen, sifting through ideas on how to put our lives back together. They all waved back.

"Going with Dak for awhile." I rubbed hand cream on my hands and neck. Forced a smile. "Zoonawme's walking the dogs. He'll lock up." I hesitated for a moment. Our family looked like broken china.

"My car's over there," Dak said. We walked out into a dark night. A black sky was dotted with glittering stars. From the high altitude up here on Big Butte mountain, over a mile above sea level, city lights below twinkled in the atmosphere like a Christmas display. Being submerged in a personal fog over the years, I wondered if I really appreciated the magic Butte performed after dark.

"Please, Blessed Mother, make this meeting short," I muttered.

"Speaking of meeting," Dak said. "What seemed a coincidence—Jeep meeting Dr. Freida during a legal matter in Chicago—now appeared to be planned by fate." He ground a key in the ignition several times. "I'd tell you to buckle up, but this beauty of a Rolls Royce is too old to have seat belts."

The engine started with a popping sound.

"We could take my car?"

"What? And push it uphill? No thanks," he grinned, until his serious side showed up. "MP's got a lot of explaining to do. I'm starting with the coffee pot fiasco."

"Zoonawme told me Nurse Chambers was involved, but you've said nothing since you interviewed her."

"She did purchase the pot for MP. She denied tampering with the mechanism. Also agreed to take a lie detector test."

"Give me her handwriting. I'll tell within minutes if she'd be your main suspect."

He turned the focus as we stopped for a red light.

"You realize your friend Jeep and his wife are related to you?"

"My God!" I gasped. He was right—Orla's my sister. Jeep's my brother-in law, except they don't know it yet.

"The window on your side rolls down, if you want air."

"Does it roll up again?"

His mind focused on MP's meanness. "I want to believe Dacsu coming to Butte was a coincidence, but—"

"Mike would call it divine providence."

"I don't believe that either." He thought of his rough childhood—abusive, cruel father and passive mother—there wasn't room for religion in his heart. He aimed his severe hatred for a father's authority at God. "I'm not a believer in miracles or God." He leaned in to turn a sharp corner. "Like Zoonawme. I put my faith into the environment. The elements."

"O.K. Pope Agnostic," I snapped. "Can't get Slippery out of my mind. How he saw me from the back of the plane and told LB he was hired to rob me."

Information overload, I thought as the car backfired with a loud noise.

"Makes me queasy to recall Mary O'Donovan's courageous flight to Butte. Her connection with you. And finding your daughter," I chatted without stopping. "I get goose bumps at how my job in Berlin wasn't taken because of a fluke. Who knew I'd end up looking at life in a different way. That I'd find a family. I guess everything did happen for a reason."

His phone rang. He turned it off without checking. We stopped with a jerk at a crosswalk. Black smoke billowed inside from a faulty exhaust. As I rolled the window up to stop choking, I thought I heard a dog howl. I wouldn't recognize a Banshee if it bit me. We turned right. A sharp corner. I tilted.

"Where are we going?" I finally asked.

"Anselmo mine yard. She said she likes the view from there, over the city."

"What? That place is pitch black, dark—pitch, pitch."

He wasn't listening. He concentrated on his meeting with MP. "I'll do the talking when we get there."

"I need to go to the bathroom." A full bladder was always my immediate response to seeing Megan Pat. I crossed my legs, and my fingers. "Dak? . . ."

The Anselmo was located in an area of trendy renovations. Where homes on the west side went for a premium. But, the mine hadn't operated for quite some time. More of a museum piece than a place of business. Where daytime workers kept Butte's mining past alive by recently starting to restore a gallows frame, one that was transferred from the Black Rock mine when it closed.

I was weaned on the uniqueness of Butte's history. Strange how, not knowing where I came from, and that I didn't have a history, everything historical bored me. But, visitors salivated to view a site that contributed to the largest mining operation the world has ever seen.

We turned left towards a place where lights don't shine. After the moon went to sleep, there was no darker place in the world, than an abandoned mine yard situated deep within the Rocky Mountain range.

"Why meet at the mine?" I felt sick. Why'd I agree to come?

"Megan Pat didn't say," he said bluntly. "Other than to suggest we needed privacy. She was right on that point."

"You holding up O.K.?"

We ran over a box on the road. He stepped out to check if some kid put a cat—or a bottle of Ketchup in it—and drove on. "This shouldn't take long. Just enough time for me to wring her neck . . . and she knows it."

"Heavenly Father, stop her from being killed," I prayed out loud.

"Faith in a heavenly father. Never an option for me," he said with certainty, turning on a gravel road to the mine. "I knew, *intimately,* who my father was!" His anger fixated him on his own past.

"Funny," I commented. "The whole lot of us are going to make some therapist wealthy by the time things are ironed out."

Brakes squealed, the car sputtered, as we coasted without an engine. He pulled a choke out. He tried starting it a couple of times until the engine cooperated. "Yup. Freudian stew.

Mother, father, daughter, sister, brother," he quipped, unemotional.

"Dak, when're you getting a new car?" My kidneys knew he hadn't missed a pothole.

"I think the mayor has the hots for me," he laughed. When he smiled, the most handsome men in Hollywood would have to take a back seat. "She ordered the car. Her way of thanking me for not stringing her kooky kid on a flagpole."

"Will he do time for manslaughter?"

"Too young. He'll be punished, though. Then released to his mother's custody."

"Why not to his dad?"

"That SOB skipped out of town before the kid was born. A little male guidance, and he'll turn into a better person," he said with compassion.

"You? Compassion for a kid?"

He hunched his shoulders to the wheel, to steer around large boulders laying across the road. "Truthfully, I'm starting to feel excited to take on the role of parenting Dacsu. I'm getting older. I'd retire if I could afford it. But, a man in his mid-forties that has to shell out to three ex-wives—"

We arrived. Parked next to Megan Pat's over-priced, highly polished, steel gray Mercedes. A midget show piece. Unless one of them was driving, Pen Doodle and Spirit dog would never fit inside. A door creaked as I eased out.

"I think I see her," he reported, scooping a flashlight from the trunk.

My face drained, stomach flinched. I held his hand as we cautiously edged around the yard looking for a foot path. I wanted to run. "You stick to me like gum on a theater seat!"

"Over there." He shined the light.

I could barley see her sitting alone on a bench near the front door of the Hoist house, boarded and closed. Where the only wheel churning was inside my brain, telling me to disappear before one of her personalities could do damage to me.

We were twenty minutes late.

"Hello, you two," she chided in a pleasant voice. She'd dusted off her best personality. "You sure got here fast. Thank you both for coming."

You'd think we just had coffee together, and she met us to bring dessert.

"Why the cloak and dagger, MP?" he asked.

"Dak, come closer. Alone, if you don't mind?"

The warm evening suddenly turned cold. I piddled behind a rock, buttoned Hummy's shop worn sweater to my neck and waited. She's a lot smaller than me, I thought, wriggling impatiently near the car.

"She wants to talk to you," Dak said. She's really upset. She knows how tight we are. I think her plan is to get you to soften me up."

"You can't be serious?"

"I need your help. I don't think this will be a problem. After all, I'm right here. Besides . . . you're a woman."

"And, you're a man. So what?"

"She's crying buckets over there. I get all flustered when a woman cries. You knew my three wives. Criers. Wailers. Tears got them all my retirement money. I'm feeling sorry for MP. Please, Caitlin. See what you can do—I'll wait my turn to thrash her." He dug in his jacket pocket. "Oops, sorry, I left the flashlight over there on a bench."

"You're not going to leave me?" I said in panic.

"No, I'll be standing right here."

MP lit a tiny pathway from a distance. She seemed farther back than before. Far enough away that the light appeared to shine from the head of a pin. My heart pounded. I walked on eggs.

Closer. Until I saw her beautiful face.

Serene, calm . . . and dry!

Not one tear in sight.

I knew then, the only thing in her sights was me. I started to yell for Dak. "Hey—"

"Dak," she feigned a sob. I recognized a messianic tone in her voice. She called out to him like an angel. "I'd appreciate it if you'd get us a blanket from your car . . . and some Kleenex, please."

Dak clearly didn't know much about women.

He retreated with only the stars to guide him, and fell over some sharp boulders. "Ah . . . damn!"

"Megan Pat?" I walked slowly. Like a lamb to slaughter.

Suddenly, I turned at the sound of footsteps behind me.

"Thank God, you're here Dak."

I should have realized Dak had to walk to his car without a flashlight. He'd have to come back the same way. Slowly.

Without warning, MP came at me from behind like an iron wrecking ball.

She surprised me with a choke hold. Started barking orders like a bulldog. Her assassin personality.

"Yes, *Red* . . . I've decided you need surgery. Not your heart! The brain! Yes, your pea brain will fit nicely into your super-sized navel. Stand still, fatso."

Red? Fatso? "Look . . . I see Dak coming over here."

"He's too far away by now," she said somberly, her mood changing to an enforcer. I helped her drag me behind a building. Her headlock would have snapped my neck if I didn't move my feet.

My worst nightmare began.

How do you reason with a psycho that's gone over the edge?

"He'll come looking for me," I promised while struggling.

She put her mouth to my ear. "Been trying to get rid of you since grade school!" Her expensive perfume lingered on my neck as she spun me around. I wanted to peel off my skin and send it to science.

I screamed when she pulled a small handgun from her designer jacket, jammed it into my side, and ushered me across the yard.

"Move . . . as if your life depended on it."

I'd cooperate. I knuckled under when I wanted to knuckle over, and kept going. Maybe the weapon was real?

"Please help me, Blessed Mother . . . please . . ."

Chapter Thirty-five

"Ugh!" I whimpered, stumbling over loose boards and trying to keep my balance. She used the flashlight for herself. Pushed me harder. I plowed into a dirt mound, faltered, but kept moving. A few seconds later, I tripped and fell over rusted cable. Tearing skin from the palms of my hands, and opening large gashes on my legs—souvenirs from beneath Mike's place during the earthquake.

"That won't do," she said, shifting from enforcer to physician. "Most likely, you've picked up nasty bacteria from oxidized cable. Can't allow your open wounds to be infected with copper poison, like your Uncle. I can fit you in next week . . . oh, sorry, dear, that'll be too late."

One of her personalities had to be on an Opium diet.

I couldn't see much, but I saw her eyes glaze over.

"Ouch . . . ouch!" Her gun pressed hard against my back. "You're hurting me."

"Wrinkling your clothes, too, eh? I hate that no one in this town wears high-priced apparel—other than trampy Rose." She ran her fingers over a costly turquoise stone fastened to the front of her expensive jacket. Twitched. Then, tore off my sweater, stomped on it, and shined the light in my face. "I hate freckles. Mostly, I hate that you share a loving relationship with my man."

"Please! You've got this all wrong. Dak and I are just good friends. Let me go!"

The more I struggled, the harder she pushed the gun into my back.

"You always were a pathetic sicko."

"Ouch! Stop it!"

"You and Dak have been in love all your life. I'm going to fix that tonight." I don't know which one of her showed up, but she forced me to wiggle through barbed wire, recently strung to close off an area that led to an open mine shaft. She walked cautiously as she followed me. All the while her hand was gripping the gun.

I appealed to her softer personality. Slowed my speech. "Megan Pat. You've got a great reputation in Butte. Don't ruin that."

"You saw to that, *Red.*" she said, poking me in the back.

"Ouch! Stop hurting me. I don't know what you mean."

"You brought Dak's pilot friend, and his daughter to Butte."

"You're wrong."

She tomahawked me in the stomach with the gun, and laughed.

I reeled in pain. Tasted blood swirling in my mouth. "Please . . . stop hurting me." There'd be no arguing with a madwoman. I didn't dare faint.

Out came her sneer. I'd seen it all my life. Just before she did something terrible to me. What else could she do to me out here? She's not going to ruin her career by wasting me.

"Don't count on your Indian to save you. I put an emergency call to him that your sweet, little office was burning. He must be half way to Copper Dust Forensics by now."

About the only thing she's afraid of is mice. She twisted at the sound of a mouse scampering by her feet. It ran across the platform . . . she shot at it.

"Oh, God! Your gun is real!"

"And licensed. To protect myself from people that're jealous of my wealth. I'm in a class of my own. I could buy the entire State of Montana with my pocket change. People like you, that can't rub two nickels together, wouldn't know about that."

I thought I knew all the faces of fear. But, squinting down the barrel of her gun, brought up a new one. The crack on my tail end tightened. Shoulders stiffened. Dak was nowhere in sight. Survival was up to me. I welled up a temporary bravado. "Did you tamper with the coffee pot that was sent to me?"

She slugged my chest with her elbow. Stuck the gun in my face. "Your Indian chief foiled that plan. Showed up before it caught fire. He's such a meddler!"

"You hire the McDoon twins to rob me?"

"Those two idiots. I should have hired a professional."

"What were you looking for?"

She seemed amused as she loosened my blouse from my slacks. Rubbed cotton material between her thumb and her forefinger. "Hmm . . . Ms. Early Rummage Sale—"

She also seemed preoccupied. Expressionless. A slightly more approachable personality came out. I seized the moment. "Are you responsible for burning down my house?"

"When I left, that inferno was hot enough to roast both your dogs." She yanked my hair until my head snapped back.

I couldn't fight her, but I could keep fighting down my vomit. I held back an urge to try to take her gun away. "Why'd you do it?"

"Stupid Slippery and Sledge were supposed to steal a box of papers and get out. I should'a cut Slippery's other leg off when he came to the hospital." She paused. Another personality came forth. A clever Dirty Harry that goaded me past the Dry where miners once showered after a shift. We both tripped over a piece of timber, earmarked to build a shaft. "Blame your college roommate."

"Judge Ava Foil?"

"That fag stored incriminating documents about me in your basement." Her eyes darted to my heart, thumping like a rabbit's foot. She took my neck pulse. Grinned wide.

"Where're you taking me?" There was no breeze. No sounds from the city. Except, for noisy crickets that didn't let up anymore than she did. "MP . . . please let me go!"

We came to a platform, near the edge of a mine shaft being renovated for tourists. I dropped to my knees and brushed against a rusted steel cage currently being restored. Visitors on a tour would get a thrill dropping down to the six hundred level. I wasn't a visitor. *Dak . . . where are you?*

"I know you and that sneaky red skin call me MP for military police, behind my back." She failed to push me forward.

"Uuf!" I sprawled next to boot marks stomped on the landing by a miner.

She dug her heel in my back. Knocked the wind out of me. Her, *whoever,* was having a good time. A madwoman has no limits on strength. She boosted my over-sized frame up with one arm, and pressed the gun hard against my heart.

"Dak . . . Dak! Help me!" I screamed wildly hunching my shoulders. My voice sounded like sandpaper.

"Save it! He doesn't know you're on the other side of the yard from him."

He had to hear the echo of a gun shot in this quiet place. Sound ricochets off tin and steel, and chambers into an echo in these mountains.

Scheming was my only weapon. "Ava told me not to worry. The box was filled with outdated records for a genealogy project."

"Sure, Einstein . . . and, I own the Brooklyn Bridge." She heard a board squeak. Turned abruptly to look for a mouse. Her grip loosened. I broke away. Clamored to my feet and started to grope towards the railroad tracks that led out of the mine yard.

I've heard an insane person has heightened hearing, and razor sharp reflexes. She tripped me at the top of the platform.

"Assume the position, butterball." Her fingers tightened on my blouse. She argued with one her other personalities for a minute. Then toggled me closer to her face. "Ava's info was proof I didn't attend college the first year I was away from Butte. Can't have that kind of news blabbed all over town."

Her voice felt like cold steel on my neck. "I don't follow?"

"I had Dak's baby!"

"Hey . . . your business is your business."

"You'll never share a baby with Dak. I saw to that when he was in for hernia surgery." She threw a heavy right hook to my nose, leading with the gun. "If McDoon goons hadn't failed

. . . your charming two-by-four mansion would still be there. Cost me plenty to set Sledge up in Helena. Slippery was more obstinate. He wouldn't move away . . . but he'd stupidly run away . . . from the law."

I swayed from dizziness. Cuts and open sores stung like a swarm of bees were biting me, over and over. A dog barked. I had visions of Spirit dog rushing in to save me. This wasn't the movies. I was in a state of shock as I squinted at the gun. This was real life, I told myself.

In desperation, I reached up suddenly, and punched her in the stomach. A weak punch, at that.

"Ooph!" she snorted. Then, "Wham!"

The butt of the gun cracked my left cheekbone with such force, pain ratcheted through my head like a lightning bolt. I saw stars that weren't in the sky.

"You look at me," she demanded, releasing the trigger guard of a revolver—a .357 Magnum identical to the one Dak carried. She cocked the hammer, rotated the multi-chambered cylinder around an axis, and pointed it at my heart.

So . . . it ends here, Blessed Mother?

God, forgive me my sins!

Chapter Thirty-six

"I'll sell this as an accident," she promised, relaxing her shoulders. A great weight had been lifted from one of her personalities. "I'll tell Dak, and the police, you snatched my gun from my bag, and was going to shoot me."

The only strong thing about me, at this point, was a Herculean smell of my under arm deodorant. "Please, don't point the gun at me. It might go off."

"It will go off!" She prodded me with her weapon to inch me closer to the shaft. "I'll say we struggled . . . you fired a shot just before you fell down the shaft!"

All of a sudden a shot rang out.

Then, pure silence. Even the crickets stopped yelling.

I didn't know what dead felt like. If a bullet penetrated my stomach, I felt so sick already, I wouldn't notice. Maybe it lodged inside my chest. Maybe dead wasn't so bad after all?

A few seconds later, another shot rang out.

Although my eyes were smeared with blood from my cheek, I saw her clutch her chest, and sway. She groaned. Her body jerked. She held onto a railing with one hand quivering. It appeared a slug had entered her chest.

Where'd it come from?

I heard her gun drop. She staggered backwards, toppling over me, towards the mine shaft.

"Help. Please, Caitlin . . . help me!"

"What's happening?" I narrowed my eyes. Darkness blended her in with the black frame of the gallows. "Where are you?"

"Caitlin . . ."

"MP."

I squinted tighter to see her silhouette slumped close to the edge of the shaft. I fought to stay conscious. "Hang on." Every muscle within me ached as I crawled. Blindly. Slowly. Leaving a blood stained trail as I snailed her way. "I can barely see you."

"Caitlin..."she begged.

I never wanted her dead. I crawled to her voice. We were both down. I felt her sleek, curvy legs dangling helplessly over the edge. I also felt weak. Nauseated. Afraid. I corded my arm around hers. Her fancy, blue linen jacket was stained with black suet and blood. "I'm trying!" I said. My legs felt like water. I attempted to wrap them around her tiny waist to keep her from slipping further.

"Lift me away before I pass out." Her arms folded over her stomach. Her voice faded to a whisper. It was the first time I'd heard her wail in pain. She sounded like a calf being branded. I'll need medical—"

By now, my head was spinning like a top. I was too exhausted to squeeze an orange, let alone squeeze her to safety with my legs.

She clawed at my arm. "Pull me up, damn you fat head."

I felt her starting to slip away.

Barely able to breathe, I held onto her jacket. Until it tore.

This can't be happening! Please God. Help me save her.

"Ohhh . . . Caitlin . . ." Her voice rattled in pain.

My shoulders felt lighter as her warm body slid from my grip. I was shocked to hear an echo of her voice dim with each second that passed as she fell down the shaft.

Amid a deafening silence, I prostrated myself on a splintered wood platform, next to a lunch bucket, pick and ax, and a can of chewing tobacco. A weird thought came to me. Tomorrow, when the worker that left his stuff came on shift, life would go on as usual.

"Someone there?" A voice called from a distance.

Closer by, I heard someone else running this way.

"Cat Woman," Zoonawme said, dashing towards the platform. Smoke drifting over the front sight of his single-chambered pistol. Sweat dripping from the trigger. "You answer me, damn it!"

I would learn later, that he had followed the scent of my cherry hairspray, to track his way in the black of night, across the yard to the gallows frame. To where he found me, laying near the shaft. Beaten. Injured. Frightened. And, grateful to be alive.

"My dear Zoonawme!" I cried. "How—"

It hurt his back to kneel beside me. He untied his red, western bandana to wipe blood from my face, and stopped when I screamed in pain as he touched my cheek. "Where are you hit?" His heavy voice carried across the yard.

"I'm not shot, I—"

"That your voice Keno Savvy?" Dak called out from the opposite direction Zoonawme came from. "You with Caitlin and MP?" He limped over the yard's obstacle course without a flashlight.

"This way, " Zoonawme called out. "Platform."

Dak came closer. Drew his model 19, .357 magnum. Positioned himself in a caveman squat, his right arm stretched stiff holding his weapon. "Anybody hurt? I heard a shot earlier. Another one just now."

"Here," Zoonawme guided, flashing his light. He stomped a huge spider with his cowboy boot. "This way."

"She was going to kill me," I whimpered. "She was really going to kill me!"

"Who was going to kill you?" Dak grilled, approaching us. "After I left you, I heard a shot. Started to run to where I left you and MP. Who in the hell is after you and her?" He holstered Mr. Smith and Mr. Wesson. Crouched beside us. "You had my flashlight. I fell while running. A pile of broken glass caught a big slice of my leg. Took me awhile to stop an artery from flooding. Who shot you? Is MP all right?"

"Cat Woman hasn't been shot," Zoonawme said, shifting his weight. He lowered his head to angle closer to Caitlin. Looked down. Saw initials carved in a platform board—*EE.* Beside that, an eagle's form had been skillfully whittled out. He nodded at his cousin.

"I can see you're bleeding, girl?" Dak frowned, swiveling his head around the construction debris. "Where'd Megan Pat go?"

"MP laid off the first shot. . . at a field mouse." I siphoned strength from both of them, like I've done all my life.

"Say, what?"

I rubbed my cheek. Bone chips moved under the skin. More blood oozed out. "She did this to me."

"Why? I don't get it? She was afraid to face me tonight. Not you. Where is she?"

"She was never afraid of you. She was obsessed with love and passion for you." I supposed all her personalities felt the same. I pointed in the direction of the shaft. "Megan Pat's down there. I'm so, so, so, sorry!"

Zoonawme's gargantuan arms lifted me to my feet. He steadied me. Dak held me up on my other side. The three of us edged cautiously, silently, toward the hole, and looked down.

"Oh . . . my God!" Dak shrieked. "I thought I saw someone waving a gun, and I fired a warning shot this direction . . . from back there. How in the hell did I hit her?" He held onto the side of a cement mixer, his mouth stretched. "I'm a skilled marksman, and—"

"I murdered her!" Zoonawme confessed, reaching for his gun. "You didn't do it, Paleface!" He checked the safety. Turned the barrel of his .40 caliber towards himself. "I sensed she was going to shoot Caitlin. It was dark. I wasn't trying to kill anybody when I fired."

"Slow down friend," Dak encouraged. He gestured his hand.

"I intended to warn her to stop terrorizing Caitlin." He handed the gun by the butt, over to Dak.

"Wait! Let me think," Dak said, wondering how Zoonawme knew Caitlin and MP were at the mine yard . . . on the platform, no less? "MP shot the first bullet? I fired the second? You saying you fired the third?"

"I fired the fatal shot!" He stared squarely into Dak's eyes.

"Where'd you come from? How'd you know to come here?"

"When you didn't answer your cell, Dak, I followed you. I overheard that MP asked you to meet out here. She'd be the last person to dirty herself in a mine yard. I suspected a set-up."

"How'd you know to shoot at MP? It's pitch black out here."

"Blackfoot ears. I heard a gun cock. Came forward immediately to help."

"You might have shot Caitlin . . . did your Indian powers tell you that? You might have shot Caitlin!" he said with an edge.

"You really don't know much about women, Paleface. Little sister's never held a weapon more dangerous than a water gun. Sharp night vision. I saw one person down. The other was pointing a gun. I knew!"

"Please stop your arguing." I leaned on Dak. "MP didn't die from a gunshot. Both shots might have injured her all right, but she was alive when she fell. Her gun fell down the shaft. She died because of me. I just couldn't hold her—"

Dak lowered his head. He felt certain his bullet killed her. He stomped at some scrap wood, in disgust. Spied a 158-grain bullet from his .357 Magnum, imbedded in a piece of railing that shattered. He'd only shot once. As quietly as possible, he kicked the rail down the shaft. Then he mumbled. "It's all my fault." He pulled his hair with both hands and grimaced. "If only I hadn't left Caitlin with MP, this would've never happened. Thank God you're alive." A long pause. "There must be a God to thank for Zoonawme's cunning sixth sense. Our lives would never be the same without you, Caitlin!"

I crumbled into his arms. He called an ambulance. Then, he dialed Needlepoint. "I know you're off duty. LB's at dinner with Dacsu. We need assistance, immediately. An accident victim—a body—at the Anselmo mine yard." He listened to a question. "No, it wasn't a homicide. The victim had been shot . . . twice. Lost balance. Fell. Presumed dead."

He never let on that his bullet didn't hit MP.

He slapped his hand over his firearm cartridge. It has a larger charge and casing, and was more high-powered than other gun cartridges of the same caliber. He knew Zoonawme's semi-automatic fired a complete cycle. Ejecting a shell casing, and reloading another round from the magazine.

"If you were out to kill someone, friend," he told Zoonawme. "You'd have peppered the scene like a machine gun."

Dak's phone rang. "That's right, Costello. An accident. Call the coroner—"

Suddenly, he stopped, tears pooled in his eyes.

Megan Pat was the current acting coroner.

Chapter Thirty-seven ✍

Butte's grapevine worked fast. LB heard what happened, and rushed over. "You don't have to do this tonight, Boss," he said with solace, knowing Dacsu's mother was at the bottom of the shaft. He was saddened that the two women had never met. "It was a moot point that Duggan's came for the body. They could bring it up, all right. But, a mine-safety crew said there's a serious problem with acid at the bottom of the shaft."

"Acid? I thought the restoration people cleaned that up?"

"Super Fund got stuck on hold for awhile. It's going to take time to bring up the body . . . if there's one left. They assured me that nothing down there can withstand such horrible corrosion. Don't hold out hope—"

"Enough evidence for an inquest?"

"Just you three's testimony." He waved the ambulance to leave with Caitlin. "I left Dacsu off at the Finlen. You given a hint of a thought as to how we tell your daughter? She's a tough person, but . . ."

"Not yet, I was—"

All of his staff showed up to help. Cindy wrote his statement down.

"I fired a warning shot," he told Cindy to write down. Although he never loved her, he felt responsible for Megan

Pat. They had a child together. "Megan Pat must've caught my bullet. I'm the only one on the force that loads bullets that expand on impact. My revolver fired one round for each pull of the trigger. I pulled the trigger once, and she caught the bullet."

He handed his gun over to Costello.

"Don't record that, Cindy," Costello ordered.

"I give the orders," Dak replied.

"Not when you're involved in the accident." He turned to Cindy. "Most likely four feet of acid's pooled down there. It'll be impossible for forensics to verify that a bullet killed her." He handed Dak's gun back. "If there's a her, to find." He wished he hadn't said that. "Did you write down that Caitlin felt sure MP was alive before she lost her balance? She said they were talking when Dr. Megan Pat fell."

Dak held his hand over his heart without speaking.

"Boss, is there anybody else you want us to call?" LB asked.

"Yes, LB . . . please call Father Riley."

There was a long pause. MP was Catholic. A major contributor to the church. She attended Mass on Sundays. She just snapped, he thought. Dak didn't believe anybody's God punished someone that lost her mind. He didn't realize it until that moment. His moment of discovery. He'd always believed there was a devil. He imagined his cruel father to have been possessed by such evil. Through MP's death, he understood an evil person doesn't know what they're doing. That his father's goodness was destroyed by too much alcohol.

"Satan was brutalizing me . . . it wasn't my father that went after me," he mumbled to himself.

"I didn't hear you," LB said. He watched Dak's face. It looked different somehow, and he couldn't put his finger on the change.

Something strange happened to Dak Sullivan.

His heart was opening to Christ.

"Did I hear you right, Boss? You want me to call Father Riley? . . . for the victim?" He tossed his head towards the hole.

"For me . . . call a priest for me!"

Chapter Thirty-eight

Three years later on a sweltering July afternoon, long after Butte recovered from the quake—the second single greatest catastrophe ever to befall Butte—next to the Granite Mountain mine disaster, the O'Shaughnessy clan were slowly healing their long suffering emotions. They attended a grand scope wedding, along with five hundred other people.

"Pin this on my lapel, Cat Woman," Zoonawme said, handing me a rose. He scanned my long dress, and form fitting bodice, that showed off some lost tonnage. I felt feminine when soft green chiffon flowed every time I moved. "Zakhooa would definitely approve."

"Achoo," I sneezed, all the way down to my matching high heels. I moved away from a yellow and white, Daisy floral arrangement in the center of a long table, filled with enough food to feed Africa. "What's in your other hand?"

He handed me a Cashier's check.

"So much money! Made out to me? Why?"

"I sold Eagle Eye's estate. He'd want you to have it."

"Not a chance!" My face flushed.

"Face it, little sister. You're tied to my cousin in spirit through eternity. Besides, we're family."

"Good, you keep it—all in the family." I slid it the pocket of his black tuxedo, next to a bright red hanky. He loved the color red, and he loved weddings. Especially this one.

"Crab pot," he joked.

"Pip squeak."

"Sod Buster."

"Side winder."

"Side winder?" he roared. He pointed his finger at Spirit dog and Pen Doodle, barking at the back of the reception hall. "Take this money. Upgrade Copper Dust Forensics' equipment. We could use a good cell phone system. A better chair for my back."

"Cells! How did those bulky gadgets ever catch on?" I saw Dak standing next to Orla and Jeep. "Our former Sheriff looks so handsome in his tuxedo."

"Not my type." He moved closer to me as Aunt Rose elbowed through the crowd, adjusting her Maid of Honor, orange silk suit. She was sending arrows of disapproval at her sisters, hibernating at a back table. She had no patience for a woman, or anyone . . . of the 90's, that didn't feel liberated. She dipped into a punch bowl heavily spiked with Old Country Grappo—homemade, 100 proof firewater—a special vintage liquor fermented from imported grapes. Made to keep dark Italian skin soft, and their love life active.

The former red head plumped her black dyed hair, piled high like a public sculpture. "Way'd bay drenken teh theh bride en groom, tes proper en fetten," she toasted.

I toasted. Wet my finger in a glass, and ran the taste slowly over my tongue. "Geesh . . . and, I thought Irish Mead was strong enough to blow up England. I changed my mind."

One teaspoon of that high octane, Italophite anesthesia, bootlegged to every basement in the city from the Italian sector, could see me through a kidney transplant.

"Ded yeh see Dak? Himself talkin thengs oover weth Fr. Riley, now." Aunt Rose swung around. "Finden Jesus . . . thet's hes miracle."

Zoonawme and I locked eyes. We'd discussed my miracles just yesterday. "Here's to the assassination of my inner enemy, a self deceptive opinion, that I'd been targeted by God for pain. And my—"

"Quiet Please." Sticker Noon clanked a spoon on a glass. Except for a few soft whispers, mouths munching pasties, ears attached to a cell phone . . .most everyone in town had one . . . the room silenced.

"Here's to Africa. Here's to bald heads. Here's to the nuns," he toasted.

I held up a thimble full of Grappo to a room full of smiley guests. There's a distinct togetherness among party-goers during a toast at a wedding. A subliminal bonding. Nobody remembers the toast. It's the bonding that matters. "And, to all of you!"

They clapped, and cheered for themselves. I gazed at my family, standing together in a group like a bullet-proof vest. "How I love them," I told Zoonawme.

Aunt Rose butted in with another toast. "Caitlin's eye-openen adventure begen en eh dimension oov tyame thet shay actually belonged en, now dedn't et, child?" She bottomed-up. The crowd joined in. I wet my finger.

Her odd statement about time felt appropriate, I thought. WWII. Berlin. Flight 411. Gunner. Erin. Slippery. It all began with my parents. Everything that happened thereafter, led back to Dr. Freida, I mused.

Just then, Orla walked gracefully over with Jeep on her arm. Her full length, ice blue, strapless gown, flowed elegantly as she stepped closer. It was harder for me to get used to being a twin, than it was for her. "You know, dear sister," she said, speaking with the voice of a nun. "It was all a divine set-up. If you hadn't found documents in Mike's basement . . . and survived the earthquake . . . we wouldn't have proof that we're twins, and that you were the blood match that I needed for my surgery."

"Aunt Rose knew. So did Father Riley," I answered bewildered.

"Yes. But, if Dr. Freida and Jeep hadn't met in Chicago, no one would have found me," she sighed.

"Somebody should write a book about these experiences," I chuckled. "I'll never remember all that happened without a refresher course." For sure I'd remember Eagle Eye forever.

"Another toast," someone bellowed.

"Thanks to Eagle Eye," I said, raising my thimble to honor a man that saw something in me I couldn't see in myself. It choked me up to think that we cashed in rare gold coins, and silver dollars that appreciated mega much over the past forty-plus years. The money belonged to Mike, and he donated all of it to pay for both my sister's medical bills—and mine, I thought to myself. "We should build a shrine for Mike's generosity," I added.

Orla came over and squeezed my cheek. "Your reconstruction didn't change that we look exactly alike." She brushed her short red hair, cut exactly like mine, against my face, as she turned to hear a lively three-piece band starting to play "*Through the Years.*"

Jeep asked Aunt Rose to dance. He made it a point to know her as a family member. He respected his new aunt. He couldn't resist tickling her large earrings, as they joined a crowd on the dance floor. "My dear, newly found, vulpine aunt, these diamonds are compressed crystallized carbon," he teased her.

"Spake eh lettle slower, lad. Aye can't oonderstand yeh." They bumped into LB and Dacsu, swirling like Fred and Ginger, and dancing over to the head table.

"Time to throw the bouquet," Dacsu suggested. Single women bunched, and waited to catch good luck. Aunt Rose prodded her sisters, sitting at the table drinking Grappo, and eating bite-sized pasties, to get in line with her. They laughed. Waved her off.

She yanked me into the line. "Yeh'd bay cetchen theh flowers, straytt away." Dacsu kept her back to us. She threw her bouquet high into the air, in the direction of giggling women of all ages.

"I have it!" Elsie from Bruce's Donuts shouted, dashing to Zoonawme, and asking him to dance. Irish tradition. The lucky catchee would choose a partner and lead off the next waltz. Elsie secretly hoped she'd waltz him into marriage. "Me next," she murmured to herself.

Father Riley and Dak were engaged in deep conversation when I broke in. "You looked nervous walking your daughter down the aisle," I said to Dak.

"I haven't recovered from Dacsu inheriting millions upon millions," he replied. "Can you believe she was Megan Pat's only living relative? Such irony. MP never wanted to see her own child, yet this beautiful person," he pointed to Dacsu. "Fell heir to all of her possessions."

"You think her and LB will live in Butte?" Cindy broke in, holding Needlepoint's hand.

"Hard to tell," Dak said. She set me up for life. She'd better come around to visit her old man. He stooped over. Fed the dogs mystery meat. Tapped Judge Ava Foil on the arm.

"What's your guess?" he asked her.

"Hmm? What? You ask me something?"

She was wearing a tailored tan suit, and standing next to her attractive partner, a lawyer interested in environment. Informing Jeep about legal aspects of an extensive program. Preservation of precious genes of a declining river-dwelling population.

"I think LB'll leave for awhile," she said. "Money brings out the travel itch. Then he'll come home. They always come home."

"Heard you were asked to run for State Senator?" Dak smiled.

"All I'm running for is a fishing pole," she grinned at her partner. The bomb that detonated her car to pieces was placed by a disgruntled employee. She felt safe again. "You've got the right idea, though. This retirement stuff is one addiction I rule as favorable for my team."

Dak ran his eyes from Cindy to Needlepoint. "They make a good team, on and off the job. But, you know these office romances, especially cops, in the end they never work out." He goes on to say that Costello's wife divorced him and that he left town last year.

"Heard Nurse Chambers bailed, too? After you put out an arrest warrant for her, for attempting to kill Zoonawme at the hospital parking lot, why, she—"

The band struck up a loud tune. "*The Wedding Song.*" They sounded more like a full, twelve-piece orchestra, than a back-yard put together.

LB and Dacsu danced alone, whirling out of step as guests stuffed money in the bodice of a long, white Satin gown that Captain Mary O'Donovan gave her as a present.

The music ended. Crowd clapped. The groom waddled to the podium and seized the microphone. One of the traits he fell in love with Dacsu for, was that she accepted him just as he was. Overweight, and completely in touch with his inner self. The kind of a practicing Christian, Dak aspired to become.

Dak's face beamed proudly at his son-in-law. His daughter. Curiously, after retiring, he'd been filling his time coaching a snot-nosed, neglected kid—the mayor's son—by training him in horseshoe pitching . . . and the merits of good conduct.

"I'd like to introduce Dacsu's parents from Chicago." LB's blue eyes sparkled as brightly as his wife's violet eyes. "And, my own mother, of course." He waited for applause to stop. "Also, my, umm . . . my new wife's father . . . umm . . . make that my ex-boss. No! Dak's my father-in-law . . . times like these really call for a score card."

LB left the podium to step into a long line forming at the Men's Room. Break time. Servers filled guests' glasses with Champagne for another toast. People discussed arthritis, puberty, taxes, and Megan Pat. About her accidental fall, as the paper stated, just as she was assessing the Anselmo mine to make a sizeable donation. So the grapevine was fed.

Food handlers, a group of neighborhood women that volunteered to pour coffee, began to serve cake.

Me? Stay away from sweets at a party? A slice of a cake gifted by Town Talk Bakery—a five layered, chocolate and white creation, iced with love—tasted like a bite from heaven.

LB introduced other visitors. "We'll miss seeing Caitlin's twin around town," he told Orla's parents from Chicago.

"She promises to visit often," I spoke up, tears flooding my eyes. "Our *Mom* insists." The sound of "Mom" resonated happiness among the O'Shaughnessy clan.

Father Riley didn't agree that we laid to rest our feisty chromosomes of dispute.

"Those women will be going at a three-way brawl after Rose downs another Grappo," he predicted, tripping over Aunt Nell's oxygen tank. He dipped into the punch bowl for an umpteenth time.

I looked up. In came a surprise!

Mike surfaced from his hotel. He waved at the family, and spoke in Latin—almost as his second language. Father Riley, a bit slurry, decoded. "Greetings and love to everyone. Uh . . . something close to that, anyway."

Mike complimented the twins. We looked exactly the same after Orla gained weight for her surgery, and I lost some before my cheekbone reconstruction. Mainly because I found out that I was actually a couple years older than Hummy had told me.

Mike felt uncomfortable in a crowd. I followed him outside. He lived on a tight budget. No insurance when part of his building was destroyed. He'd given us the treasure money. It embarrassed him that Dacsu paid, what seemed to him, a fortune to restore his dream.

Now, he holed up in the Rocky Mountain Springs Hotel because he enjoyed being there. Soon, his bed and breakfast would be ready for guests. Dacsu's kindness restored his belief in himself—no matter how much he blabbed private stuff.

A Fox Trot began to play. Orla took me aside. "When I come back, will you be ready to tell me about our brother, Sam?"

"Yes, I will," I answered. "I'm ready!"

Jeep and Zoonawme walked over and asked for a dance. Both of us twins accepted. A Tango played, and we all sat down. Laughing. Giggling. Smiling. Orla took off her shoes to dance the next one with her husband—Chicago women had as much trouble with their feet as Butte women did. Zoonawme guided me to the floor.

If compliments didn't scare him away, I'd tell him how handsome he looked in his western-style Tuxedo. He requested a Marty Robbins' tune. He was as light as a feather on his feet. We pretended Marty finally arrived at Rose's Cantina.

"All of the loose ends in my life were solved." I stretched my neck to whisper to him.

"That's not true!" His face tightened.

"Do I need to wet my finger?"

"You have a responsibility concerning Erin . . .your father's whereabouts. He needs to be sent on his journey by the family. Your call."

"What would you do?"

"I'm a Blackfoot. I'd bring him into the family."

"I'm sure Dak would agree with you . . . if I told him. He's had such a full plate . . . then, his retirement."

"We both love you, little sister." He paused. "Your problems have always belonged to us. Why don't you come with me to visit Zakhooa next week? She might shed some light."

"I haven't ridden a horse the past three years," I said, trying to keep my enthusiasm down. I felt overjoyed at the invitation. As close as we were, it was the first time he'd asked me to accompany him.

By now, it was four in the afternoon.

The food and drinks kept coming. Music played on. They tell me Ireland was the same. Italy, too. Keep the generosity flowing long after the bride and groom have left.

After the flowers have wilted.

Perfect hosting for as long as it takes. . . . until guests are carried out.

A warm yellow sun was shining through stained glass windows of the church hall. We watched the bride and groom brush popcorn, showered on them by guests, off their travel clothes and prepared ourselves for a full night of more toasting.

It was comforting to see Dak growing closer to the mayor's son. They stood side-by-side, waving at the car that carried his daughter and son-in-law to Yellowstone National Park for their honeymoon and admiring the sign they pasted on the back:

Don't Call A Cop—He's The Driver!

One of the three bartenders hailed me as the newlyweds drove away. "Phone call for you, Caitlin."

"Hello? I'm a little busy now," I said. "Can you call back next month? . . . what did you say?"

The voice didn't sound familiar, but I listened. At first.

"No!" I broke in, just as another toast was being applauded. It was hard to hear. "I refuse to accept a job that'd take me to Egypt . . . huh? . . . well, of course I'm the best damn forensic handwriting scientist in the biz. Highly expensive, too." I played into someone's joke. Everyone in Butte knew I'd work for nothing if I felt like it. "No. I can't recommend anyone else." I hung up.

"A prankster?" Zoonawme asked, standing beside me.

"It might have been an archaeologist from Egypt that dug up some ancient goat skins," I laughed. "He said the Geneva Historical Council recommended me to decipher and analyze symbols etched into the parchment. Information that could change the history of the world."

"Don't answer any more calls," he suggested, spinning around to see Dak. He was passing a large tip to the caterers from a stack of envelopes. He was disbursing the stipend to the entire serving team. "He'll come over to give me an envelope for the women volunteers."

Other than Elsie fantasizing she had a chance with Zoonawme, most single females in the building—and a few married ones—lusted after Dak. He wasn't going to approach them with money.

It seemed to me, the party had just begun.